PRINTED IN THE UNITED STATES OF AMERICA

ISBN: 0984966609
ISBN 13: 9780984966608

Library of Congress Control Number: 2011918991
Charlton Productions, Portland, OR

To
Ruth

THE VERY LITTLEST
DRAGON

"Tink"

JUST FOUR STICKS
PUBLISHING DIVISION of CHARLTON PRODUCTIONS
Portland, Oregon

PRINTED IN THE U.S.A.

Table of Contents

Author's Acknowledgement

There are many misconceptions about how a writer brings a novel to life; some may be true in some cases, but others are wildly wrong.

One of my largest personal stumbling blocks was the ideal of a writer, alone, hidden off somewhere away from people, performing one of the most intimate inner-personal acts a person can undertake short of training to run marathons. Yes, this book did involve over 3,000 hours buried in a dark basement office at all hours of the day and night; but I wasn't exactly alone; if the computer was on, the flow between Laura and myself was "on".

The other "people" were the shadows of the personalities of people I interact with over the course of a day, or through my lifetime. It is these bits and pieces of a character that helps bring it to life for you, the reader; because they echo from people you may know in your own lives. That is the true magic about fiction stories; they resonate in our own lives.

The other groups of people, who are there in the background, are those that somehow, actively help you get through the gestation and deliver a healthy, happy book to the market. Sometimes this group is a small, tight knit group, and for other writers or books it is a collective of many people doing many things. With *The Very Littlest Dragon*, things were on the larger side; but different.

From the start, this book was about custom picture framers. Collectively between Laura Reynolds, the illustrator, Mar Griswold, the primary editor and me, we have over a hundred years of experience in the custom framing industry. More than a half dozen other picture framers worked hard as test readers, (trust me; not an easy job); and many other picture framers from around the world, in the tight community of less than forty-thousand, were asked for their input about certain images or bits of information that helped tell this story.

Finally, there was help via Kickstarter.com.

> **"Kickstarter is the largest funding platform for creative projects in the world.** Every week, tens of thousands of amazing people pledge millions of dollars to projects from the worlds of music, film, art, technology, design, food, publishing and other creative fields. **Each and every Kickstarter project is the independent creation of someone like you!"**
>
> *--- Kickstarter.com*

The result of this project on Klickstarter, community and organizational out-reach was: over 100 supporters, from four continents, and seven countries. The majority are custom picture framers who have probably never meet Laura Reynolds or myself. But from now on, they are all part of a larger family.

Below is the alphabetical list of supporters, and where noted; why they supported this book. From Laura and me, thank you all, so very much.

Americana Frame, Sharlene & Jim Stacy
Ambiance Photography - Karen & Rick Barletta for Molly
Amy McCray, Hickory Hollow Framery
Andrew Watkins
Anne LeBouton
Ashley Sutton-Daniels
Baer's Portland Husky Friends
Barbara Pelton
Beaga, Jogga, Shootie and the gang
Becky S. Florence
Beth and BJ Willinger
Beverly & Paul Keyser
Bill Zimdar and all the great people at Frames Unlimited
Bob Doyle
Bonnie Surguine
Bronislaus Janulis, Framewright
Bryan & Kristi Nelson
Buttercup & Delilah
Carrie & Jose Escobar
Cassy Adamson

Cathy Coggins (aka Chickie Coggins), Needle Craft World,
Kissimmee, FL -Purveyor of Fine Needlework Goods
and Framer Specializing in Needlework Treasures
Charles Penninger
Cindy Kimble for Grandchildren
Cookie Dodd, just because
Cornel Rosca, American Choice Fine Frames
Couture's Art Gallery & Frame Shop, Dick & Allora Couture
Darlene Lemley
Dave & Jan Kukkola-Miller
Dave Makielski
Derrick Dodson
Don Pettigrew, Valdosta, GA.
Donna Green
Douglas and Ann Ward
Edith Antl, Framinggoddesswhobelieves
Elaine Nelson
Eleanor Hunting
Eli Wilner, Master Frame Purveyor NY, NY
Ellen "Bossy Ellen" Collins, with thanks
Fingers, Pickle, The Rock and Cheese Caso
Floyd & Ruby Miner for Branden Williams
For Jenna & Lucas, love Papa Joe
For Miranda and her love of dragons
For My littlest framers, Cat, Mimi and MG , with love,
Sarah Bernard, Art'ique Frame Shoppe, New Orleans,LA
Framah aka: Ralph Fahringer
Honda Miria Rose Van Swart
Jana Kutter
Jared Davis
Jeff & GeAnn Rodier - Art & Frame Outlet, Myrtle Beach
Jeff Kaufman The Frame Station
Jeni & Scott Bushur, Home Accents Frame Shop Effingham, IL
Jim and Colleen Siman, Fastframe of Johns Creek GA
Joanna Klick
Joan & Ray Breda
John Barlowe - Frame Shop Art Gallery & Gifts

John Keglovich
Joyce Briggs
Julie & Lee Palmer
Karen Green
Karen Haverstock, Haverstock Creative Designs, Bedford, NS, Canada
Karen Short
Karen White
Kerri Marshal, DVM
Kip and Joan, Framed in Tatnuk
Kirstie & Jeff
Larson-Juhl
Leo Nicotera
Leonard Deles
Lucas Anderson
Lynn Fey-Duncan
Mar Griswold, State of the Art, custom picture framing and cat rescue
Mark Steinberg at Artrageous Custom Framing, New York
Mary Ann Miklich, Classic Corner, Pueblo, CO
Maryanne & Eldon Maldin
Matt Stanley & Family
Matthew & Emily Tuttle
Mary Henry
Melody A Brunetto
Merry Mary, Most Brilliant and Wonderful, Queen of Her World, Gentle Nag of the Universe and BFF
My sweet boys, Jonah and Tanner Wassell
Neil Zellman + Ginny & Maya
Nich Wattanasin, InterNich LLC, Boston, MA
Norton Taaffe
Pam and Jack Flynn
Pat and Eric Erickson
Paul Snider (The Picture Frame)
Richard Christie, who's framing inspiration is Anastasia Krasnobaeva.
Rob and Barbara Markoff

Rob Clark
Russ Wood; Grey Owl Framing
Sadie Cassavaugh
Sara Applegate, Applegate Gallery & Custom Framing, Vienna, VA
Sarah Charlton, Angel
Scott Purcell, CPF
Shana & David Keiser, Fifth Avenue Galleries, Columbus, Oh
Shari & Duane Hunting
Shayla Grumble
Sherri Marx
Sister Mimi Caso, Private Framing Collector
Starfish Framing and More, AJ, Mary, & Scout, Lincoln City, OR
Steve Breda
Stewart Garrett
Sue Hartford
Teri, Chris & Jake Oelrich
The Andrews Family, IL
The Callewaert family
The Canada Family: Brent, Gillian, and Penny
Tom & Kathy Ellison, for Adam
Ty Okamura, in loving memory of Cookie and Piggy-- best cats ever
Vivian Kistler, picture framer, teacher
Wally Fay, Sunshine Frames, Jacksonville Beach, FL

"Boomer"

Prologue

The young blue-green dragon, with lavender highlights glowing on her cheek wings, rested serenely against her bonded mate H'n, a large "obsidian" dragon. It was the distinct crimson edge markings on each of his large scales as well as similar red highlighting on his facial features, which the smaller blue dragon Q'Int had always found attractive. The two had married or bonded a few years before and were now relaxing as they watched over their cherished first clutch of eggs. Two eggs rested in the shallow heating bowl before them. As usual among dragons, the two eggs looked nothing alike. The much larger one was almost black in its deep red color and the smaller was, well, kind of plain tan beige with a strange greenish tinge to the shadow. But then, in their dragon world, nobody was worried about egg color or size; Q'Int had come from a medium sized egg, powder blue with red spots, and H'n had arrived in what could have been confused with an ostrich egg - large, white and covered with gritty bumps. So it was with parental patience and dragon curiosity that the couple observed the eggs as they wobbled and twitched with the usual birthing alarms.

BOOM! The top half of the larger egg exploded. The attending parents looked into the egg to see nothing but the darkened rim of the hole as if something had passed through so fast it had scorched the shell on the way out. As they stood there, scratching their heads, another sonic boom sounded and suddenly, floating between them, was a small (well maybe not so small) baby red dragon.

Their first son smiled and gently flapped or feathered his wings in the air as he skulled in place. All three smiled, and then the smaller reached out as high and far as his wings could reach, and with one great stroke, disappeared in a burst of speed and sound - BOOM!

"I suppose," the father said, "that our new son should be named Boomer." His eyebrow tendrils stood on end as he also made his eyes dramatically very wide open. "Although," he mused, "a little quieter inside the house, would be nice." They both nodded their heads and wriggled their upper wings in mirth.

Just then, an almost not-there sound came from the smaller of the two eggs. "Tink, tink, tink." The sound was cautious, delicate, and hesitant. The expecting parents stared at each other in curiosity. "Tink" came from the egg and then stopped. The father lightly tapped the egg with his one extended claw. "Tink, tink" the tip of his great shiny black claw sounded on the hard shell. "Tink, tink" the sound responded from inside. The feathery midnight black right eyebrow rose on the father's face as he cocked his head to listen, and looked sideways at his spouse, as if to say, "What do you think about that?"

Q'Int mirrored his gaze with her own signature single raised eyebrow. That same lovely raised eyebrow that had first attracted her mate to introduce himself to her at that gathering so long ago. She smiled and wiggled her upper wings.

Suddenly there was a last "tink" and an ever so tiny hole appeared in the large end of the egg. The very smallest of claws, more like a tiny black thorn, poked out of the hole. The parents both blinked at how truly small it was, that tiny needle tip of a claw, extending out of the hole in the egg and probing about, as if testing the air.

A flash occurred, streaking its way over the top of the egg at the same time as a small clap of thunder like "Boom!" rocked the egg. The eyes of both parents opened wide as they gazed at the egg, now split by the sonic boom into two large cups. In the center stood the very smallest tiny little dragon, they had ever seen. It scrunched its ruddy greenish dirty moss colored face and sneezed. "Choo!"

The littlest son of theirs batted his eyes as if he did not believe he was out of the egg. Just as suddenly, his brother appeared (quietly) and nuzzled his neck and wings as if to say, "Come on, let's fly and play." Therefore, they did. The larger red, and the tiny much much smaller mossy, er, um, well, muddy colored new dragons flew about the house as the parents watched and silently wondered what the future would hold for these two totally different dragons.

Chapter 1

Another day of "why"

Just as the cover of a book conceals the story within, there are many ways that the deeper truths can be obscured from knowledge or view. A forest of tall old trees, for instance, with reaching limbs and a verdant canopy hiding a cottage nestled in among the trunks and hostas with its worn thatched roof covering a space that is somehow several times larger on the inside than the outside. Or the not so small office in that quaint bungalow cottage, the one that smells of age and comfort, from the many shelves of books that fill the walls, to the large well-worn leather swivel armchair to the large oak desk that is so old as to appear almost black. The fact that the desk's top is almost clear of items may seem the most telling of mystery, but actually the story would begin with that lone coffee mug, the one with the thin crack running down its body just to the left of the handle, and just under the little dragon's left wing.

As one of the youngest workers in the Paws & Claws Fine Picture Framing Atelier, Tink sat in his favorite spot with his arms folded along

the porcelain rim. His chin rested on his wrist, and he found himself staring out of the office window with his wings draped limply around the rest of the large coffee mug that always sat on Guff's large business desk that overlooked the small patio facing the forest. One may think that Tink might be contemplating the fact that a full ninety percent of the store's business came walking out of that forest, even though there was no visible path, trail, track or road; but that was the farthest thought in the small greenish brown dragon's mind this warm late spring day. Tink's mind was filled with the word "why" and the addendums behind the "why" had grown. He now had the question of his abilities, or lack thereof, to add to his "Why?" pile of soul-searching questions which tormented him in his idle hours, or so it seemed most days. He knew he was known as the "all around guy", which really meant he was the guy all around the shop doing the bits and pieces of work that were, well, small stuff; stuff that anyone could do if they were not all busy doing the "real" framing. This left Tink to scrape spilled glue, pick up trash, hold this, push that, fold those and roll these, how many of these do we have and where did those get put away wrong in what shelf or room or under, over, in or on top of? Tink was all around the shop doing the little things. Moreover, it was not exactly a little shop to be all around, since it was bigger on the inside than it was on the outside, an important feature when it came to the shop's location; in amongst the forest trees the way it was.

The morning work at the Paws & Claws Fine Picture Framing Atelier ("Atelier" is just a very fancy word for "workshop") had been the usual helter skelter like any other Wednesday morning, except it just happened to be Tink's 50th anniversary as a picture framing dragon. This, if anyone stopped to think about it, could result in at least some cake, or chocolate or even chocolate cake and café mochas, that is, if anybody thought about it. But, in a frame shop full of busy dragons, such events come and go, and work goes on. Although the framer who directed most of the work was Guff, it was his dragon workers that created the most amazingly special picture frames that made Paws & Claws so renowned.

The Atelier sat nestled at the edge of the very large, deep and sometimes even darker forest. The shop owner was the Master Picture Framer, Guff, who happened to be a very large grizzly bear with a penchant for

3

custom Hawaiian shirts and bright red rubber clogs. Most of the dragons that worked for Guff had been with him well over a hundred years and each dragon possessed one or more very special talents. Dragons made the very best picture framers because of the mass of skills that a framer needed to acquire. Many years of training were required, beginning with apprenticeships and then more years as a Journeyman or Fellow in the Craft, before their peers could consider them a Master. When there were several framers in a shop, many simply specialized in just a few skills, like most of the dragons at Paws & Claws.

The team of dragons was a remarkable combination of several different types of dragons. Skell, a Nordic dragon, sported very shiny black horns and an extra-large wingspan that was tipped with growths of iron diamonds that he used to cut or etch glass and mirrors as well as work metals as need be. His color usually matched the metal that he was working with, and then sometimes when he was daydreaming about his youth flying in the fiords of the North, his wings could become almost transparent and his body scales would turn a shade of silver like a cloud or mirror; even though he swore there was no chameleon blood in his line.

Dvarkowalzitine, "Dvark," commonly called simply "Dee" for short, was the most common dragon in the atelier, and the most Skilled, for he was the Master Painter and artist of lines and embellishments. Born in the eastern slopes of the Russian Ural Mountains, Dee grew up at the knees of some of the most talented icon painters of his time. His mother was a duel breather, and she could breathe temperature-controlled flames from her nose while blowing a chilling breath from her mouth. She had taught this skill to her son. She also used this talent on her garden's bulbs to put them to sleep or warm the earth of her flowerbeds to force an unseasonable blooming – a talent Dvark seemingly missed acquiring or at least did not find of any use.

Aside from this skill with his flame and breath, Dee also had diamond-enhanced iron claws that could be used to engrave anything, including steel. Most frequently, though, he used his controlled flame to etch glass or gold in many kinds of patterns that he would design or maybe see in a book that Flith the Archivist would then research. This makes him the "go to" person for special patterns such as maybe the floral paisley in the running field of a picture frame that was popular

during the early Renaissance in northern Italy or Tuscany, not the floral patterns of say, the later periods. The "field" is that wide flat strip running down the middle of a fancy picture frame; and the floral paisley just happened to be his favorite to do because,as he always liked to say in his heavy Slavic accent, it made him think of his mother and her large flower garden back home, although no one could remember him ever taking a vacation or going to visit.

At the other end of special is Twill. Twill is the most unusual of all the dragons besides Tink because instead of skin, like Tink, or scales, like the other dragons, Twill is covered with dove gray blue feathers made of glass - not the hard glass of a window, but a soft and fluffy downy kind of glass like the spun glass of insulation. The feathers are made entirely of hollow glass so thin that it is soft and pliable instead of brittle; unless of course something (or *someone*) makes her mad, then all bets were off as to how hard her feathery shell can become – glass, metal or diamond? Her eyes are the ice blue turquoise of the inside of glaciers, except when she is angry, when they flame to the raging red of a brilliant ruby or a warning sign; not something you would ever want turned in your direction. Her "flame," if one can call it that, is a very transparent light blue like the blue where the sky touches the distant sea. There is no heat, but where it touches, a thin layer of glass will appear. By making several passes or staying in one place, she can "pool" or "pile" the glass into a shape that is as solid as any other glass, except it is unbreakable. It is called Dragon Glass, and one of her favorite things to do is to build hollow shapes in the air that become Christmas tree ornaments. These are colorless and can be painted or just catch the light.

Much beyond that, Twill is a general mystery. Some think she was possibly French, which would account for the almost French blue color, but that was definitely *not* the other language that she was known to mutter to herself as she applied gold and silver leaf to frames, which was not her favorite job. Definitely not French!

No one would be so rude as to be nosey about her background. As for her age, one could merely hazard a guess. Even Chang could only say that she was at Paws & Claws when he arrived over 150 years ago from Mongolia.

Of all the special talents, Chang's is the least obvious. His talent as a wood carver is amazing to watch just in itself, as he wields his chisels, saws, hammers and rasps, molding the wood to his will. The many tendrils of his face that surround the crossed blue and brown eyes are as prehensile as a monkey's tail. So instead of the time wasted in looking for a wayward tool, or picking up and putting down tools, this wingless Snake dragon has his whole toolbox of tools floating at the ready about his face. His tendrils seem to anticipate his needs and will reach out and gather up the tools that he will be using next or even two or three steps into a process. His hands are thus always carving the wood and always with the next perfect tool for the job. As he carves, his powerful forearms, something most winged dragons do not have, bulge and ripple from the power applied to shape the wood. The reds and oranges of his oversized scales seem to flow and ebb in intensity from dark to white-hot flame depending on his exertion and the power he is embedding into the work. But what is not seen and only occasionally overheard is when he talks to the wood.

Chang's true special dragon talent is two-fold: first, his crossed eyes actually see in many different ways. He sees what the wood is doing, he can also see the stress that is in the wood from how it grew, and occasionally he will use another way of seeing, which is the "colors" of temperatures, to know when steaming wood is at the perfect temperature to bend a stick into an oval or circle. Second, with his ability to talk to the wood, Chang actually talks the wood into doing what he needs the wood to do. Sometimes that does not always require the assist of a sharp tool or steam, just a sharp mind and a sharp tongue.

Born in the mystical forests of the far east of the frozen lands of Mongolia, and the only hatchling to a gypsy wood-charming dragon, he had learned about asking the wood to shape while still barely as tall as his mother's first knees. Chang was an outcast, even among his own people, because of his crossed eyes that seemed to hex the young dragon into running into doorways, or flying into buildings or trees. The young Snake dragon believed he was cursed. But a lucky happenstance of an accident and chance meeting of someone who recognized his eyes as being able to see on so many levels changed his life. Instead of confusion, his "disability" led him to see his calling and skill. As he became older, and some say as good at wood whispering as his mother, he was sent west into servitude, into the Black Forest of Nells to apprentice under a not so nice wood artist wolf named Pzztzill. Only after years of

7

this long hard service, did Guff the bear hear of this young dragon and offer to take the "good for nothing lazy worthless tramp of a dragon" off the wolf's paws and parsimonious payroll. Since that day, a very long time ago, each morning as he walked through the door, upright on his massive hind legs and standing almost as tall as the bear, Chang would nod to Guff and say, "Thank you".

So as Tink sat curled in Guff's large coffee mug, he was scrutinizing the dull mossy mud-brown dirt color of the mottled nubby surface that was his skin. He did not even have any honest to gosh dragon scales. Not one that he had ever found, not even a pre-growth ridge where scales would one day appear; he just had bumpy skin like a plucked turkey. *Just plucked turkey skin - yeesh*, he moaned inwardly.

The sunshine oozed through the leaded glass office windows, and fell like a warm mantle on his long neck and tiny wings. It felt almost as good as his mother's biscuits tasted, fresh out of the oven and smeared with warm honey. Sometimes when the sunshine was just right, the windows were just dirty enough, and it was later in the day, Tink could almost swear his skin looked more bronze or gold than mossy mud-brown. And that was why he always liked to take his late afternoon break sitting curled in Guff's mug on his desk by the window. He did not remember when he had started sitting in his boss's coffee mug, or even why he had started. Had he asked permission? Had Guff stopped drinking coffee? Or was Guff just being polite?

Nevertheless, little Tink, so very little Tink remained to wonder why, at eighty-three years of age, had he still not found his "talent or special ability." He had been asking this question for years, along with the old questions of, "Why am I so very small?" and "Why am I the color of mossy mud?" These questions made sense to Tink; but one that would make more sense would have been, "Why am I small enough to fit into my employer's coffee mug, and why does he let me sit here instead of drinking coffee from it?"

And if Tink had been thinking that question at the same moment as Guff shuffled quietly past the office door, he might have sensed a small flash of a dark brown eye glance out of the side of a fuzzy face, and the very smallest hint of a knowing smile crinkling in the right corner of Guff's mouth. Guff walked up to Twill who noticed the unusual touch of a faint smile in the corner of his mouth, and they looked back knowingly

towards the office door and the tiny brooding dragon. The large hulking softy rolled his eyes above his recent affectation of half glasses perched down his long ursine nose, and shrugged his huge shoulders causing the surfers and grass huts to roll on his Hawaiian shirt. Only the quick eyes of a dragon such as Twill noted that the surf had changed and one surfer had kicked out, where two others had wiped out and disappeared into the waves.

"If the boy frets much deeper, he's going to crack the bottom out of my mug," Guff worried softly as he handed Twill a couple of orders. "Maybe you can get him to help you with these orders for the next few days." They looked over the sheets at the specifications on the different frames needed.

"I'll need Dee to do some engraving on these six dedication frames. I'll loan him Tink to hold the frames. Tink just loves hearing Dee's stories for the nine millionth time." They both chuckled quietly in their conspiratorial jest at Tink's expense. But the truth be known, Tink never seemed to tire of listening to Dvark talk about his homeland and his mother's garden and cooking. It was so exotic and different, and too, it drew out a side of the rough edged Russian that made him softer and more like a "lovable uncle." Tink responded well to this side of Dvark, and Dvark let Tink know that he secretly liked to think of Tink as a favorite surrogate nephew. Over the past thirty years, the two had become a solid team that produced some exquisite examples of engraved and incised frames. "But first," continued Twill, "I have a more important errand for Tink to take care of," *and I think the fresh air will do him some good*, she thought to herself.

"Tink, dear," Twill called, and the tiny brown green dragon floated eagerly in front of the matriarch of the shop's work room. He fluttered with almost no movement of air as he skulled the space in a perfect hover. This talent he had learned from his much larger twin brother and none of the other dragons would admit their inability to master this maneuver. "For the tinctures on these areas of this series of frames we will need some grindings of jolat root, mixed with the skins of black walnuts. The jolat root will have to be brought in by your brother, as I know we are completely out right now and at this time of the year it will have to come up from South America, preferably Brazil. The walnuts, however, are ours for the gathering over in the Nordal Valley on the west slope. I'll draw you a map. Take a sack; I saw quiet a number of these gems lying about since they have recently started to fall." She tilted her head and gave him the cold look of one eye under a cocked eyebrow with her soft feathers sticking stiffly straight up for a more dramatic fun look. "Be careful and only touch the skins with the tips of your claws, or they will stain your fingers for months and your mother will have my hide for a feather duster."

Tink began to giggle at the thought of Twill's beautiful blue glass feathers used by his mother for dusting, but stopped, as "the eye" suddenly got very close. "Are you still here?" she cackled in a mock Halloween witch's voice. Then she was laughing at empty air as Tink raced to fetch a bag.

Twill turned and looked across the shop at the muddle of dragon wings and tails, hands and flames all gyrating in multiple colors and du-ties as picture frames were being made, painted or gold leafed, stained or tinctured and finished so that art could properly be housed and pro-tected for display on the walls of their patrons. She thought of the many dragons and one hedgehog that had come and gone during her almost 200 years working for the big bear in his magical atelier. She smiled at the family that was now a cohesive beating heart with the sole goal of beauty . . . until her quick eye spotted a practical joke in the making by a certain pair of young dragons. Other than the fact that one was blue and the other was green, they were "TWINS!" The retort was explosive as cannon fire and had the effect of everything freezing for a split second, then two small bodies streaking for cover.

"Now, if those two grandnephews would just grow up . . ." Twill thought as she slowly stalked the room proceeding to restore proper working decorum. Out of the corner of her eye, she noted Tink's tiny body with a bag in tow disappearing out the window, without a map for direction. This meant that she would not see him until morning - clever little guy, she thought. Not that he was lazy, but she now knew that he was aware of the blackberry field that was ripe right now, and expected she would find his muzzle and hands stained not from the walnuts but a well-deserved gorging on blackberries. Maybe he will pick a bunch for his mother. A fresh baked pie would be nice, she thought, as her claws clamped down with a green ear in one and a blue in the other. "Boys, I have work for you. Lots of work to be exact," and marched deeper into the rear of the shop with two drooping bodies, more like wet dishrags suspended from each hand, green in the right and blue in the left.

The large pear shape of the accountant M'Ree waddled by looking over her fire red glasses. *Fudge,* she thought (channeling something the twins were thinking), *Oh yes, it's been way too long since I made fudge.* She exhaled a very deep dark chocolate with raspberry compote-scented sigh, as the herd of sheep, which was what her enlarged lower body resembled in motion, picked up just a little more momentum with the thoughts of a chocolate reward now securely on the close horizon.

The front door opened, but nobody or nothing entered, the door simply stood open. Guff looked up expectantly and then finally quizzically. He slowly put down the frame samples he had been putting back in their proper places on the display wall. A good long session of choosing the right frame and matting had left the frame design counter cluttered from one end to the other. Now he simply handed the few samples in his hand to Twill and saying nothing, walked out the front door, which slowly glided behind him and closed.

Guff stood in the shadow of the overhang from the roof. The deep shadow usually supplied him with the deeper light in which to look a farther distance into the dark reaches of the forest, but today it would seem to be no advantage or even needed. Guff just listened as the light breeze whispered in through the pine trees, barely moving the tiny petals of the daisies in and among the hostas of the near forest. Rolling his eyes up into his head, his lids closed and his superb hearing became even more acute, more attuned and more sensitive to what was quietly happening under the hostas, between the daisies, and in the detritus of the forest floor. Guff was witnessing the start of a new life; one that he had been waiting for almost two hundred years now. The time was here, and he could not be more proud than if he was the parent.

She was coming - soon.

Chapter 2

An All-Around Tink Day

"Dee! Tink!" the bear huffed his way back in the workshop. "We need an inscription incised into this frame." So much for a stolen early morning break, thought Tink as he slowly climbed out of the coffee mug.

His job would be to hold up the frame so Dvark could cut the engraved letters with his directed pencil sharp flame. Tink had been trying over the last year to breathe fire, but all he could muster up was a pungent smoke wafting from his nostrils that made him sneeze. So, for now, he just held the frames for Dvark and a few of the others; and Dvark would always say, "Da, you getting gooder at holding the frames, ten more years and we be a good trio: me, you and frame." He said this every time they worked together and every time he laughed. And every time Tink felt the weight of holding the frames for another ten years listening to Dvark's grammar, which, now that he thought about it, had an amusing tendency to fluctuate back and forth between almost perfect English and a capriciously unconscious reverting to his Slavic roots.

"Tink, I think this time you hold it for a bit more angle so I can open up the cuts for a wider incising." The smallest pencil-thin flame shot from Dvark's nostrils as he blew a thin steady stream of cooling air from his mouth so the wood would not catch fire, or even turn a singed brown. Tink, for all his boredom, still marveled at the skill that it took to cut with the flame one hairbreadth in front of the cooling chilled breath. Many times Tink had watched the power of that breath as Dvark had blown on his tea in the summer to make it iced without ice cubes. Something Twill tried occasionally, but only succeeded in turning the tea to ice, or glass; but she was getting better.

"Dee," Tink asked as the older dragon examined their work. "Why do you think I'm so small?"

A single whirling bronze eye slowly levitated until it peeked over the frame, as the matching eyebrow tendrils arched into question marks. (Another one of Dvark's special talents that made him unique and a cause for his own amusement.) "And at the cusp of childhood, this bothers you why?" Dee's eye whirled even faster and redder if that was possible then lowered back to examining the picture frame; Tink heard a soft *humph* followed by a low chuckle.

"It's not just the size, but also the color," the small dragon whined while muscling up against the back of the very large gold frame six times his size. He had become very adept at arching and curving his wings into "flying buttresses," which was a little shocking to some dragons, and a very interesting curiosity to some of the older ones, as well as to Guff, since it required actually bending his bones. "I'm not even green." The small mossy mud-colored dragon picked up the tip of his right wing and braced it out another inch and against a deep gouge in the bench top giving him even better leverage. "Even the Terror Twins are at least blue-green green," Tink continued his whining complaint, more to himself than his mentor and fire carver on the other side of the frame. His small brown tail curled left across the workbench as he braced for the weight that he could feel was increasing as Dvark dug deeper with his flame, scooping out the curled leaves of the pattern in the frame.

A mumbled distracted voice on the other side of the frame muttered "Please to go tell Twill and Skell they are no good; and must become green to be so." Tink, listening intently for critical instructions from the Master Framer, rolled his eyes at the comment as he also noticed the tip of Dvark's tail begin to swish and twitch; a sure sign that Dee was having fun and laughing at him and his "silly" worries. Tink slumped inwardly in his resolve at the still unanswered questions. The two would work the rest of the early morning in the silence Dvark preferred.

While some of the dragon workers preferred to sip coffee and relax for the morning break, Tink relished his time sitting in Guff's mug for the morning break because of the special light that usually did not quite make it into the forest until later. But then there were the special times like today that the time was shared with Guff at his desk, discussing topics other than the shop. A favorite subject of all dragons and this bear in particular was food, more specifically, the food that Tink's mother loved to prepare. Especially her forays into the latest recipes for rice balls, rolls and fish balls, which were a staple in most dragon households.

"So if she washes the nettles in the lemon juice and spring water, it takes out the toxins?"

Tink nodded as he sipped some more coffee. "That is what she says. I don't know if there is another secret to it or not, but it sure does add a nice zip to the green roll with the brown rice."

Guff, eyes rolled up and to the right, thought about what he knew of nettles and how tough they were to get out of bear fur, as well as what happens when they work their way to his skin and why there is a reason they call them 'stinging' nettles. "Hmm, sure will be nice to get a chance at biting back a nettle or two," the big bear grinned with the right side of his mouth and winked at Tink as he sat on the bear's large knee. "In fact, I happen to know a rather large patch in the east area of the forest and it would make me cry if it got used up."

Tink and the big bear chuckled as they sipped the last of their coffee. Tink watched with the side-watching fovea (focal points in a dragon's eye) of his left eye, as three of the surfers on the large wave near Guff's shirt pocket could not handle the shaking of the bear; they wiped out and were consumed by the wave on his ever-present Hawaiian shirt. Tink did not know how the shirts did that, but he did find the shirts and the dramatic changes in their scenery to be a good indicator to the bear's mental state. Although lately he had been mixing the shirts up a bit with some new patterned shirts with dragons on them, and as if that was not enough, one shirt was of all the dragons that worked at the Paws & Claws Atelier. Tink thought about that shirt as he drifted back to work via dropping off his small coffee mug at the "Rocket Fuel Station" (coffee urn). There just seemed something wrong with a shirt that depicts the dragon workers doing the work that they were each doing at that moment, even when they do not always do the same thing. It was a nice shirt and all, just a little unnerving for Tink.

"Tink," a plaintive call came from one of the back rooms. Pu, one of the Snake Dragons and the Fabric Master, had earlier dropped a comment that he would be fabric wrapping a large liner this morning. Not that he had specifically mentioned Tink's name, but as sure as his skin was mud brown green, he knew that at one point this morning he would be 'playing with Pu', and getting all wrapped up in his work. Tink chuckled at his own little humor, as he loved the turn of a pun, not for serious humor but just for fun.

"Coming Pu," Tink called as he popped over Jeeter's head as he was winding his way through the main workroom with a hundred pound sack of ground talc stone called whiting, a staple in the creation of large gold ornate frames. Tink just did not think that the Paws & Claws used *that* much whiting. Every time he saw Jeeter, he had a large sack of whiting on his shoulder. Tink pictured Jeeter going home at night carrying a sack on his shoulder, which made Tink laugh just as he entered the Empire of Pu . . .

"Something about fabric you find funny?" a very serious Pu asked Tink as his nose radar tracked on the very small dragon hovering in the air.

"Nothing about fabric, Pu; I just was thinking about . . ." Tink felt that both of Pu's forward hunting fovea were trained on him and that he was being evaluated as prey. Tactfully he attempted to shift the subject to Pu's empire. "So, you had mentioned that there was a rather large liner that . . . HOLY CARP EARS!" he shouted as he spotted the 8" wide moulding on the liner that filled the wall upon which that it was leaning.

"You weren't kidding about it being large!" Tink's head whipped back and forth from Pu to the large liner, "Do you even have fabric wide enough for something like that?" he asked, looking askance to Pu for illumination.

Pu was looking at the liner but now re-focused on the small dragon slowly hovering closer as he sized up the liner frame. Tink looked again at Pu then started to look back at the frame but his brain finally stumbled on the deep furrowed brow and disgusted look on Pu's face as well as the dramatic flaring of the articulated nostrils. "Oh, yes," he responded with chagrin, "of course you have fabric that will fit. What was I think-ing?" He smacked his right palm to the jewel in his forehead.

"Good eye, junior dragon," retorted Pu as he spun about on the ball of his left foot, stopping with a strategic slap down of his large, long and very prehensile tail. "The narrow measure is just 118-3/4" and the fabric is 120", maybe." Ever the mentor, or at least teacher, Pu now whipped about to face Tink and like a magician pulling a scarf from a hat, his left hand produced a collapsible measuring stick from his pocketed apron and began waving it about, using it now as a pointer on the various fac-ets facing them in this project.

Tink wanted to roll his eyes, but knew better; even if Pu was looking away, he could never be sure he was not somehow being watched. Tink fully understood that after 50 years working at Paws & Claws Atelier, there were mirrors and fragments of mirrors, as well as eyes, every-where. Especially when you least expected it.

" . . . And so with the scoop pulling down much of the excess fabric, along each side there runs a half inch of un usable fabric that is called selvage, so, the fitting will be very . . ." Pu whipped around and turned his targeting on full focus and brought it to bear on the tiny mud green dragon. "Are you paying attention?"

Responding physically to "the look", Tink backed off a bit as he responded by shaking his head as he reiterated the problem, " . . . so the fit is going to be very tight and tricky," he finished with what he hoped was an ingratiating smile.

The silent look was held for almost the count of five, "Yes, well, go heat the rock box to about 200 degrees . . . oh, yes, I'm sorry. I forgot. You have no flame." Pu shot him a short look, putting Tink back in his place as he stepped to the door and asked Dee if he could come lend a hand. "And while you're in here, could you help me place this magnificent liner up on these four work benches."

It was rare that Tink felt totally useless, but in the case of such a large frame, the two large Snake dragons each standing a full five feet tall, but with tails and all were close to 125 pounds each, as well as very muscular and scary strong. Tink simply stood back and watched the ballet of moving a frame that was larger both of them together. On the way out, Dvark stepped over to the box made of soapstone and blew a flame into the box until he knew the heat in the stone was the desired temperature.

Tink, having performed this routine many times over the years, knew that the next step was to place four or five "mice" in the box so that they would heat up. The mice were nothing more than sewn cloth balls filled with rice or field corn. Tink placed a matching set on the cold or cool slate floor. The mice were used to "iron" down the fabric to the wood liner frame that Poul, the glue-blowing dragon, had blown down a day or two before with an adhesive that was special for fabric. The application of the hot mice reactivated the adhesive, applying the cold mice from the floor set the adhesive.

Tink had learned many years before that a metal heat iron was only suitable for use with certain fabrics; many others take on a glazed look if an iron is used. Like the silk they would be applying this day that was too thin to have Poul flame down the frame with the glue. To try to lay the fabric on the wet adhesive would make for a nearly impossible task; better to wait and do the process dry with the mice. Today, Tink's job would be to shuttle the mice back and forth into Pu's hands as he slowly and perfectly applied the fabric to the frame. The term "Master" was not thrown around lightly when it comes to the application of fabric, but it perfectly described the Master, Pu.

Lunch would be late in coming, as once the process began of shuttling the mice about the fabric room, the workers could not be interrupted until the task was completed. Tink was fascinated listening to Pu's unique form of communication, which consisted of squeaks through his nose, ticks from his tongue, and the clicking of his unsheathed claws. Especially upon examining his own claws, Tink found this even more intriguing because he knew of no other dragon that had retractable claws like a cat.

Dvark stopped in several times to maintain the heat temperature, as well as marvel at the other Master, at work in his Empire. Dee, seemingly casual, would lean his dark form against the door-jamb, and with his forearms folded across his chest, watch intently as the yellow Snake Dragon with the red ridge trim flowed like a flame colored stream, winding its way from outside the frame to up on the tables and inside the frame, getting each and every thread straight as a laser line. His sheathed claws tugged and urged the fabric to form to the frame, and be the perfect fabric Pu knew it could be.

During the late morning, others would glance in for a moment to see the Master dance his fluid dance, with such a large frame; Jeeter even came in quietly and gave the fabric a very close look, and when he felt Pu had stopped, looked up and said only, "Exquisite." At which they both nodded, and returned to their respective jobs.

The lunch fish balls were gone, and the last of the sweet sauce licked from the inside of the little container, and now a small resonating thrumming was echoing from the mug on Guff's desk. The large bear, fighting off a nap himself, was enjoying Tink's company and the sunshine pouring through the wall of nine-lite Tudor windows all the while he was trying to catch up a little bit on some important personal paperwork and correspondence. As much as Twill chided him for not getting an email account, Guff felt that he could leave that for other generations. What little communication he needed or even wanted to do, he would do the same way he had been doing it for almost 200 years - pen, paper, and an envelope or other means.

Finally, the rhythmic rumblings of the Tink mug symphony were too much for the ursine inner beast and with the pen capped, the paper straightened, and all stowed in the proper drawers, the desk now cleared was ready for the best ursine use. The red rubber clogs raised off the floor, crossed on the corner of the desk, and Guff was sound asleep before the chair had reached its fully reclined position. The sunshine melted its way through the ancient wavy glass as the healing balm of slumber salved the two beasts; the master and the . . . well, apprentice would be a misnomer, yet Journeyman would also not describe the small "all around guy" that filled the porcelain mug near the window.

"This looks to be grand, Jeeter," Dvark offered as he examined the frame in his hands. "The panel was yellow bole over the gesso, was it not?" he asked as he examined the flat middle panel of the picture frame's profile, to which Jeeter merely nodded.

As Dvark ran the back of his right index claw along the burnished gold leaf, he admired the workmanship, "Your burnishing of the gold is trackless and totally uniform, Jeeter. You have come a long way since I have come to work here." They both quietly chuckled at the old joke between a pair of the oldest employees at the Paws & Claws. Jeeter had actually been in residence long before anyone else could imagine, but as anyone will tell you, he is not very talkative.

As Jeeter walked away, Tink, refreshed from his nap, once again looked and wondered about the two large scars running down the dragon's back where wings should have been. This enigmatic dragon, who probably said less than twelve words on his most talkative days, was the one person Tink wished would tell him his story. Jeeter was a wingless "right" dragon with a flame red rudder on an otherwise all green body, except for the ubiquitous tan-yellow chest and belly plates. He moved like a wraith or a shadow, always restocking supplies just as you need them, and making gesso or composition castings for some of the frames, and yet, he never seemed to be talking with Twill or Guff over the jobs that need doing; he just went about his day.

"So my little Tink, what do you tink, Tink?" The older Russian dragon laughed at his own joke or pun, as he pointed at the frame on his workbench.

"It's beautiful, Dee, but I thought you were going to etch a pattern into the panel."

"I will." The large blackish brown dragon smiled, "So, now it would seem it is time to awaken the educated beast of the wall." He nodded his head dramatically backwards over his shoulder at the blank paneled wall. He stepped one foot toward the panels and reached out, knocked twice, then once, then three times. Turning his head, he winked at Tink, "Always the secret knock; always." Over the many years that Dee have been working for Paws & Claws, Flith had been known to ignore any other knock, thinking it was only something knocking against the wall, so Guff had worked out a "secret knock" that was agreeable to all. Dee felt his entire being fill with both excitement and no small measure of trepidation - this happened every single time he knocked that secret knock. No one ever knew what to expect once the panel opened and the way was revealed - every visit was like the first time, nothing was ever in the same place twice, and to add to the thrill, this was to be Tink's very first visit behind the wall.

They both turned as a tall but narrow section of the age-darkened clear pine, plate and rail paneled wall collapsed back into the wall itself, and an eerie yellowish light flickered from the now exposed opening. Like two nervous excited children on Christmas morning when it is still dark out but they just have to peek, the two dragons stretched their necks to peer around the corner to see if they could see any of the secret Fiefdom of Flith. Flith was the company's archivist and researcher of historical information, so any frames that needed to be historically accurate were historically accurate.

Tink had never been invited to visit the library/archive/research room where Flith (for all intents and purposes) lived - Flith himself was rarely ever seen out and about in the shop. In fact, Tink had worked for Paws & Claws for over ten years before he realized that Flith might just work there; and another four or five years before he found out Flith's name and what he did.

The illumination was a low yellowish light that glowed through what appeared to be many veils or sheer drapes hung almost *en masse* down a short hallway that ended in a bend so that nothing could be seen. The air had a smell of incense, barbequed spare ribs, roasted raisins, old leather, and burning candles. Both dragons caught the other with flared nostrils and half-closed eyes as they sucked up the air of mystery and the aroma of adventure.

Remembering why they were here, Dvark offered, "Flith?"

A pallid visage, almost a skeleton of a dragon's head, popped around the corner, blinking many times. Flith presented the ultimate expression of the pure absent-minded professor. His black horns, uniformly miss-aligned ear wings (one up and the other sticking straight out like a cowlick), one eye open much wider than the other, and one wing up and folded tight with the other dragging draped on the floor added to the wild effect. He looked as though he had just been startled awake, as he may very well have been. "Yes?"

He paused seeming to catalog who he was looking at or what they may want, as he stuck the two middle claws of his left hand into his mouth and sucked at the nails, thinking. "I'm sorry; is it June yet?" He blinked and then realizing he was sucking on his claws, withdrew them and hid the offending limb behind his head, which now made him look all the more like an errant child caught with his hand in the cookie jar.

Dvark's shoulders sagged in disappointment. "Um, you were looking up the proper pattern for the panel on a Neoclassical French frame?"

"Classical?"

"Neo," Dvark added, "French." Tink watched Dvark's eyes turn black as obsidian and hard as diamonds. *This was not going well . . .*

"Late 16th century, early 17th," Dvark added pronouncing each syllable with a breath of air for punctuation.

Flith blinked as if seeing the two dragons for the first time. His head slightly bobbed up as if to see better, the ear wings realigned as the eyes trued even, and then his whole frame oozed around the corner and into the hall separating the draping. "Dvark?" he asked curiously, "Tink?"

"Yes."

"Oh . . . oh happy day! I was just working on some patterns for you." He suddenly stood erect and a huge smile stretched from ear wing to ear wing. "Please, come in, come in," as he waved them into the small and narrow space. He suddenly realized that he and Dvark could not occupy the same space, so he turned saying, "Well then, follow me," and he led down the curious passageway in the wall and disappeared around the corner.

Dvark looked at Tink with big exaggerated eyes and rolled them as a comment to what just happened. Tink in response shrugging innocence, offered out his right hand toward the passage, as if to say "there is no way I'm going in there first."

As they began separating the drapes in the few short steps down the passage, Tink could not help but think about a certain book he had read many long years ago called *Alice in Wonderland*. After 50 years, Tink and Dvark were discovering that the building had its own version of a rabbit hole, along with its own Mad Hatter. Three more of Dvark's strides confirmed this.

Tink turned the corner and immediately ran into the back of Dvark's head, who did not notice. Tink recovered and climbed up on top of Dvark's head, grabbing hold of the two long shining black horns. He pulled himself up to see and almost fell over backwards.

They were standing in an anteroom with a massive desk half buried in stacks of books, globes, charts, maps, and a golden bird-less bird cage with three small books and a plumb-bob inside (Tink didn't want to know). They stared in amazement at a stuffed wombat that looked like it was being used for an ottoman, and a huge stuffed (Tink hoped) great horned owl stretched out in full flight, hanging from the ceiling, a large swivel chair, and in its own niche, a large brass and silver hookah. Stretching back into the dark were floor to ceiling book shelves, making up a library that most small towns would vote bond issues upon. OK, maybe only kill or wreck mayhem over.

Standing next to the desk stood Flith with his tail arched up high, and a globe lantern suspended from the tip near the rudder. "Anyone for tea? I was just putting on a pot of orange pekoe with a hint of blackberry mint." He offered, "Dee, Tink. It is very good you know."

Dvark broke the spell and stepped one step forward, "Um, Flith, we really came for the pattern for the frame-" His head bobbed up about a half of a neck worth and his ear wings flared. "Blackberry mint? As in lower Siberia blackberry mint?"

Turning, Flith happily clapped his claws, "Of course from lower Siberia silly, the northern stuff is totally inedible you know." Looking back over his shoulder, he looked for Tink who was now shamelessly hovering up and down in the stacks of book selves. "Tink, Tink, join us in tea?"

"No thank you," returned the muted answer.

"Well," started Flith, patting the cozy onto the steeping pot. "We'll just let that steep as we go over these patterns." Turning to the desk, he rolled out several schematics of patterns. "I wasn't sure about the location you were focused on in France, as well as the Neoclassical stretching for almost thirty years, with the two schools of classic emphasis of Roman as well as the Greek to draw from, so I kind of made up some rough sketches of different areas and periods to go over . . ."

Dee had long since stopped listening and his eyes were jumping from one fovea to the other as he marveled at the detail and polychromatic play of the subtle hues that Flith had penciled or inked into the patterns. He looked up with newfound admiration for the little known fellow worker that hid in the wall. "You drew and painted these?"

Timidly, with a soft draw of air, the archivist admitted, "Yes."

Astounded, Dvark asked, "When? I only asked you for the research a few weeks ago." He leafed through dozens of pages containing many intricately drawn, detail rich patterns, each one more exquisite than the one before.

"Oh," Flith shrugged as he quietly poured the tea into eggshell cups that were almost clear in their thinness and translucent splendor. "Oh, here and there, I find time." Setting down the pot and resetting the cozy he looked up and away at the ceiling, "some days, some nights. I don't know. It all just gets done somehow." Handing Dvark the cup and saucer he settled down in his chair. "Sorry I don't have any honeyberry scones to offer you, but I ate the last one a day or so ago." Closing his eyes, he sipped in the nectar of the tea.

"Dee!" Tink came shooting out of the back, coming to a hover inches from Dvark's nose and teacup. The dark Russian dragon was also relishing his tea along with long lost memories from his youth. "Dee."

One eye opened to examine that which was ruffling his smoothed countenance. The tiny mud green dragon floated patiently in midair doing that irritating hover thing with no visible movement of his wings that drove Dvark or Chang nuts because they could not figure out how he did it.

"Flith has a whole shelf of books about Celtic patterns," Tink bubbled, "with those 'twisty-beasty' things of rabbits and foxes and bears, oh my, they are so very. . . very . . . well, just very."

"Oh, you like Celtic patterns, young Tink?" Flith slowly fought his way back to the present and injected himself into his realm of knowledge and experience. "You know, the Celtic knot as chiseled in stone, precedes the tying of the Gordian knot." He leaned forward and the lantern still hanging from his tail appeared to glow brighter as his eyes also seemed to glow. "You know, the Romans had a set of interlacing knot patterns of their own . . ."

Outside of the wall, in a much different reality, Guff was looking for Tink. As he poked his head into the Empire of Fabric he noted that Pu was standing in the middle of the room and directing a modest sized greenish-blue dragon folding fabric in one side of the room, and a bluish-green twin rolling fabric in the other end of the storeroom. Guff smirked to see "The Twins", Green and Blue, or in their proper dragon spelling, G'Rn and B'Lu, put to constructive work where there was no room for mischief.

"Yes sir?" Pu asked as he noticed Guff.

"Oh, I was looking for Tink."

Pu simply pointed at the one wall not lined with shelves. The wall that was the backside of the matching wall in the great workroom; in theory, the other side of a 6" thick wall should be Dvark's work bench area; but Guff knew better, and as he listened very carefully, he could hear a muted version of Flith lecturing on something in which he was well versed: history.

Smiling, Guff nodded to Pu, who returned the gesture, and walked back into the workroom. Scanning about, Guff realized that the end of the workday had come and gone, and most of the crew had "flown the coop" as it were.

Too big to squeeze through the mysterious passageway to invade Flith's domain, as much as he really would love to sometime, he knew he needed to break up the education that he also knew could be captivating for many hours past the passing of daylight, as Flith had no track of any time or other concerns. Stepping to the passageway of the cloistered panel, he simply called out for Tink and Dee.

Tink was immediately to respond, and Dee was slower and more reluctant, as expected.

"Tink, if I could see you for a few minutes in my office," Guff jerked his head, granting him permission to precede the bear, "and, Dee it's after hours, so you can either return to the wall, or go home as you wish." He looked at the old friend with a smile and an arched eyebrow. "It's your choice." Laughing, he left the pattern master to his own demons, as he guessed that Dvark, as usual, would be drawn back in to den of Flith, as a bee to a flower; and he was not very often wrong.

"Tink, my little buddy," Guff sank down into his favorite chair. "We need to talk about what we can expect this year as the summer winds down." He reached out instinctively for his coffee mug, but suddenly remembering Tink's favorite resting place, he moved the mug in Tink's direction.

"The end of summer, sir?"

Guff got up and rummaged about in the shelves a moment then excused himself, returning with a mug of steaming coffee. "Yes, the end of *this* summer." He resumed his seat as Tink climbed into the empty mug on the desk.

"This is the year that the Fairy Princess will be revealed, and we have quite a local community of affluent fairies in the area. In as much as they are always looking for ways to leverage their position, I expect that we may see an uptick in the fairy traffic as well as maybe the gnomes and some humans." Guff scratched behind his left ear as he cocked his head and looked sideways at the ceiling.

"Fairy Princess?" Tink was confused but intrigued.

"Sure. I believe this is the year, and it's always about the end of the summer or early fall sometime; I forget when exactly," he sipped his coffee. "It's not like it's really often enough to really remember these things. After all, it's been almost a hundred years since the last time."

"Fairy Princess?" Tink was stuck on a concept or title . . .

The sonic boom rattled the windows and Guff heard a few of the smaller forest denizens cry out with tiny "eeps" and rustle for cover in the under forest, bushes and forest duff or detritus of rotting foliage. "Sounds like Boomer is in a hurry," the bear laughed.

A streak appeared in the courtyard. "Tink!" The fire red and orange medium sized dragon hovered just outside the office windows, "Oh, hello Master Guff."

"Good evening to you too, Boomer." Laughing lightly, Guff acknowledged his smallest worker's sibling and another dragon Guff considered as a friend. "What is on the agenda this fine spring evening, boys?"

Tink looked to Guff, to Boomer and back to Guff.

Boomer answered instead, "We playing team drop-ball down in the pasture. Some of the other subsonic messengers and I, and I wanted to know if Tink is off and can be my partner?"

Guff smiled at the thought of how dragons play ball. A neutral dragon tosses a ball weighted in such a way as to cause it to erratically fall from the 10 or 12,000 feet, through two sets of players. Whichever is lowest on the score gets the higher flight "perch", and if they miss the flittering ball, the next team gets a try as the ball continues to fall. Guff guessed it would be fun to watch if you could fly and actually see everything. He also guessed that was the reason it never caught on for national television broadcasts. Chuckling and waving his paw, he released the two dragons that disappeared into the waning afternoon.

Continuing to ponder the upcoming event and the resulting business ramifications the Princess matter could evoke, he thought that he should maybe leave himself a note to talk it over with Tink, and if nothing more, Twill, as she would be the most affected.

Leaning back in his chair, he listened to the buzzing that was coming from the blooms just below the windows, as well as the many sounds and smells that wafted his way from the forest. His large head rolled lazily on the back of the chair as he looked out through the rippling glass windows. The eighteen dragons and one hedgehog on his shirt slowly faded and disappeared as the general color of the shirt shifted to the midnight blue of night. Guff's eyes drooped shut as he slowly began to hum to himself.

Chapter 3

A Day of Fairies

The leaves in the undergrowth rustled along the perimeter of the forest around the small stone patio in front of the Paws & Claws Fine Framing Atelier. The rich carpet of the hostas' wide deep green leaves were pushed aside as a rumpled once-red stocking hat moved from plant to plant in a winding path like the fin of a shark among summer vacation swimmers.

Tink's chin rested on the ceramic mug's rim, mossy gray brown on aged white that almost looked like a reflection of his skin. His eyes were open, but the back patio was not what he was seeing. His mind was replaying the torrid visions gathered from the day before: clutching his brother in a death grip as they hurtled through the air at blinding speed. Tink had never ridden much on his brother's back like some of their more adventuresome friends; he was just a more "go slow and safe" kind of dragon, at least until yesterday when the call came from a good family friend from far away. Their clutch of eggs was about to hatch, and they had requested Tink and Boomer to be there as witnesses.

Even as the dragon flies, three thousand miles is a long way, except for Boomer who, flying many times the speed of sound, daily flew that far most mornings as a Rapid Messenger.

The flight had started routinely and over territory that was familiar to Tink, but as they rounded the Steel Mountain and turned east, Boomer had decided that Tink could handle a little speed and had pushed the limit of their two bodies combined. If it had not been for his brother's forethought of providing Tink with goggles, his eyes would have flattened from the air pressure. As it was, the view was a little psychedelic in that at sometimes the air compressed in such a way that the light refracted and the landscape colors changed from greens and blues with brown to oranges and purples with gold and silver flashes. Although enduring the fast ride was an extremely scary experience, by the return flight after the hatching of the twin girl dragonesses, Tink had started to settle in and enjoy the colors and sights.

Now from the safety of his mug, wrapped in the warmth of the sun tumbling through the window, the visions were friendly and mesmerizing. The color combinations were realigning into combinations that may someday grace a picture frame or a mat around pictures of his brother's travels. Tink's muddy brown eyes rolled and tiny flashes of gold glittered though the pupil in bursts that were briefly visible and then gone, all unbeknownst to Tink.

The glaze in his eyes flashed away as he glanced up at the hostas' movement. Uncontrollably his nostrils flared as if about to throw flames or sniff the air for strange smells or danger. The last large leaf moved up and away from the patio, exposing a gnome in an unusual bright orange one-piece jump suit and a rumpled dirty once-red stocking hat that matched his muddy red clogs.

As the largest of the three Neffel triplets stepped out onto the patio, his head snapped up and focused on the slight movement of Tink stretching his wings in the window. Ned raised his thumb to his fuzzy ear and stroked it upward in a gnome salute as a hello to his friend Tink. Tink wiggled his eyebrows as much as he was able - not much, but enough for the eyesight of a gnome.

The hostas behind Ned shook slightly once again as Nat and Norm joined their bother in the sunlight. Tink waved as he noticed that there was a package under Norm's stout right arm. The dourest of the three just scowled at the tiny dragon sitting in the coffee mug warmed by the sunny window. Slowly a little twitch jerked at the corner of his mouth as he recognized his friend that he had not seen for several years.

As the three passed across the patio to the front door, Tink, in anticipation of someone's needs, began to climb out of his private domain - but he found himself stuck. He wiggled his back claws, and they worked and he could feel the smooth ceramic of the mug; so, that was not the problem. He pushed down on the rim of the mug with his arms and tried to help with his legs, but still no good. Next, he tried to turn around but the base of his tail was stuck securely. A very quiet and tiny "Help," escaped from his mouth accompanied by a puff of frustration from his nose that had the smell of North Forest stinkweed. "Glue," he thought. "Twin trouble!" he exhaled in a low (for Tink) rumble. It was not the first time he had been the recipient of the Twins' special talent for practical jokes and stunts.

A silent long blue flame that smelled of Wintergreen and Spearmint flared from around the corner. An ice blue nose followed as a precursor to the swirling irritated icy blue eye of Twill. "What are you doing Tink?" she whispered, "Guff has called nicely for you three times already." She flowed around the door into the office like an arctic stream, thick and chilling, her body, wings and tail oozing and swelling into a large tableau in front of Tink still stuck in the mug.

"The Twins!" Tink moaned with disgust. "Glue, I think - but I can't see."

She leaned into Tink and pulled him forward so she could look at the base of his tail. "Hmm," she rumbled like a distant avalanche, "You're going to need to stop by and see Dvark on your way up front," as she released an icy blue flame that was colder than any ice. The glue shattered and released its hold on Tink's now frozen backside.

"Ow, but thanks," Tink called as he disappeared in search of Dvark's hot flame, leaving Twill to shake her head at the Twins that refused at ninety-four years old to grow out of their childish antics. Then she chuckled about seeing Tink flying off with his entire backside frozen in the shape of the mug.

"TINK!" Guff barked impatiently from the front counter.

"He's getting mad son, you'd better hurry," Dvark chided.

"I know, but quick, unfreeze my bottom," as he flipped over in mid-air to present his backside.

Dvark, on seeing the shape and blue chill started to chuckle but then quickly blasted the offending sight and a last jab of a pointed flame sent the tiny dragon on his way. The time for mirth would come later as he "discussed" the frozen flesh with the creators of the "blue bottom."

****

"Tink," Guff started, "I know you remember the Neffel brothers." He cleared his throat to accent his meaning that Tink "had better remember." "Well, they have a project that I think you should be involved with as it will require diminutive hands the size of yours to get the detail just right."

"Ned, Nat and Norm: Mister, Mister and Mister Neffel," Tink's eyes twinkled and whirled in delight of their longtime friendship as he gave a dramatic little bow, "It has been entirely too long since you graced Paws & Claws doors and garden." His joy was mirrored in the three bushy bearded faces, as the gnomes' heads bobbed up and down like a calliope with appreciative peeps and squeaks.

Tink stood beside Ned as he looked at an exquisitely painted image on a tiny bisque plaque. The scene was of a very famous and special mountain to dragons called K'Tng, or The Kell, meaning The Dragon's Heart. The sky in the painting seemed to change color as Tink moved. Tink lightly braced himself by holding onto the edge of the table, and the painting continued to change, and the sky darkened as the mountain shone with a golden glow of day's last light as the sky erupted into a riotous evening sunset high in the upper reaches of the Himalayan Mountains. "It repeats every hour the same scene of that day on The Kell."

"Is it magic?" asked Tink.

"No," started Ned.

"It just knows," added Nate.

"Or so we think," finished Norm.

"It's our gift to the new Fairy Princess when she is revealed and weds," continued Ned.

"So we want it special," added Nate.

"So we thought we would ask the advice of a dragon we trusted," completed Norm.

"And so we thought of you," they chimed together in three part harmony.

Tink just looked from one to the other blinking and finally, with his face begging for help, he looked to his Master Guff. Tink had never designed anything on a frame, much less a whole frame or even close. He was overwhelmed and did not know what to say or do.

"Humph," Guff commented, "I suppose that Tink might want to consult with one or two of the other dragons as to what would best exemplify and complement the soul and center of their universe," as he adjusted some of the corner samples on the wall, fidgeting at being in a position of subjugation instead of that of the Master. "Maybe Twill or Dvark might have some nice input as they are kind of more from that region. Ahhemm . . . sort of . . . well respectively," fidgeting now with the mat samples. "And of course, there is Chang who is basically from right next door, so to speak."

Before the conversation could become any more strained or uncomfortable for especially Guff or Tink, a tiny gust of wind opened the door, allowing the entry of a band of fairies. Fairies dressed in some of the finest clothes Tink had ever seen. He had heard of cloth woven from spider web thread, but he had never been so close to see the shimmer of the multi-hues rippling across the cloth as they walked or gestured with their hands.

The three brothers turned as one and studied the squadron of royal courtiers, for it was obvious that was exactly who they were. The large room seemed to become a bit colder than it was just moments before, as the gnomes and fairies reacted to an ancient feeling towards each other that nobody today remembered or understood. The room continued to literally fill with fairies of all colors of skin, eyes, clothes, shoes, hats or what Tink thought may be hats, for certainly those long thin white feathers weren't really growing out of the side of that lady's head.

Tink's eyes continued to get larger and larger as he experienced his first real look at such an enormous gathering of fairies in one spot and so close up at that. The brothers turned back to Tink as one. "We will leave now,' started one, "Please let us know what you derive from your consulting," continued another, "We will look forward to your thoughts, Tink."

The three lifted their red hats, and swept them down across their legs as the Neffel trio bowed as one. Then turning, they wound through the throng of fairies and out the open door still flowing with more multi-colored denizens of the deep forest. And with the departure of the gnomes, the ensuing surge of colors floating in the air or standing on the floor seemed to change color and harmonize in hues of pastel morning on a dew strewn pasture with soft pinks blending into gold and frosty blues with undertones of fresh yellow green tips of new day grass. The colors melded and blended with a distinct ebb and flow except the taller couple in the center of the charge of winged visions. These two were quiet, reserved and colored in clothing and head wraps as shiny black as the heart of volcanic glass. Deeper than a moonless night sky, yet with tiny specks of twinkling lights as certain as a thought during sleep or a shadow, caught out of the corner of one's eye; definitely something Tink had never seen in his brief eighty-three years of life.

As the two silently stepped forward presenting a largish (for them) package to Guff, Tink quickly made his excuses and fled toward the workroom with a still slightly "frosty" tail floating behind him. Guff watched with his one eye narrowed, assessing in curiosity, but also knowing that the answer, most assuredly, rested with the Twins.

"Jeeter, Dee, Twill, front please." Guff's call released Tink from returning to work holding frames for Dvark, as he would probably be busy with the fairies for the entire afternoon. Therefore, Tink grabbed his lunch pack and escaped into the back patio, too afraid to look at the mess in the bottom of Guff's mug, seemingly positioned there for his comfort.

As Tink settled under the shade of a hosta leaf on a smooth flat quartz rock, he had no way of knowing that Twill's ministrations were more concerned with cleaning the evidence out of the cup than releasing Tink. After all, it was the burden of an aunt to look after great grand nephews, no matter how distant they are or unknowing. Therefore, Tink settled down to a favorite summer lunch that his mother occasionally loved to spoil him with: fresh baby spinach wilted with tiny carrot starts, pickled beet cubes all wrapped in slivers of cucumber and dipped in plum sauce.

Tink slowly chewed his first bite and savored the tiny charred bits of sweet nettles in the plum sauce his mother made. In his school days, the contents of his lunch pack could trade for far more food than he could ever consume, but as was his nature, he shared instead and made many of the fastest friends that anyone had ever made across many groups and type of students.

"I think that sauce is one of the most wonderful smells I ever happened upon around here," a voice amongst the hostas pronounced.

Tink stopped chewing and thought about the voice. Searching through his mind, he decided he did not recognize the voice. He slowly turned to see if perchance he could spot the person speaking among the plants. The hostas were silent. A light breeze gently moved the leaves and stems ever so slightly but was not enough for Tink to catch a smell of anyone. He was beginning to think that maybe he was only imagining the voice and started to open his mouth to take another bite, when it spoke again.

"I once heard that such a smell used to be inhaled near the school, but only during the warmer seasons, when the children ate outside," the voice continued. Now it had Tink truly curious.

Not feeling the least bit threatened, Tink commented, "It might even smell better if you were closer or even chewing on some," he invited.

"I thought you would never ask!" the voice shimmered past his right ear as a musty and slightly battered looking pixie ducked under his wing and plopped down next to him. He blinked at the rapid movement and thought - what a day of firsts this was turning out to be!

Tink looked over his lunch partner. Her pink top with a graphic stylized daisy was more dirt and plant rubbings than pink cloth and if he were to describe the original color of her leggings, his closest guess would be at peat or just mud. Having never seen a real pixie, much less up close, was not sure if they usually had wings with battered edges, and what for the entire world looked to be moth holes in the membranes. Her hair was sort of a mouse brown and hung limp and stringy from under a wide paisley patterned headband, and down about her head and shoulders. A good washing would help a lot, both clothing and body, he thought, but would never say aloud.

Tink decided that her face, and especially her nose, was somewhat cute, in a "roughhousing about the muddy garden with your brother" sort of way. Nevertheless, her eyes were limpid blue as the full moonlit frozen fiords that he had seen from his brother's back the night before. He felt like he could just fall into them and swim about and be refreshed and be welcomed to do so. As his mind wandered lost in her eyes, those eyes were busy appraising him as well. Mossy mud dull and of nothing special, but his mouth looked capable of a warm and friendly smile for a friend and his eyes were afire with the wonder of life.

"And what do you think about sharing your yummy lunch with a dirty pixie?"

"So," he swallowed, "you *are* a pixie."

"Duff," she said as her grimy right foot gently kicked at the rotting leaves on the forest floor.

"Yes," Tink nodded in agreement. "It is the cycle of life. Green leaves turn brown and fall to the forest floor where they rot with other vegetation and become duff. Duff rots further, becomes fertilizer, and breaks down into the earth providing minerals and nutrients needed for the trees to grow new green leaves." He turned to look at the dirty face of the pixie. Her mouth began to open as if in shock.

"It's true," he flustered.

"No," she laughed, "Duff. It's my name."

"Oh," he said softly.

Tink slowly chewed a veggie ball dripping with plum sauce. His eyes whirled with tiny flashing flecks of gold as he stared at nothing and actually thought of nothing either. Just slowly chewing, and as he did, his mind slowly turned a page or slipped a cog or did something that brains do.

"Duff."

"Yes?"

The silence was long and in the time of his thought, the tiny fire beetle crawled half way across the small stone laid patio, three boring beetles became lunch for the red-shafted flicker woodpecker, and the pixie next to him started to hum quietly. Not humming as if it was a song, but humming like a freezer humming late at night out in the garage - distant and cyclic but somehow reassuring.

"Why?"

"Why what?"

"Why name a child after the droppings of the forest floor?" Tink's eyes had stopped their whirling but one or two of the tiny flecks of gold remained. Duff recognized this as something that had not been there a few minutes before, but did not know why.

"You don't know anything about pixies do you?" she asked with a smile, delicately taking another veggie ball from the bath of plum sauce and dropping it in her mouth. She chewed as she studied the tiny dragon face studying her. "We all get named from parts of the forest. A pixie might be found under the lip of a rock and his name drawn from that rock. Nobody is as simple as "stone" but maybe Gneiss, or Malachite. My mother was Brook and my father I think was Blaze, the mark light-ning makes when it wraps around the outside of a tree.

"You think his name was Blaze? You don't know for sure?"

"Hmm, not really," she pursed her lips, "I'm also not really positive my mother was Brook; but it's something I like to tell myself. It helps me with my fear of water," she said wiping her hands on her leggings, and smiling shyly out of the upper corner of her eyes at Tink.

She continued to explain the nature of how pixies are not actually "born" as in a mother giving birth to a baby. It is more as if they are "found" in and around the forest - in a peapod, or cleft of a rock, knot-hole in a tree, or even in the duff of the forest floor. The "homed" ones are "found" and raised by other pixies who become their "parents". The rest are reared pretty much by whoever finds them. In Duff's case, a pair of chipmunks for the first few years, then there was a grumpy old badger, a deer fawn for a summer, a clutch of partridges, and for the last many years with a soft and kind one-eyed old slider turtle in a mud hole down by the creek. Not exactly what one would think of as a stable home, but for a pixie, not at all unusual.

Tink sat eating slowly, listening to Duff and learning more about the forest within several miles than Tink had ever learned in the last seventy-five years. The difference between Tink's world of flying over the giant hosta leaves, and Duff's world crawling and walking under the cool green spread of those same leaves was like the difference between daylight and the dim world of dusk, where everything loses its color and there is no uniform light.

As Duff spoke, she also hummed. Not like as a human or a bear would hum, but more like a cat purring. The sound came from some-where deep in her body, from a place that was not controlled or even considered. In fact, it was not even clear if Duff even knew she was humming. Moreover, if that was not strange enough, there was a har-mony coming from the body next to her - and dragons do not hum. Well, they could in their throat, but they would more likely just sing as Chang did, and Dvark was asked repeatedly not to do. However, Duff and Tink were definitely humming, in harmony, and neither heard it. They sat there, eating veggie balls with plum sauce, the very smallest dragon and the dirty pixie with the tattered wings.

Only one other soul heard their hum for it was vibrating within his chest as well and he knew what it meant. He slowly closed the window in his office so he could better listen to the humming in his chest. Guff smiled at the knowledge of the very powerful secret that nobody else at this time knew, but had everyone guessing. He leaned back in his great comfortable chair, gently closing his eyes and dozed while listening to the hum in his chest: a hum that was two hundred years coming.

Chapter 4

A Quick Trip of Brotherly Bonding

Tink was already tired as he dragged himself out into the patio walking, not flying, with his tail trailing heavily through the dust on the flagstones. In order to keep the caustic fumes away from him as Dvark "aged" the large gold frames they were etching with acid and scorching to make the acid rot the gold. Tink had stood braced by tail and one wing, holding the frames and continuously fanning his other wing for the last three hours.

It's one thing for a dragon to fly for three hours over say an ocean or cold mountain range, but it is much more stressful to stand bracing against the thrust of the wings for three hours. Combine this with the sheer physical strain of supporting a frame that is eight or ten times your size and weight and it is a whole different matter. Dragons are incredibly strong for their size, but there is a limit, and Tink felt that he had just found that point.

The entire shop had been working on a huge order until late the night before and started back up in the chilly hours before dawn. The wood chips about Chang's table were deeper than most of the smaller dragons if they even dared stand close to the maniacal tool-wielding dervish. The twin troublemakers, Green and his brother Blue were now both so completely covered from painting and sanding the white dusty gesso under coating, their names should be White and Whiter, if anyone had the energy to tease them. The shop was buried in the work and so totally focused that it took the keen fuzzy nose of Guff to smell the trouble starting - singed dragon flesh. Not yet a full burning, but getting close; so Guff had called mandatory nap breaks. The immediate result being two large thuds as Pu and Pol collapsed in the fabric room where they had been wrapping mats and liners in fabric all night in order to keep up with the rest of the crew.

Too exhausted to fly across the ancient slate flagstones of the patio, Tink dragged two wings and dragged his tail (which was sound asleep) behind him. With each step, Tink knew he was closer to the mug that Guff had thrown out under the cover of the hosta leaves in the forest edge. There were still a few small chunks of the Twins' glue left in there, but Tink's tail base seemed to be getting used to them. After all, if it had not been for his having been glued into Guff's cup as a mean practical joke, Guff would never have thrown the mug out in disgust. And, that would mean that Tink would still be suffering the indignation of occasionally settling down into that last bit of cold coffee. A decidedly rude awakening when all he sought was a warm spot in the sun

Tink moved the overhanging hosta leaf up and out of the way as he ducked under. His nose leveraging over the rim of "his" coffee mug as his rolling eyes inspected every detail including the ever-present crack just to the left of the handle. His right hind leg and left wing tip caught the rim and he curled into a small ball that rolled over the edge and plopped down into the mug in one twisting roll of a move. The first puff of dust came out in a muted snore as his jowls landed gently on his left arm that ran along the rim. He was sound asleep and never noticed the small foot sticking out of the dead brown leaves composting on the forest floor behind the hosta stems. Tiny dirty toes twitched once, then again and then they were still. Under the leaves, Duff the pixie's quiet little snore first synchronized and then harmonized with the deep thrumming that resonated from Tink's mug, a most curious duet.

The sun warmed the edge of the forest and the wee creatures came and went about the business of keeping the forest running smoothly. Squirrels were gathering and burying nuts, ants were moving bits of nutrient back to the nest, beetles were changing one nutrient for another and the larger animals went about their labors as well. All of the forest was busy and vibrating with life and activity except under a certain hosta next to a tall Douglas fir tree near a clearing that was the patio entrance for an amazing picture framing business. Under that canopy of leaves, the harmony of tiny snores melded and made those in earshot happy. And a bear with very good hearing twitched his fuzzy round ears and pulled back as the large warm smile confirmed where his special employee was, and with whom. He took a long sip of good strong coffee from his new mug as the thought flickered through his mind about how it was going to be a very long day for both him and Tink; even though Tink probably hadn't remember it yet.

A nap, Guff thought, what a great idea as he gently set down his now very personal coffee mug that was actually too small for Tink to sit in and he glared at the now smaller cup as the coffee level began to rise. Guff shook his head and the coffee retreated and disappeared as he swung around in his chair, and lifted his thick shaggy legs and the ubiquitous red clogs up to the desk. A low rumble seemingly starting from the feet and sounding for all the like of far off thunder, rolled through his large body as it almost became one with the chair.

"Guff, I've been going . . ." M'ree started as she waddled her sizable girth through the office door with her eyes focused over her bright red stone rimmed eyeglasses at a claw full of receipts. "Oh," she quietly exclaimed, as she halted. For M'ree, this was an amazing thing to watch, as it more resembled a bumping and jumping small herd of sheep than a single entity coming to a halt.

Guff's left eye slowly opened about three quarters of the way and instead of the usual twinkle was a hard marble of deep red. "I'll wake you in about an hour . . . or so," she apologized as her flock, with tails now set to reverse course, started jumping and bumping backwards as she maintained eye contact over the rim of her red stone rimmed glasses. The door followed her silently and as she just cleared the jam, she heard a very tiny click and then a hollow thud of a bolt shot into a lock. *"Funny, that,"* M'ree thought as she waddled back through the shop, *"I don't remember there being a lock on that door."* Her tail tip kept rolling and unrolling in agitation as she slowly shepherded her herd of sheep towards her bookkeeping lair and a much-deserved reward of chocolate morsels. After all, it had almost been two hours since the last reward for finding those fudged numbers in the billing. "Mmm, fudge; now there is something I haven't made in at least a month…" Her stomach rumbled, as much in sweet anticipation, as from the old dragon gas that the crew worked hard to ignore as she putt-putt-puttered by.

In the corner of the shop Dvark and Chang, who never seemed to need sleep, were quietly arguing or debating, depending whether you were an "Old School Russian" steppes dragon or the more philosophical "Old School Tibetan" dragon. The subject of their discussion was color: the flame-rotted gold had turned out to be more "verdigris" (greenish) instead of the "oxide" (reddish) that had been desired.

"I know my recipe and it had absolutely no vinegar or toad gall in it." Dvark barked more at the universe than at Chang. He knew that it was not Chang's fault, but something had happened and this was how the two old Masters could work things out - by butting the two most knowledgeable heads together and listening to the ringing of iron on bronze.

"Verdigris does not happen in the absence of a caustic acidic maturate. There had to be one present, yes?" Chang's long red and orange tendril eyebrows flailed wildly in the air with his agitation, which was matching the flaring and twitching of his tail tip. If he hadn't been a Snake dragon, and actually had wings, they too would probably been wildly moving in and out in his agitation, as were his large oversized scales that were his "flight propulsion" slowly pulsed in and out creating a slight breeze of body heated air.

The two quietly examined the tiny flecks of the rotted metal. The green was definitely the corrosive aftermath of an acid with native oil; but what, and where did it come from? Each was lost in his own diagnostic dialog as the languages diverged and melded in and out as need be. From years of close proximity to his friend and his habits, Dvark instinctually ducked and weaved to avoid the two chisels and a gilder's knife that the Asian had forgotten he had still in his tendrils' grasp as they waved about slicing the air at the end of each sweep. The quiet buzzing of dead tired dragons hummed through the workbenches as the young dragons had found their safe haven in cabinets and under tables, as was their nature, and succumbed to the nature of exhaustion.

The quiet afternoon ended when a far off clap of thunder followed almost immediately with a more localized sonic boom as something crashed through the sound barrier directly, but high over the Paws & Claws Atelier. Two bright red eyes, whirling eyes, flashed open and then slowly returned to the deep bottomless brown twinkling with stars as the large furry body reformed into the known bear. The low rumbling voice announced, to himself, "Mail's here."

The lock on the closed door ceased to exist as Guff reached the doorway that was already standing wide open as an archway. Floating in mid air, the medium sized fire red and orange dragon appeared unfazed at the sight of a dissolving door and the sudden appearance of the for-midable bear. But then, this very special courier had witnessed more strange things in his career than he would ever talk about. A simple door trick in the frame shop where his twin brother worked was an everyday occurrence to him.

"For you, sir," as he handed Guff a small envelope, "I believe it's a summons, sir. I've been instructed to wait if there needs to be a reply, sir." Guff was always amazed at Boomer's ability to just float in midair with no apparent movement of his wings. He knew that somewhere in the young dragon's wingspan, a very small movement was going on at such a speed that even his vision could not see it; but he did perceive the very slight breeze escaping from the ultra fast body.

"Thank you Boomer," Guff started as he passed a single claw through the edging of the envelope causing it to pop open. "Tink is out front in the hostas. I'm sure he heard your arrival and is awake now, and would be happy to see you." Guff started in a dismissive mutter as he began reading the missive. "I'll have a reply for you in about ten minutes." Before his paw could rise to dismiss the dragon, there was a "pop", and air was all that was left of the super-sonic courier dragon who was already out the front door. Guff turned with a 'humpf' and shuffled back to his desk re-reading the card. This was what he had anticipated, but not expected in quite the same way as it was turning out.

He slowly sank into his large squeaking armchair and the door began to refill its opening like sand in an hourglass. The left fuzzy ear twitched imperceptibly and the now tar black marbles of eyes slid slightly, looking up into the deep furrowed eyebrows. The door's progress paused, for the span of three beats of the large heart, then as the eyes resumed reading, finished sealing the portal including the click of the lock. If one were to breathe in the ancient oak of the hand-hewn closure, one would smell whatever hundreds of years old oak should smell like.

Boomer stood chuckling at the sight of the dull burning red eyes of his brother. "It must have been a long night or long day?" Boomer asked rhetorically as he lifted the hosta leaf just enough higher to shuffle under the shade himself. He shouldered into the dank humid forest earth and filled his scent glands with the heady musk of the decomposing leaves and other plant matter. "Mmm, it smells so good here," he muttered, savoring the rich earthy coffee smell of the ever-rotting forest floor.

"Thank you," tinkled a tiny voice from under the rotting dropped leaves and detritus about a nearby hosta.

Boomer twitched and smiled. "Good morning to you too, Duff," he spoke to a voice he knew existed, but had never heard, from a person he had never seen. In fact, a person so very bashful, that of the small number who even knew she existed, only a select few had ever seen much less met her.

The very red eyes burned dully under half closed lids. A smell of burned rubber seemed to be coming from the tiny wisps of smoke or steam that wafted about Tink's nostrils. He stared at his hyper-energetic brother who sat smirking at him. "What?" as Tink nodded his head up which forced his eyelids even further into his now blurred vision as he faded in and out of the waking state. Deep dark mud green bags hung below his eyes and his usually proper mouth hung open and askew from his exhaustion.

"You really don't remember, do you?" His brother asked as much as stated as he stared down at the pitiful puddle of dragon in the dirty porcelain coffee cup with its large crack. "Well," he said rising up through the hosta leaves, "I hope you are in a lot better shape at 4 o'clock when we leave for Finland." His sonic boom punctuated his statement and his disgust but barely even ruffled the low rumbling snore that echoed quietly but deeply from the bottom of the cup as if there were a large cavern hidden within the dark portions of the porcelain.

A blue jay flew through the opening between the forest and the building, hunkered in the shadows of the taller trees, and noted the strange polyphony that emanated from the hosta bed below; one of a deep rumbling and the other a soft higher pitch with a whistle squeak at the end. If the bird could have smiled, it would have maybe even chuckled as it recognized the two noises for what they were and from whom. Instead, it offered a loud cracking caw as it whistled through the tight turns between the trees and was gone.

Behind the nine pieces of glass in the window sash, cracked open to the office, a deep brown eye under a heavy lid burned with an intense smoldering heat as the rumble below uttered a blessing, "Sleep deeply, my friend, for what you are about to do, you deserve it and may you make it through the night." And, the lid slowly fell and the earthy rumple of a sleeping bear melted the light about him, and the shop slept.

Already far beyond the influence of the sleepers, the flash of the red winged messenger streaked through the sky and past a jet liner where only a small boy noted the passing of the dragon as he was watching with his nose pressed to his window. Boomer slowly turned a spiral as he thought about the delivery he was about to make, and the long journey that would take place that evening.

The wedding was taking place in the top of Norway; and Tink and Boomer had known about it for a month or two, but just three days before, they had both received word that by personal edict, the two brothers were to attend. No RSVP necessary - they were being commanded to attend. But even if they had left the minute they had received the invitation, Tink would never have been able to fly that distance in the remaining four days. And then there had been the many messages that Boomer had been required to carry and deliver because of his supersonic speed and ability to fly great distances.

Boomer had thought this sudden flurry of messages was just make work which seemed a little frivolous, but many had turned out to be very highly respected and even higher placed recipients and senders alike. Something was definitely happening or at least coming to a head. He just wished he could maybe figure it out. Not that he would tell anyone, but just to know.

As mad as he had been about his brother's forgetting what they would have to do tonight, he too had almost forgotten. And his lapse would require him to make a stop by the leather smith before collecting his brother at the frame shop. Boomer turned one more lazy roll ending upside down which allowed him to dive that much faster as he dropped at twice the speed of sound and pulled out right in front of the front gate of the large white building, startling the many guards on duty there. Captain Jake Morrow dropped his hand from his side arm and stepped out of the guard shack. "Damn Boomer, can't you ever come in just a little slower?" he chuckled in mock anger, "One of these days I might have to change my pants, you scaring me like that."

"Sorry, sir," offered the young dragon who was twice the officer's age. "This one is important, and I think I'm supposed to wait for a reply, sir."

"We'll get it right up to the office, son. Want some coffee; or would that just slow you down?" the officer asked with a grin, as he passed the message to a runner.

"It's one of those days and a bit of the black would be just the right balance for the hour, sir." Boomer answered in the ritual.

The two moved into the tiny kitchen section of the guard shack. "How long have you been carrying messages Boomer? Fifty, sixty years?"

"Seventy-one come July, sir."

The dragon floated in the air sipping the extra strong brew favored by the naval officer; and in a show of how much he was enjoying the dirt thick flavor, Boomer's ears curled and uncurled.

Captain Morrow laughed to watch Boomer's ears, as he knew the motions were as unconscious and uncontrollable as a cat's purr. "I see you like my coffee too," as he winked with first one eye and then the other, a favorite signal of friendship among dragons. "And, seeing how you have been bringing messages here to the House for longer than I have been alive, we'll stop with the 'Sir' and leave it at a simple Jake and Boomer. Do we have a deal, son?"

Boomer snickered with a tiny lick of flame slipping out of his nostrils, "It's a deal 'Old Man'". And they both laughed. The humor in the dichotomy of the disparate life spans was not lost on the two long time friends. The staffing of the guard shack had originally turned over in an annual cycle. But nearly twenty years earlier, a young lieutenant fresh off of his introductory sea duty hadn't even flinched at the sight of his first dragon, nor had the close proximity to the small sonic boom caused him any alarm (unlike the other new guard who had fainted dead away as Boomer suddenly appeared in front of him). The "Old Man" had been on extended duty as liaison ever since; and on occasion, he was even rewarded by some of Boomer's mother's famous dragon fire cookies.

As he flew his last leg of the day, Boomers internal clock was warning him that he would be a couple of minutes late getting back to the frame shop to pick up his brother, but he knew that picking up the harness would be even more critical.

The harness chaffed a little around the rear wing ports, but with Tink attached, that would allow a bit of a drag and take the edge off the rubbing. They had a bit of practice with the new idea for the harness with some short flights a few hundred miles or so, but nothing like the several thousand miles they would need to travel before dawn.

Boomer had enjoyed the previous times when the two brothers had traveled here or there. It gave Boomer some mental relief as he flew over the same mountains and plains that he flew over every day, which after 80 some years had become a bit mind numbing; but with those trips, he was now sharing his life and the world with his brother.

Tonight, though, he thought of the first ride he had given his brother because Tink "was so slow." As Boomer chuckled and smiled, the wind caught in the slightly open side of his mouth and the next thing he knew, he had a huge inflated jowl that had swollen almost to the size of his head and was causing him to turn. He bled off speed and dropped out of supersonic until he could force his mouth back in to a closed shape and return it to the needed rock hard seal. What nobody but Tink and their mother knew was that the secret to Boomer's ability to fly at supersonic speed was not the speed, but his ability to breathe and see at those speeds.

When they were just new hatchlings sleeping at their mother's chest, Boomer had a curious snore as he slept. One night his mother, by the light of the full moon, carefully examined Boomer to see if she could find the reason his breathing had a slight whistle to it. What she found was his mouth was all but welded shut, and a flap of skin drawn back and covering them completely, although facing forward, sealed his nostrils.

Alarmed that somehow he was unable to breath in this condition, it took a few more breaths for her to realize that the whistling breathing was coming from his ears. Boomer was actually breathing through his ear canals and it was the small ear hairs causing the whistle.

It was several years later that Boomer actually realized that not every dragon had four eyelids, and could see through two of them. His brother had two, with one that he could semi see through which was fine up to about 700 miles per hour. Tonight, however, Tink would have to hunker down and keep his eyes tightly shut and his head in the special cone that would allow him to be aerodynamic enough to crash through the 3,200 mph, Mach 5 barrier to get them to the farthest reaches of Finland. The two brothers would be traveling a very long way to the world of the Ice Dragons; and, some very special close friends of his, who were getting married over the following three days in the tradition of Dragon weddings and gatherings.

Chapter 5

Going North

Tink never remembered his pillow being so rough.

His fuzzy brain struggled in mud, in an effort to maybe start the process of opening the door to the possibility of maybe thinking about considering at least conscious thought as a prelude to half opening one eye to the world and trying to figure out what was that stupid water sound; did someone leave the bathtub running?

As he rolled his head over onto the other side, the normal pool of damp drool-soaked feather pillow was not there. In fact the soft cotton had been replaced by a cushion of . . . Tink slowly elevated one eyelid to a blurry landscape not of his bedroom of the last eighty some years, but a stretch of . . . sand? "*This can't be right,*" he thought, reclosing his eye. The grainy texture started to make itself very clear what it was, as was a burning sensation along the side of his face, which was somehow exposed to the late morning sun. Now his eyelid rose so that he could look down along his long nose to see what was causing the burning sensation. "*Nothing,*" he thought; "*there's nothing there.*"

Well, not exactly nothing; because the whole side of his face was prickly and burning and felt like, well, it felt a whole lot like several other places on his small body. And as he slowly pushed himself up off the sand looking ever so much like a wet droopy mop, he started feeling patches of raw skin abraded and sensitive to the sun and breeze. "Ow," Tink muttered. The fog in his mind was slowly moving about, but not exactly clearing, as he looked around.

"Where in the world am I?" was all he could get his mind to ask as he took in all of the landscape around him. The ocean looked, well, like an ocean looks. Is there a difference in appearance between an ocean and a sea? The tide was rolling onto the beach in foot high waves, which for Tink was more than a little intimidating, as he was a dragon who had never been this close to the ocean, or any large body of water at all for that matter. So the tide wasn't going to reveal anything for him. The sun was not cool or cold, so Tink ruled out Norway or Finland or maybe even Sweden; but it was not hot either so Spain, Portugal or the Mediterranean were out as well. As he looked behind him, there were just low-lying sand dunes topped with sea grasses and no large looming mountain, so that removed Gibraltar from the running. He was starting to feel like the living incarnate of the "Where in the World" board game kids liked to play. But he had no secret card to give him the answer.

He tried moving his wings, "Ouch!" He was stiff and sore, with patches of fire here and there, as he rolled his head over to look closer at the burning sensation on his left shoulder. His fine detail lens clicked down into place, and it was the first time he had ever really been aware of his vision changing, and why. He looked up and the lens roughly glided back into its hiding place at the rear of his orb. He sat down in the cool sand, hmm…. at least that did not hurt. He looked back at his shoulder, the lens slid back out across his eye, enhancing his vision. The little bumps of his skin looked like much larger bumps and it looked as though coarse sandpaper had been taken to his hide and knocked off the head of every bump. Staring back at him was a field of open little red volcanoes of raw meat and pain; and as the breeze hit the nubs, the nerve endings were aggravated even more. Now Tink rocked back a bit more on his tail and looked at the sand around him, as the lens slid back into its pocket only half way and then stopped.

Through half of his vision, as the other half was a wild blur, he could see the trench a small projectile had plowed through the damp sand the night before. Coming in from somewhere low over the water and landing more like a meteorite than an 80-year-old dragon. As he sat looking at the only evidence of destruction that he had left on the landing field and the ample body of evidence on his own self, he now totally observed, "Ouch." And with the saying realize that his mouth tasted like the burnt remains of Dvark's burnishing mud, and he began to cast about for some water or liquid that he could drink other than sea water.

After trying to walk for a few yards, he decided that he would need to fly, and with a great gritting of his teeth, he spread his wings. He proceeded to throw himself into the air with one great swoosh of his wings and next thing he found himself lying on the sand whimpering in pain as a knifing fire seared up his left wing and into his body. "Oh dear trees and rocks," he cried. The littlest dragon curled in a ball and then rocked back and forth, "What did I do?"

As the pain ebbed, he slowly uncurled from the fetal ball and began to examine his wing. There was no evidence of a broken bone or tear in the spandrel webs. Slowly he rolled the wing over, and there, sticking out of the upper surface was a small stick. A splinter from a bit of sea flotsam that had become lodged in the abraded skin, right in the middle of the widest part of his wing, and right where he could not reach it. Tink sat down hard in the sand and in sheer dejection uttered a final offended call of surrender, "Ouch."

Meanwhile his brother was having troubles of his own and his nose was about two June bug toenails away from the much larger nose of their mother, a common large green-blue with curious streaks of red that would appear when she was upset, usually from interrogating children who she did not think were quite telling her the whole story. "But mom, he was there on my back when we flew up out of the Oslo area. I do know that for sure because he made the comment about the fireworks over the castle."

"Then where is he now?" As she spoke, each word was punctuated with a throbbing pulse of the red streaks.

"I don't know," whined the courier, on the verge of tears. "We were tired, and he might have fallen off as we went south. I just don't know. In 72 years as a courier I have never lost a single letter or package, and now, I have lost my own brother." He finally crumbled to the reality and folded in on himself and lay at her feet. "I just don't know where."

She looked down at him with the duality of the two hearts of motherhood. The tearing apart of your heart for your hurting child, and the tougher love that means to kick them into rising to the occasion and doing what is needed. "Well then, if you won't go look for him, I will!" as she strode for the door. Her husband "harrumphs" and turned the paper's page in feigned indifference; for he has learned that there are times it is best to just let his partner handle the challenges when it comes to the boys.

Boomer dragged himself up from the floor, "Mother, you wouldn't even know where to begin." Slowly he skulled the air, but was not himself as he was bouncing around a tiny bit, just enough that his mother could tell how exhausted he was. "It would take you at least a day to even get in the area, and I can be there in an hour."

His mother, now blocking the door, gave him the most chilling "Mother Look," a look that could freeze a hot summer heat wave, "You're exhausted, go to bed and I'll wake you at 3, with a breakfast. Now go." The topic was now motherly settled and closed. The red courier slowly rotated in the air and skulled his way to the room he shared with his brother.

She could not be sure, but it sounded like he had even started snoring before he had cleared the door much less settled on his pad. Her heart was breaking for her exhausted son, and that she had another son who was lost somewhere between here and Norway; a rather large area to search by anyone's standards. Especially when looking for a rather small ruddy green dragon no larger than a coffee cup. As she set her alarm for 2:30 in the morning and settled down next to the now quietly snoring hulk of her husband, she was thankful for the strength she had gained from him these past hundred years, but her mind was on her smallest and (deep in her secret most secret of chambers of the heart, not of blood and muscle but that which beats with the soul of a mother) ever so slightly favored son.

The sun engaged in its fiery silent storm that ended each night sinking into the western ocean causing the sky to bleed, the clouds to flame and with one last muted shriek of protest in the form of an iridescent flash of deep sea green light, and was gone. The sand cooled, as the birds sought their roosts from the chill sea breezes and fluffed their down to bulk their forms in a ritual that the small dragon neither knew about nor could join. As he lay on the sand, he thought of his warm place in the sun in a mug owned by a large shaggy friend. And if he were much younger, he told himself, he may have even allowed himself to cry.

"How did I come to be here?" was his last chilly thought as his little body shivered in the cooling evening on the heat-stealing sands by the ocean. He was not unobserved. A short distance away, near the top of some tall sea grass, in the sliver of the new rising quarter moon, the beast panted softly. In the scant moonlight, one glistening drop of drool traced its way down the very large canine tooth above the large pink and black spotted tongue. After all, it was close to dinnertime.

"Scout, venez ici, vous oaf grande. Le dîner est en attente." [Scout, come here you big oaf, dinner is waiting.] The man in the wool jacket, corduroy pants and tall rubber boots grabbed his crushed hat in his right hand and waved it at his dog's tail that was not wagging as it usually should. "Qu'est-ce que c'est?" wondered the man as he topped the rise. In the last light, he saw a small bundle of something in the sand a few meters away, and followed his dog down the small slope to the beach below.

"Pourquoi, c'est un dragon." It is a dragon, the Frenchman exclaimed to himself and he squatted down and felt for life. "I think we have us a guest, Scout," then, as he looked closer, "Mon dieu, an injured dragon guest," he corrected himself as the dog sniffed closer at the blood around the wound. The man gently lifted the small soul up out of the sand and cradled him as best he could in what was left of his arm, without hurting the punctured wing any more than it already was. He turned, his rubber boots crunched in the damp sand of the beach of Les Hemmes, France, just west of Dunkirk, a beach famous for a failed invasion attempt during World War II. As a small boy, he had run dangerous yet vital errands for the French underground and had lost half of his face and a hand as he pulled his older sister to safety from a burning building. As the small form instinctively burrowed deeper into the muskiness of the man's rough woven aromatic wool work jacket, his benefactor turned to his companion dog and confided the sad insight, "And once again Scout, it would appear that the sands of Dunkirk are not kind to an invader."

Overhead, unseen and almost unheard was a fluttering of black wings in the inky night sky of a Leach's petrel. A small nocturnal bird who was a few hundred miles away from where he would normally be, but his duty that night was that of watcher, and tonight he was especially attentive. The small dragon had nosed in for a very hard landing earlier as the petrel had taken over from a gull. He thought to himself that it looked as if the dragon was not even aware he was landing and had made no attempt to lessen the impact by properly flaring his wings or pulling up and promoting a stall at the contact. But the human had found him, and was taking him back to his home which was next to the black walnut tree near the small swelling in the creek that ran down and out to sea near the old metal building. So it was time to pass the information along, and as he increased the flapping of his wings and turned, the increased sound caught Scout's attention and he glanced up and noted the small dark bird hurrying off in the night as if on a hunt, or a mission. Turning slowly, the battered old dog hobbled after his master and new guest; his three legs carrying him as fast as his ten years were capable of in the chilled night air. "*Mon du,*" he thought with his tongue flapping up and down, "*An injured dragon, what next?*"

#

As the sun was only a dim scratched line of golden light in the far off eastern horizon (a light that would not widen enough to reach Boomer for another hour or more), the red dragon flew upside down in a sub-sonic sweep. His eyes scanned with the wider side-ways central or search fovea, for the heat register that was semi-unique to his brother. The night chill helped, as the 110-120°F heat range Boomer was scanning for should stand out like a large torch in a dark room. Or that was what he was hoping. The kind of torch or bond fire that had lit up the wedding night in Norway as two of the oldest of dragon families finally joined with the marriage of Thor and Chil just mere hours before.

Boomer thought back on how they had gotten here in the North of France, with him looking for his lost brother at the crack of dawn. Boomer had returned to Paws and Claws to collect his brother. The good news about dragons is that they usually do not pack anything for a trip. So it was just a matter of Tink receiving permission to leave earlier than usual, but as Guff had left much earlier as had Twill, Chang had not been sure if he or Dvark was supposed to be in charge and whether they could OK the early departure of a worker. Just then, from out of the back M'Ree waddled, and with a subtle wink over her ubiquitous fire red stone glasses, asked Boomer to please deliver a very important envelope that absolutely could not wait. Since Boomer was rigged with the harness instead of his courier pack, he would just have to take Tink to hold the envelope addressed to Thor and Chil. In a flash, with Tink barely settled in behind the bullet shaped shield, Boomer had cracked the first of five sound barriers they would break that night, and he was still going ballistic vertically. At 22,000 feet, in the very thin air, Boomer rolled over, dove through the second and third sound barriers, and had just leveled out at 18,000 feet above sea level as he broke the fourth. He would be over the ocean and in colder thicker air as he broke the fifth speed barrier at 3,702 miles per hour which he would maintain for the 9 minutes it took to transit the cold English Channel and then over the North Sea where he would drop back to his usual cruising speed of 1,540 miles per hour, his most comfortable speed between the sound barriers 2 and 3.

By the time they had crossed France, the harness had loosened enough to become somewhat comfortable and did not chaff anywhere Boomer could feel. The shield was working perfectly as was his brother's ability to maintain the small arch of his wings, extending the slipstream and actually providing all the lift they needed so Boomer's efforts could be converted to propulsion and speed. It really was working out quit well. Just as long a Tink could stay awake and not fall off.

They had zoomed past a jet liner just before Calais, France and Boomer could have sworn he recognized a familiar fuzzy face in one of the windows. But the visuals at Mach 4 and recognizing something traveling over a thousand miles per hour slower just did not make any sense and besides, his chance at hitting Mach 5 was rapidly approaching and he had to focus. Later at the reception as the large ursine figure in a tuxedo stood beside where Boomer was hovering and whispered, "Very impressive flying," he knew that Guff was not referring to his ability to hover.

#

As the sun had been just starting to creep up over the northern reaches of the great Siberian expanse, Boomer had flared his tail tip to slowly bleed off the tremendous speed he had been able to maintain in the continually cooling air. The cooler the air, the denser it is and provides a better lift as well as more for him to push against. With Tink's wings arched just right, the lift had been almost perfect to allow Boomer to devote all of his effort into what would be considered a continual shallow dive, resulting in a much higher speed with less effort. The term "synergy" flittered across his mind as his right wing tip rotated three degrees to start the sweeping lazy right turn over the huge bay of Nordkin; or locally known as "az Északi-fok öble.

As they completed a last sweeping turn, two much larger dragons fell down from above and dropped into synchronized flight, Boomer and Tink became an escorted cadre for the final slow approach. It felt almost like hovering in place, allowing Tink to rise up out of the shield and take in the breath-taking landscape of the bay and the fort-like crag of Kinnarodden, the northern most point of land in all of Europe. The large golden-red dragon escort on their left chuckled, "Uf da, Boomer, you're about two hours earlier than we thought you would be."

Now allowable at slow speeds, Boomer's nostrils retracted and the stone-like lock of the upper lip on the lower jaw loosened. "It was a great flight, Sekar. The air was nice and cold and fat; I'm just glad I didn't freeze Tink to death." He chuckled, "You are back there aren't you brother?"

The small head rose above the shield and instantly became worried about the rapidly approaching great crag of a mountain. They were obviously flying directly into it. "Yes, I'm here; just a bit stiff and cold." His eyelids all snapped open as they kept gliding straight at a particularly hard looking outcropping of cold stone and ice with only a modicum of softening snow.

"Tink, meet Sekar and Tuk, Thor's wing mates. Sekar, Tuk - my little brother Tink."

The two large dragons nodded their leather helmeted heads and chuckled as Tink let out a quiet, "Eep!" as the four slid straight into what Tink's eyes told him was a solid rock wall. The entrance to the palace mustering yard and the general entrance for all dragons was actually a continuous vapor that acted as a disguise.

They alighted in front of the largest black dragon that Tink had even heard of. Its head was at least twice the size of Tink's wingspan. Its eyes were glowing with a deep dull unblinking red. If it were not for the slight movement of the gigantic wings, it could have passed for a statue. "Flight Master Ki," Boomer addressed, as he bowed his head and with a wing tip to his little brother's head, Tink followed suit. "We come in peace, and beg passage to attend the festivities for which we have been summoned."

"So, this is the little brother we have heard so much about." The dark gray polished granite floor seemed to vibrate and Tink looked about him as the sound truly seemed to be emanating more from the stone walls, ceiling and floor than from a thing of flesh and blood. "We will have to watch such a small one very carefully." The giant head lowered to within a short arm's reach of the tiny dragon, making him very aware that he would be less than a bite-sized morsel for this great dragon. Then very quietly the great dragon reduced his voice to almost a whisper, "Welcome, young Tink, to the Palace Kinnarodden. May your stay be as fortuitous for you as your presence is for us."

Rising back to his original official stance, he snapped a slight military nod of the head over his left wing, "Sekar, escort them to the aerie quarters and see that they are made comfortable. They probably would like some steam and a rest before this evening's event. Especially Tink, he looks a bit cold still; the steam will do him good."

As they started up the low winding stairway, another crew of dragons pierced the veil and landed in front of the black giant for review; but Tink was still too overwhelmed by all of the surroundings to pay attention to them. The grand stairwell alone was larger than the entire building of Paws & Claws, and certainly wide enough to accommodate the three of them as they walked up the slowly circling stairs; even if they had walked wing tip to wing tip, they would not have brushed the polished walls that glowed with stripes of light. Fascinated, Tink walked close to the walls trying to discern the source of the glowing bands. They were not evenly spaced or even true bands, more like splotches of glowing rock that were stretched into streaks. The entire tunnel was covered or included with the glowing stone in such a way that the entire space was illuminated, but without a true obvious source.

Boomer finally noticed that Tink's fascination had finally brought the little brother to a halt as he picked at the clear glowing stone where it was set against the dark granite. "It's quartz," Boomer started, "the entire Palace is lighted this way."

"But, how?" Tink asked as he resumed his ascent.

"The Great Fire in the belly of the Kinnarodden Mountain is eternal. In the chamber the pure quartz lining does not burn and its tendrils reach out through all the rock of the mountain providing a constant light. Tonight, I will show you a sight you never dreamed possible." He turned up the stairs, "Come on, I'm tired and sore and need some steam."

"Boy," Tink grumbled to himself, "A guy flies just a few thousand miles and suddenly gets grumpy for some reason." He flexed his wings and arms trying to work out the stiffness and kinks from holding the same position all night.

A bright red face flashed within one scale's distance from his own only this one was breathing a stench of rotted rock and burned rubber, the signature of his brother's irritation. "I heard that, tiny brother," he flared in a manner that may have intimidated any other, but it was the same familiar bluster Tink had experienced over the last 80 years. "And, just remember, you are never too old to be tickled until you giggle like the little field mouse that you are." Then he disappeared in a pop of the air rushing back to take the place the dragon had occupied a fraction of a second before.

The officer Sekar just rolled his eyes as if to show his exasperation at the "brothers". He waved his left claw, and called, "Come on, I'll show you where he went," as they continued their climb up through the great mountain's interior.

"Who built all of this?" Tink marveled, still dragging his sensitive claw tips used to fine details of picture frames, along the smooth walls feeling for the joining of the solid stone and the clear glowing stone and finding none.

"I don't think anyone knows. It has just always been here." The guard answered as he began to recount the stories of his growing up in the great hall. Dragon memory of living inside the great stone goes back many generations for more than a few thousand years to before the Fairy Wars at least. The 'Rodden had always been the home for the North Clan. There were other smaller enclaves, but this was always the center, the seat of power and governance.

They turned around a last sweep of the stairwell and stepped out onto a wide and deep ledge in a great cavern. Sekar stepped forward and spread his right wing out across the expanse of many miles of open air space in a stone cavern with a ceiling that was an easy mile above the floor far below and said to Tink, "Welcome, to the North Clan Hive." Tink gazed out in amazement as he watched hundreds of dragons soaring, spiraling, tumbling, or just flying to and fro about their daily errands, the air was alive with more dragons than he had ever seen in one place.

"It...it," he stuttered, "It's amazing." His head continued to bob and swing as he tried to track everything at once.

"From here on out through the rest of the day it will get fuller and fuller as the guests arrive for the wedding. So you really came at a great time while it's not busy." Diving off into the air, he called back to the tiny wide-eyed dragon, "Come, let's get you settled in, and some steam to warm you up." As Tink broke his awe and followed the large dragon in his headlong dive, thinking about what it was that he was really doing - flying inside a mountain. Dvark will never believe him and he laughed at the thought of telling Dvark an amazing story instead of the other way around for a change.

The steam was just what Tink's tiny semi-frozen body had needed, but he could not help but marvel at the sight of hundreds of crystal blue to deep midnight red dragons perched on shelves within the steam fumaroles. Flith the Archivist at Paws & Claws would have called this sight "eye candy," a visual delight that was approaching that of sweet tasty candy or at least some of M'Ree's homemade fudge or any other chocolate concoction she could possibly invent to entice him. Not that she was "sweet" on Flith or anything like that, just that there could be some rumors . . . but back to the steam tubes.

Sekar had lead Tink by falling down through most of the large tunnel then turned off and back up a slightly smaller fumaroles that would be even warmer, and for some reason carried a sweeter scent. They found an open shelf large enough to accommodate not only the much larger dragon and Tink, but within minutes, showing off flying upside down and backwards, Boomer found them. The object of his display close behind; a very small young dragon, that was almost transparent with only a hint of ice blue, hovered with blinking eyes upon seeing Tink. Boomer settled down on the far side of Sekar with no shelf left, leaving the child to either skull the air, or land next to Tink. Graciously, Tink spread his wing in offer, and she accepted.

They sat side by side both with large eyes slowly blinking and taking in the matching size of the other. In his 83 years, Tink had met a few children smaller than himself, but not many and not that much smaller than him. From the day he had hatched, he had grown less than twenty percent larger than his birth weight, and his height a tiny bit and his wingspan not at all. So to find a child or even a hatchling that was smaller was a very rare experience for Tink, and yet here she was, smaller than he was, but only by maybe the thickness of two or three scales. And, she did not seem to be that close to a hatchling.

She twittered. A common form of what humans do when they giggle. "You must be Boomer's little brother," she twittered.

Her voice was like a tiny tinkling frozen stream of slow thickened water tinctured with miniature bells of ice bouncing over rocks, ringing them in a cascade of little chimes. He had never heard anything like it other than the ringing of Twill as she moved when her glass feathers chimed like a wind in the leaves.

The tiny blue white dragon leaned forward looking past the stunned Tink, the large Sekar and into the amused face of Boomer. "He does know how to talk, doesn't he?" she asked. And the two larger dragons leaned back into the stone wall and laughed as Tink almost became a "red" with embarrassment. "Well" she consoled, patting his jowls, I know your name is Tink; 'Tink of the Porcelain Mug,' and I am Skth, 'Skth of the Frozen Flame' and I'm sure we will be seeing more of each other these next days, but right now I need to get back to work for my aunt, Twill." As she flipped over backwards into the tunnel and dove out of sight, Tink turned even redder to realize that someone else knew about his fondness of the mug in the garden. He slowly turned his strongest attempt at "The Eye" on his brother, which proved a waste of energy, as both Boomer and Sekar were sound asleep against the warm wall. Not having any more strength himself, Tink curled into his own special fetal curl and was soon fast asleep and humming. He was unaware that another, a mere mile away in a different part of the mountain palace was also humming in a matching harmony albeit two or three registers lower, not to mention being a lot furrier.

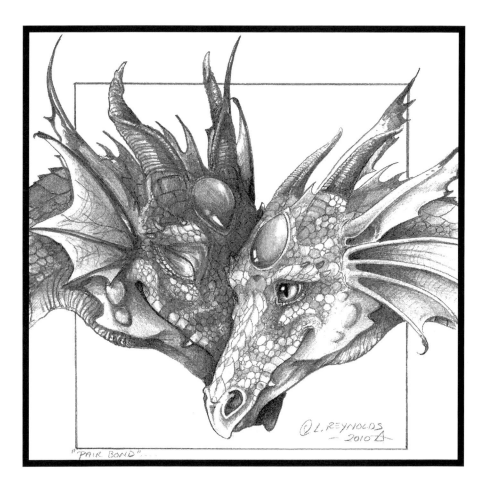

Chapter 6

Thør, Chil and the Wørld

The pinging that woke Tink sounded a lot like a small pebble tossed down the tunnels as it bounced its way down miles of hard granite and quartz crystal. The steam was a thick fuzzy blanket of white and gray playing peek-a-boo with the other wall where hundreds of different dragons - all colors, sizes and natures were shelved in the ancient volcanic vertical tunnel. The pebble pinging on the walls should have passed, but persisted. Tink rubbed the last of the sleep from his eyes and stirred, as the enormous mass of dragon bodies seemed to mimic him. The pinging now began to be centered in Tink's chest. He looked over at his brother who smiled at him.

"Remember how we used to play follow the leader and you used to try to grab my tail?"

Tink chuckled, "Well, you'd better try harder right now," as Boomer stood and levered off the edge of the ledge and began to fall in a stooping dive. Tink jumped in to the space behind his brother's tail and flipped upside down, as he dove tucked in his own fast "killing" dive. He was not much bigger than a golf ball with wings, but when those wings are inverted, they create a draft that does not lift the wings up, it "lifts" the wind down and allows the winged object to "fly" faster down than if it was just a falling object like his brother.

Tink smiled ever so slightly as he slowly flew past his brother's head, which now had some very large eyes as Boomer was seeing something that he had never seen before: his brother was out-flying him. Because of the confines and close proximity of hundreds of dragons now following the two, he was restricted in his use of sonic flight. His size and the ability to dodge others and squeeze between clusters of other diving dragons gave Tink the edge he had never had before, and he enjoyed every second of this special moment.

The bottom of the tunnel widened out into the giant cavern they had flown across earlier that day, or had that been yesterday? Measuring time without seeing the sun was very confusing to Tink. All he knew was that the pinging was getting stronger as he flew towards the huge gathering near the distant wall. Dragons flooded out of many other tunnels creating a cloud of winged bodies floating above several other non-dragons that strolled along the great parquet floor of black stone and dim crystal light. The eerie light of the gigantic space was now dimmed by the sheer mass of bodies and wings all being drawn as if by a magnet toward the pinging center of attention - on the raised dais stood an ice blue dragon flanked by two dragons as white as plaster.

In moments, which were probably more like tens of moments, but felt like a flutter of a heartbeat or three at the most, the host of bodies came to rest. As wings were tucked in and larger dragons hunkered down in deference to those behind them, the mass slowly coalesced and compacted. It did not much matter, as the acoustics of that section of the chamber were made to address a large gathering, such as a wedding. The thrones had been removed from the dais where the three dragons now stood.

Tink had wondered how Chil, a bright red and gold dragon from the heat of the South American jungles, would look with the white talc dusting of the bonding coat that now covered her. Thor, although now technically "white", was finding it more difficult to cover the radiant red trim on his large obsidian black scales. Tink was sure that Thor had practiced long and hard to subduc this red and keep it from glowing through the white powder. The two stood stoically as the Great Councilor recited the ritual that would start their lives together, bind their hearts and families, and imprint this moment forever in the hearts and memories of those attending. For this was the ancient way of the dragon to mark the passing of time - the notation of great events.

The pinging had changed and it was now a slow dull low-toned double drumbeat as the two white dragons were drawn closer together by the ritual recited by the councilor. The "Bonding" is as much about the gathering or those gathered as witnesses, as it is the ceremony. Even though everyone will refer to them as husband and wife, the proper term is "Prime Bonded" as they are the primary members of the gathering and the focal point of the bonding. In addition, it is the gathering as a whole that is being bonded. Every creature (and some would say the stone too) could feel the beat thrumming in their hearts. And it is that drumbeat of lives coming together, a pulse of the blood of two beings becoming a single heartbeat and the entirety of the gathering becomes the fortress that protects that bond and all but guarantees the endurance not only of that bond of the two, but also for the entirety of the gathering and therefore the community.

As the Great Councilor finished, she reached down with her right hand into a stone vessel that contained pure rainwater. With her wet claw she gently slapped Thor on the middle of his face between the eye ridges, and with her claws outspread, around his facial jewel. The wet claw formed a gooey white claw print in the talc. The Great Councilor again wet her claw and repeated the ritual, only this time more softly, on Chil, then leaned forward and kissed her nose, as a great-great-grandmother has the right to do. The Great Councilor turned, offered up her claws as she descended the great stone stairway leaving the two white coated dragons alone and exposed on the dais, finally holding hands and facing the crowd for their blessings to be bonded.

Tink dove and grabbed a hold on the nearest large leg he could find as he surely did not want a repeat of his first wedding storm. On that occasion he had been blown right past the bride's head and ended up covered in white for the rest of the night. A large claw reached down and plucked him from the shelter of her massive blue leg, and Tink heard laughter as the large dragon flicked him up in the air, caught his legs and held him aloft saying, "Blow for the good of the bond, little one. I'll hold you safe".

Tink began to feather his wings as if sculling backwards in the air but only gently. If he was larger, or at work, his tail and one leg would be bracing backwards as the thousands of dragons below him were doing. As each gently fanned the wind forward, the power of the combined winds was tremendous and aimed directly at the two white statues before them. As the wind hit and took effect, the talc swirled and dissipated from the couple, leaving them in their natural color, but with a limning trim here and there, and a claw mark on their foreheads and upper snouts. They were now bonded and Tink began to yell and clap as the whole chamber exploded with the same good cheer. A good Bond, a good couple and finally North and South united.

"Well little one," the large blue began as she lowered the now hoarse Tink, "At least we didn't watch you flying though the bride's whiting *this* bonding." She laughed. Tink was not sure who she was, but he knew that his jowls were more than a little red right now.

"I'm sorry I didn't ask your permission before grabbing hold of your leg, but you obviously know what happened the first time I was caught in the Bonding Wind."

The blue dragon placed Tink on her shoulder as she strolled towards the other end of the chamber where all of the others were heading. "I know you don't remember me, I've changed a bit since those long years ago. I was the Grand Councilor for Schilleal and T'Wan." Her ear twitched and her gold and green eye rolled back to see if any of this was sinking in to Tink. Obviously, it did not have that much meaning as Tink was nodding and humming to the distant music that was just starting. "I can see that I'm keeping you from enjoying the party of the bonding night. We will speak again tomorrow on the beach."

"The beach?" Tink, croaked hoarsely.

"It's OK, we will talk. Go now and enjoy." Before she could shoo him away, he was gone as a trout freed from a hook.

As she resumed her slow perambulation, she thought to herself, "I have so much to tell you, and so little time." She flexed her wings, but then let them refold, as the pain was just too much for flying. Maybe a few years before she would have been flying with the young Tink in the pursuit of the revelry, but for now a quiet walk was the mode of the day. She was as yet unaware that as she strolled she left no footprint. As she made her way across the chamber, she became more transparent and illusory until there was nothing but a few sparkles of gold glittering in the light and playing on the air currents in the cavern.

"I'm telling you, I don't know who she was, but she knew me, and I think I've her before." Tink tried to convince Boomer and Sekar over their breakfast of fish balls dipped in wild berry sauce and a stack of potato pancakes. "Remember the wedding that I was blown forward through the whiting and almost hit the bride?"

"Yes!" Boomer roared with laughter as Sekar stared wide-eyed in shock and mirth. "You wouldn't come out of your room for a week you were so embarrassed. And, it had been a great bonding that had resulted in not one but three hatching of clutches." Boomer went on to explain to Sekar about the event. "When the wind happened, Tink had nothing to hold on to and was blown straight at . . ."

"Enough!" Tink exploded, turning a lovely shade of red in the cheek flairs and up along his ears. "She was there. She saw it; and commented on it."

Sekar trying to keep a straight face as his mind played out a very funny false memory of the small dragon caught in the wind of a whiting. "Where along the beach did she say she would meet you?" Now under control and official, "It is a very long beach. There are four of them actually - the Rim, the two along the inner bay and the eastern flank. Without knowing, how can you expect to find her?"

"I don't know. I guess I will just have to fly until I do," Tink said as he excused himself and flew towards the exit not knowing that three sets of eyes followed his progress. One set twinkling with delight and mischief as they followed the little mud-green dragon across the spacious open air. Rising slowly toward the large ledge leading to the staging entrance, the small ice blue dragon followed Tink at a respectful distance.

"I see you have rested and are doing better now, little Tink." The great black dragon rumbled as the large red eye wandered in Tink's direction. Before Tink could respond the dark monolith added, "And I see you have met our lovely winter flower as well." As Tink turned to look behind, Skth dove to his other side and tagged him on the head. "Good morning to you little Skth, may your journey today be as wonderful as it is that you grace this post with your presence and beauty."

Impish in every way, the little blue twirled in the air and did a flip that shot her to the left jowl of the guardian where she gently kissed him and gave his cheek flair a tiny tug, "And, a good morning to you too, Uncle." As she rolled three more turns, tapped the top of Tink's head once more and shot out the great opening.

The great guardian mellowed just a little softer around his edges, as he watched her flow out into the sunlight. He turned back to Tink who was standing on the stone floor stunned and not actually processing what was going on or what he was feeling about the impudent child, "I believe you are what they call *'it'* and it is now up to you to catch and tap her on the head." He laughed, "And good luck with that. She practices with the young guardian patrols and few manage to tap her. I will tell you though, she does favor inside rolls to the left, so if she flairs, you won't go wrong dropping left."

With that advice, the tiny mud-green dragon shot out through the mist wall and into the sunlight in search of a small blue dot in the powder blue sky over a slate gray bay. As Tink slowed to consider his next course, he was tapped once more on the top of his head as a streak shot by from above. "You can't search with your eyes, little one. You must use all of your senses!" The voice was deeper and Tink realized it was Sekar. Just then a very familiar sonic boom sounded as his brother cleared the mountain wall far enough to experience no repercussion from the shock wave.

As Tink carved a slow barrel roll through the air in a dance of joy in the sunshine, he realized that there were hundreds of other dragons out flying above the bay also in a rite of embracing the sunshine. A slow lazy column of dragons barely moving their wings or tails circled what was called a "lift," a warm column of air rising with enough lift to push the hundreds of dragons slowly higher and higher. With the power in a dragon's flight, the added boost is unnecessary, but is more of a form of relaxation or for some even meditation as the process is slow and requires calm that some say is a "letting go" of tension or anxiety. Today Tink had a feeling that the column really was a hiding place for a certain imp and headed that way to join in, but as he flew closer to the column, he also gently climbed higher to enter above where he sensed the little blue to be hiding.

As he slid into the circling mass of bodies, he smoothly captured the lift and converted some to thrust so that he was moving not with the column, but slowly around the column. As he made his progression, he changed his eye fovea to search for the smaller blue and sort out the other colors. Unknown to him, she had adjusted her flight and hide mode to match his, yet staying slightly lower and lagging just behind, therefore in his blind spot. But Tink had played this game too many times with his brother, and so when it became obvious to Tink that she was absent from his viewing, she was probably in his baffles trailing him low and behind; a sly tiny curl pushed at the left corner of his mouth as he readied his body.

The tiny winged menace flared his wings and performed a flashing back flip, much to the annoyance of the dragon behind him who had been almost asleep in the lazy sunshine's warmth. Tink cart-wheeled off her back and stooped straight down next to her flattened tail rudder, upsetting the larger dragon's nap and flight so that it caused her to fall out of the column. The mud-green bullet shot down through the flyers sorting the colors and bodies as he sped towards the tiny blue head that kept peeking in and out between two large greens. Timing his last assault, he shot in from behind the two greens to tap the top of the head . . . of another young green.

Laughter, like tinkling glass, sounded outside the circling column as Tink tried to apologize to the seemingly surprised young green, until she too began to laugh about how he had been tricked as most of the small gathering had been Skth's watch and all had tracked his valiant attempt at tagging the small blue dragon. Pointing down towards the beach, she described the area that was Skth's known favorite area to hide along the shoreline and how to sneak up on her there.

Thanking her, and as the others wished him luck with laughs and chuckles in their love for fun, Tink dove for the headlands of the bay and the grey blue rocks of the boulder strewn beach. The arctic weather beats mountains into boulders or dusts, not the sandy beaches of gentle islands in the South Pacific. The beach may appear sandy from thousands of feet in the air, but as close as Tink flew he saw that the boulders ranged from the size of his wing span to larger than buildings. They were a perfect refuge for the arctic terns nesting and wheeling about the sky at the lower levels that most of the dragons had given over to their feathered cousins.

Tink skimmed the boulder beach, looking for that little blue flash of wing, but knew that he would probably not be seeing it by flying over the rocks. He also remembered he was looking for a much larger set of blue wings as well, but he did not he imagine he would find the elderly dragon climbing upon such a rocky landscape. She would not be found on this beach. Resolved, the small mud-green airfoil lazily flipped over and began heading deeper into what the locals called "az Èszaki-fok öble" or The Bay of Nordkin. Back at the base of the bay, the softer tides had tumbled the stones to coarser sand and arctic grasses provided food for the snow-white reindeer of the region, and he thought if he were an ancient dragon out for a walk that is where he would be found. The great stone wall of the Kinnarodden was on his left and he devoted the fovea in that eye to scan the raw beauty of the crags of granite laced with the nearly permanent veins of snow and ice. This imaged created an almost polar pattern that Dvark would want to reproduce as a panel adornment instead of the same-old paisley and flowers. Tink took a moment and committed this image to his memory and he hoped he would be able to recreate a drawing of it for Dvark to follow.

Tink chuckled to himself about how even here, surrounded by the harshest beauty nature had to offer, he was translating it into patterns to apply in picture framing. "I surly am a picture framer at heart," he mumbled in mirth.

"They say that talking to yourself is a foreboding sign that your end is very near," the tinkling voice chided him from above.

Tink rolled over lazily and flew upside down, a trick that he and his brother practiced as kids long before adults told them it could not be done. Looking up into very openly shocked blue eyes, he chided back, "Didn't your mother ever tell you not to interrupt us adults when we are talking?" As he calmly continued sculling the air and sunning his tummy, he thought how it had been a long time since he enjoyed just flying for the pure joy of it instead of getting from point alpha to point zed in the day. As he watched the little blue, he realized that he also did not have anyone to just "go fly" with. His brother was always in a hurry or gone, and the other framers had their own lives outside of work. All he had were his mug and the friends from the forest, none that flew, or those that did were birds and well, birds were kind of "flighty". He watched how the wings on the little blue pulled slightly back in the down stroke but stopped where they could take advantage of the developed muscle structure of the lower chest and transfer weight towards the tail. This was the true keel of a dragon's flight; both an aileron and a rudder merely by the flick of the flat leaf at the tip. Then there was the color balance where her scales came to the chest plates and the blue edged against the cream…

Tink flipped over and pushed his flight a notch faster as his now internally heated jowls radiated down his chest, embarrassed for the thoughts that had invaded his mind about such an obviously young child. Both fovea were now on serious work duty looking for the ancient blue.

"Does this mean you don't want to play anymore?" The hurt tinted the edge of her words, echoing in Tink's chest.

"I have to meet someone."

"Who?" Was that a touch of jealousy?

"An ancient blue that I met last night, she said she would meet me on the beach today." Tink searched the now rough expanse of sands and short grasses but found no blue walking the strand among the white deer grazing on the green grasses between the shore and the rise of the coastal moraine.

Skth surged to fly alongside, unwilling to risk watching the unsettling display of nature-defying upside down flying. "What is her name?"

Not being the persistent child, but more worried she was not being told the truth in an effort by Tink to get away, she persevered.

"I don't know, she didn't say."

Now alarmed of competition, Skth lunged ahead and stopped Tink in mid air; they hovered as Skth stared into Tink's eyes seriously for the first time. Quietly she asked, "What did she look like?" A pending sense of doom quavered in her chest and her claws holding his shoulders began to shake.

"She was very old, blue, but she was that odd deep sea old color that blues get. She had a limp or funny way of walking like her feet or whole body ached. There was a piece missing of her left ear like it had been bit, and her teeth . . . I don't think she even had any." He was trying to recall exactly but he had not really been paying attention.

"There is nobody that looks that way in the hive, I would know." Skth commented quietly as she too tried to think of who it could be.

Tink searched the small blue's face and felt that he could get lost in the depth of her deep blue pupils like a tunnel in the mountain, and then he remembered, "They were gold."

"What was gold?"

"Her eyes," he recalled "They were gold with grass green around the rim and veins like grass growing toward the center where pupils should be, but weren't; just gold, broken gold that kept floating around. In picture framing, we call it "Schabin," it means the broken or just tiny flakes scraped from previous jobs and saved, instead of the smooth surface of a fresh gold leaf. Dvark blows leaves of gold onto a frame smooth as paint, but he can't blow Schabin. If we don't have enough "scrapings" we have to put whole gold leaves onto a bed of water so we can stir it and break it up, then lay it on bole wet and just pat it down instead of rub it. But that was what the gold looked like in her eyes . . ."

Skth continued for him, "And the green grew from around the eye as grass about a stone, and her head jewel matched."

"Yes!" Tink exclaimed, "Then you know her."

"Know *of* her. It's not the same." A now worried Skth pulled at Tink, "Come, we have to talk to someone." She flew across the bay and out to sea, into the reaches of the Arctic Ocean. Tink hurried to follow her, and even though the sun was at its warmest, he shuddered that it may not be warm enough that day.

Chapter 7

Nørd M'Løree at Sea

"Where are we going?" Tink wanted to know after an hour of following the usually chatty little blue dragon, now ominously silent and quiet in her flight as well. There were no little flirty frills at her wing tips, no flips of her tail leaf, just solid grinding nonstop flight.

"To the island," she said, as if he should know.

"*What* island?" Tink asked as he pushed to catch up on her right side.

"That one," she pointed. Tink searched and saw nothing but rough seas tossed about by the freshening polar wind. White caps flecked the expanse; even the shoreline and the great mountain were no longer visible. They were quite literally in the middle of nowhere, and it did not bring Tink any comfort, as dragons do not really swim well, except sea dragons and those were just a myth. He had forgotten about M'Ree and Pu who were both sea chameleons; with Pu being a rare sea snake chameleon without wings.

The day, which had been weakly warm at best, was getting decidedly colder, windier, and wetter. Tink, in his innocence tried flying even a bit high to see if there was less sea spray in the air, but found that Skth had chosen the right height that combined the least wind and the least spray. Recovering from being blown sideways for a tumble, and struggling to climb back down into a safer side draft of the small blue, he began to wonder what he had gotten himself into. Surly, someone would miss them. A search party would come get them, right? He was not reassured when he happened to shift his vision from the forward looking fovea to the side fovea and saw the near black, angry boiling cloud wall of the oncoming Arctic storm.

"Skth!" he shouted over rising wind. "There is a storm coming." Hoping his apprehension was clear and she would turn back around and head for where ever the great protective mountain was, he snuck a quick peek back over his back to only see more angry black water shattered with white caps the size of horses, large bears or maybe elephants (he had heard that they were quite large).

"Yes." She called back with a cavalier tone. "Isn't it beautiful?" She was serious. Tink was shocked and would have been wide eyed if the wind had been a bit less biting and cruel. Usually the summer storms are just puffy things. With his central fovea, Tink eyed the icy black waters below. He knew that if even one of his wings tipped into those close and deadly waves, it would be a disaster. There could be no recovery. As the wind buffeted him even more, he thought he saw a large shadow of himself under the water that came and went as the waves disturbed his view with the increasing number of white caps. He realized that only the sun directly overhead could cast that kind of shadow; his heart skipped a beat and he involuntarily popped a few feet higher in the air; shocked at what he had seen. His "shadow" turned a barrel roll and Tink saw the ugliest most vicious set of teeth flashing in what looked like a very hungry smile, and then it was gone.

"Wha-" he stuttered in shock. "Where is that island again?" He called out as he renewed his effort to fly just a little closer to the ice blue dragon for perceived protection; and maybe just a little heat. He was beginning to feel the cold that was making him stiff in the wing tips.

"Tink, if you can't see it, you will just have to trust me that it's there." The same as the curtain of mist creating the cover for the entrance to the dragon lair in Kinnarodden, the mists of the sea hid the small island from the usual view. Skth knew the island to be large, dark, and covered with ice that was too cold even to be white or silvery. The island rose merely a few hundred feet above the turbulent agitation of stormy arctic waters but stretched for several miles as its slope of black basalt slowly succumbed to the cold depths from which it had been born. Purely volcanic, the young planet had pushed this knee above the water and created a haven from the harshest weather the planet produced, a respite called Bjørnjøya or Bear Island.

Skth flared in front of Tink as the mud green thought the blue was crazy or suicidal and taking a plunge in the black waters storming below. As if a light had been suddenly turned on, Tink saw black stone underfoot, not water, and a warm stone cave where a mere second before there had been wind, rain, and probably death to such a small dragon. He touched down lightly and was surprised by the warmth of the stone itself. Looking about, he found himself in a cave that was not that overly large, but open enough to accommodate a large dragon such as the giant black Master Ki. The walls and ceiling were smooth and polished from years of water washing over the stone. The resulting high polish reflected the two small dragons hundreds of times in the black mirror as the walls reflected each other as well.

A low grinding that was more of a vibration than a sound caused Tink to look back at the opening that was now closing like a mouth seen from the inside. "Uh, Skth?" Tink quivered. Were those lighter colored rocks actually teeth?

"Come on, or we'll be late." The blue began to walk deeper into the mountain as Tink wondered if that was what it was at all. "She'll be coming in any time now." The tunnel of the cave was not as reassuring as it began getting smaller the deeper they walked, and darker too. Tink reached out and ran his sensitive claw pad tips along the stone of the wall, which felt damp like skin in a throat. Did that wall just quiver? He hurried to walk closer to the unaffected blue who prattled on about someone named M'Løree or North or…

When they turned the corner, it was as if a shroud had been dropped from his eyes. The cavern in which he found himself was a large perfect dome with a circular pool in the middle taking up half of the space. Tendrils of steam danced and slowly undulated at the surface of the light green pool and small bubbles rose and popped on the surface here and there. In the water there were what appeared to be lights rimming the pool, but when the surface smoothed out, Tink could have sworn they were balls of flame, burning steady, bright and unquenched in the water. The light from the pool eerily illuminated the massive domed stone room and highlighted niches carved into the walls that circled the pool. Set in many of the niches were carved stone statues standing on round or square pedestals. The statues were of different species, some that Tink had never even seen or did not recognize. All looked as if they took a breath, they would be alive, each quietly waiting that time or resolved that their time was past.

As he wandered, circling the rotunda Skth watched him carefully as she sat at the edge of the pool with her hand feeling the water as if it was a fabric instead of liquid. Slowly moving her claw back and forth, gripping and extending feeling the liquid.

"What is this place?" Tink asked as he almost touched one of the statues but stopped short for fear it might move. He turned to look at Skth, now under lit by the glowing pool.

"It is many things," she started, unsure of what to tell or what she could share. "Most importantly, it is where Nørd M'Løree lives. Well, when she's not in the ocean, that is."

"Nørd M'Løree? She's a Sea Dragon?" He walked closer and squatted to feel the warm water too.

"Yes."

"I thought they were a myth." He was surprised at how "thick" the water felt, and his eyes became fixed on the light of the pool.

"They are." She spoke softly as if to no one or the wind, "Now."

Hmm, Tink hummed as the warmth and texture of the water made him sleepy. The activities of the last few days had taken their toll and fatigue was winning the battle. Thoughts of nestling in his mother's lap with his head on her chest listening to her heart beating, wandered through his mind. Flowing like streams were warm memories of his young childhood, intermixed with the smells of the forest floor, the comfort of his mug, and the soft musky friendship of Duff, perching on Guff's knee talking over events of framing. He thought about the forest and flying, blending with the sheer joy of flying high over the land and playing tag among the trees with his brother. The memories of his life meandered and wove the blanket that was Tink. A lifetime that was warm and accepting, and wrapped in the waters of the pool. As Tink became aware that a hand or claw was tenderly holding his claw he gently jerked, startled but he did not withdraw. His eyes were looking into deep pools of bubbling gold, rimmed with green sea grass as it swayed in the ebb and flow of the pools of gold.

"I'm so glad to finally meet you, young Tink." The flattened face of the sea dragon emerged from the pool and Tink now gently, slowly and hesitantly withdrew his claw as he examined a face like no other he had ever seen. The thought of a bulldog, or lion came to mind; as did the words "ugly" and "scary", as his eyes wandered from the flattened nose to the thick rubbery lips and tiny earflaps. Rising dripping from the water were short powerful thick rubbery wings with serious blunt raking claws on the hinge points that appeared well used for killing food and protection.

The large blubbery body heaved up out of the water and onto what had been a dry stone floor; the idea of a walrus came to Tink's mind. The dark gray green of her body undulated as the twin tail paddles pushed her farther away from the water and to a hollowed out area of the low rise in the multi-leveled floor. *"Those are some very powerful and judgmental concepts to be throwing about. Walrus have much larger though less efficient teeth. Mine are more like the wolf fish, who also have the refined face of a cold water dweller."* Tink realized that he had heard nothing. No words had been spoken. No sound had been made. Yet, he was hearing her speak, seeing her move, the floor was wet, but there was no sound.

"Of course not; as you said, I'm a myth." Now he heard a tittering giggle from behind him as Skth joined in Tink's dream or altered reality, he could not decide which, but he welcomed the company by someone else he knew to be real or have substance.

"Tink, meet Nørd M'Løree, Thirty Second Fairy Princess and Keeper of the Shrine" Skth gracefully made the introduction with as much pomp and circumstance demand or needed in a domed cave set in a mountain in the middle of the Arctic Ocean.

"Fairy Princess? I . . . I don't understand," Tink stuttered.

"It's a long story; but first you two need some food. Skth dear, there are fish balls wrapped in sea grass, and some of that wonderful mead would be good too. I think there might be some rice cakes left, look in the third shelf. Tink, be a dear and go with her; she can't carry it all and it's been a long few days for me, I'll just rest here." As she sunk her body in to conform to the stone hollow, her wings dissolved into her back as her lower fins separated into distinct legs with feet. The scaling shifted until it was smaller and more defined into a twinkling indigo night sky. There was a general shift and the torso became a good imitation of a sheath dress on a human body down to about a mid-calf. She looked at her feet for a moment, thinking, and then smiled as small dragon wings sprouted from just above what looked like an ankle. Smiling, her head melted into a more conventional dragon head as she closed her golden eyes and lay back against the rock as if snoozing. Soon an eerie music hummed from the rocks of the domed room, or maybe the pool, which had gone darker with the lights acting more like large stars.

"There is some of that plum sauce, do you want that too M'Løree?" Skth called from the storage room.

"Yes dear, that is Tink's favorite. And I think there is some lump crab for you too." The chamber was silent except for the music. Tink looked at Skth for answers, but she just looked at him as if he was silly for even asking.

The two dragons returned to the pool, and Tink was now positive he had just eaten something that was wrong for him before bedtime, for there before them was a human body in a deep blue dress of scales, and a powdery blue dragon's head, which resembled Skth.

"I thought this form would make you less uncomfortable," M'Løree started talking in sound, "but I see that it's even more distressing."

"No, it's, well . . . I just," Tink stumbled, with his mind trying to catch up. "I just don't understand." He collapsed.

"Come here," she beckoned softly patting the stone beside her. "Come, I won't hurt you." Guiding him with her very human hand, "Maybe this will help you relax." A very fine scaled white mug grew up out of her knee as she drew her foot up toward her and the knee rose until the mug was about eye to eye with Tink in it. She lifted him up and set him into the mug to let him arrange himself.

"How did you know about my mug?" The wonder was overcoming his fear and confusion.

"It's all part of the story I need to tell you, and we really don't have much time." She offered him some small fish balls dipped in plum sauce, just the way he loved them from his mother for more than eighty years. "But you also need to eat."

Chewing on the best fish balls he had ever eaten, Tink was very content. He opened his eyes and found himself staring at the golden pools. "Was that you at the Bonding?" He asked while dipping another ball into the sauce and then into some sesame seeds that tasted kind of toasted.

"No, that was my twin sister. She was my protector, my "Patron" and now sometimes she acts as my proxy. She makes appearances for me when I am obligated to attend but occupied elsewhere. It's kind of a longer story that we don't have time for right now. Soon we will, and I promise you will understand then; but first, a little about "the Fairy Princess."

Many millenniums ago in the early days, the fairy kingdoms were locked in bitter battle. One would think that the world could get along while the wee people went about their wars. Most of their battles consisted of hordes numbering in the mere hundreds and mainly in hand-to-hand combat with small weaponry. However, this was not to be so for long. The battles took to the air after the discovery of the power of floating boats. In addition, who better to recruit for these battles than the gryphons, birds, dragons and other winged denizens of the air? Next came the invention of black powder and other explosive agents, which lead to cannons, pistols, rifles and other forms of killing from a distance and all serving to escalate the wars.

As the wars began to devastate more and more areas, especially with the advent of a bomb called the Horath, more and more creatures became involved. Humans, drawn from their fields and their cities, found themselves forced to become warring pawns in the fairies' feuds. As feuds they were, these wars were not about land, or food, or control over regions, it had all started with the bragging rights to which tribe had the fairest princess. That is right. It was all about vanity. A king could be as ugly as a snaggle-toothed wolf fish, but if he had the prettiest daughter, he had the bragging rights, and so every few years the fresh crop of up and coming princesses would spark a fresh round of killing, burning, maiming and general disharmony in the world. Moreover, every culture and animal participated.

Finally, there was a period of almost ten years where crops went unplanted, forests were untended, and fisheries were untouched so that the oceans became over populated, people starved or were killed outright, families were not started, and children were not born or raised; the world was in a seriously downward spiral. The general population of almost every species came close to extinction. Only one sea dragon remained and she called for a meeting of every species. They were collected in a large ship that sailed on the ocean so that none could claim sovereignty. Two ambassadors from each species began to talk with all the others, and eventually they reached a decision: every species would withdraw from the battles, and all would apply pressure to persuade the fairies to end the Fairy Wars.

Gradually, region by region, the warring slowed and finally stopped. The peace accord may have been a little strained, but it was holding, that is, until the Conclave of the Princesses.

There were nine princesses that year, and all were of extraordinary beauty. Each as perfect as the others, each able to stop conversations and proceedings by merely walking into court, each of the princesses was as deserving of the final designation as the next, and none willing to concede. Just as everyone was worried another war would break out and consume the world, the last sea dragon arrived in the Conclave.

Until that time, everyone had thought that the last sea dragon had died. What was worse, for the dragons, at least, was the fear that she had taken the secret of the Kell with her. No one suspected that she possessed more than just the secrets of the Kell; she had secrets that groped into every dark corner of every species on this planet; including the power of "The Princess." For you see, she alone controlled all of those secrets and their powers. Despite the dragon belief, the Kell is the center of *all* life forms. The jewel their forehead allows all dragons to tap into the power of the Kell. Therefore, it was that ability to be in direct connection with the Kell, which allowed the last sea dragon to know that she was dying.

She entered the Conclave as the most beautiful and captivating princess that anyone had ever beheld. Upon seeing her, all of the other princesses knew that she was the one. Even their fathers crumbled and acquiesced at the sight of this radiant beauty. There was no voting, no arguments, no shifting for positions; she merely walked in, in all of her luminous beauty and strolled slowly toward the throne, and by the time she has reached the dais and turned . . . well, you saw what she looked like - a sea dragon. But by then, in everyone's hearts, she was already the new Fairy Princess.

She spoke gently to all that were gathered. She explained that the Fairy Wars must end. She explained in every gory detail how each war had reduced the lives of so many, and rendered many places on the planet uninhabitable. The destruction was tearing the world apart and it would result in the end of almost all life, save some in the seas and oceans. To remind the fairies forever of their responsibility to keep peace, she had taken control of the choosing of the Fairy Princess forever from their control. From then and evermore, the new Fairy Princess would just "be revealed" to the world. To further enforce humility upon the fairies, the Fairy Princess would never be a fairy. Drawing on the power granted a Fairy Princess, they could become anything they wanted; so if they wanted to reign as a fairy, so be it. Alternatively, they may be hatched a dragon and desire to become a wart hog, and that they could, and would always be supported in heart and soul by the fairy folk and all other species.

"So they would change and then that was it?"

"No, certainly not; they could be a fairy on Friday, a satyr on Sunday, a mouse on Monday, weasel on Wednesday and two towers of dirt on Tuesday and Thursday; or even change hour by hour or every minute or when the whim carries them. By the way, how do you like your warmed mug?" She radiated a beauty and smile that stole Tink's heart, even though he suspected it was a magical affectation intended to do just that. He also noticed that he did not have to move to accommodate the contours of the mug; the mug accommodated his contours instead. He smiled thinking, *Now if my mug could just learn that trick.*"

"*I'm sure something eventually could be arranged.*" The melody oozed through his brain as M'Løree continued with the strange history lesson. He was not sure why all of this was being told to him; surely as a male, he was not going to become a Fairy Princess? The right side of his mouth curled up at the thought. "*Not so fast, my little friend,*" the voice in his head poked.

So the Fairy Princess who was the last sea dragon and the keeper of the secrets revealed that she was dying. She did not know how or when, just that she was. Upon her death, a new princess would be revealed, and how ever long the sea dragon took from that day, to the day she died, that would forever be the time between new Princesses being revealed. And, to the day, it was 100 years and three days, and she just did not wake up, and the new Princess is revealed every 100 years; or there about.

"But wait . . . it's been 200 years now since the last Princess; what changed?"

"Has it? I don't think so. The last Princess, revealed in a time of much tribulation, was killed only minutes after his reveal. The previous Princess rushed out of the forest and was almost killed too, except for a flash of light that stunned the killers and allowed her to escape, carrying the new, now dead Princess, a badger with a heart of gold who used to cry just knowing anyone in the world was suffering. He was sorely missed. As much as the last Princess tried to fill in, it just was not the same. Princesses are needed for a time, and then they need to move on and be about their lives and jobs." The elder Princess rearranged her seating, and as she drew about her legs, they dissolved back into a shorter solid tail and fins configuration. Her knee dissolved, the mug became its own entity as she moved her hand to the mug the handle absorbed in the back and grew out and around her fingers in the front as she moved it to the rock ledge that was rising to meet her hand and the mug.

Ignoring the unsettling changes, Tink remembered something. "Hey, you said that the "Princess to Be" was a male. How could that be?" He was not sure he would want to be a Princess instead of a Prince. He was not even sure he would even want to be a Prince either.

"What make you think only females should have an exclusive right to the title?"

"Because a prince is a Prince, and a princess is a Princess."

"Ah, but, remember, this Princess can choose whatever she wants to be. Male or female, doe or buck, hen or cock, woman or man, mare or stallion - this Princess gets to choose every second of every day... So what is the meaning of gender?"

Skth tinkled with laughter as Tink grabbed his head and wove back and forth. "Oh my head hurts."

"So what happened to all of the past Princesses? This is a good question; some like Daryl the Badger were killed, others have died of old age. Some have disappeared when the time is right. Others, well, are still around, just not that active. Take me for example; I'm no longer active in the world, yet I still perform a vital function as the Keeper of the Shrine. Occasionally I get out, but not often and always in a form that gives me anonymity so that I can perform the duty I need to perform."

"So that *was* you yesterday." Tink thought more than said as his mouth was still full of rice ball and plum sauce, which he never thought he could get enough of; but today, just might prove him wrong.

"They are good, aren't they?" M'Løree reached over and delicately gathered up, dipped and casually dropped three into her mouth and as she savored the delight, she continued in the unnerving speech in the mind. *"No, that was not me. That was my sister, who cannot change forms and unfortunately has been dead these last few hundred years. But then, that is how she can get around so much, she just hasn't figured that out yet; and I'm sad to say, she may never figure it out."* Casually she popped a few more rice balls along with some lump crab in her mouth. *"You see, she never really realized her own death. She fell asleep one night and was gone. Her spirit, whoM you met, got up the next morning and continued about her duties as the Princess' Patron; and she keeps showing up here and there doing this and that, seemingly just when it's needed. The only thing she doesn't do, is come here and talk with me, even though we both need that, it just wouldn't be serving a higher purpose."* Wistfully she turned her head, looking toward a few of the urns silently standing vigil. *"A spoken word on occasion is a respite that is of great value these days."*

As the silence stretched, Tink looked to Skth for guidance. The blue was now stretched out sound asleep on the smooth rock, soaking up the warmth of the stone. Tink felt the tug of sleep in his tired muscles and the comfort of a mug as well. The events of the last two (three?) days had been physically and mentally draining and he longed for a restful sleep. The bonding celebration had gone on way too long and morning had come way too fast for him to recover from the long hard day at work before. Then there had been the long flight (even though he was not the one pushing the wings), and the very exhausting celebration; plus the flight out across the arctic ocean, which will need to be duplicated to get back. Maybe just a short nap ….

"I'll wake you when it is time. But first, you need to know and understand the obligations of the Princess Patron." The voice soothed in his head as his eyes began to droop. *"The Patron is in some ways important as or even more important than the Princess herself. Without the Patron, the Princess cannot exist. Their reveal always depends on the actions of their Patron. Always. If the Patron fails to perform the request, then the Princess doesn't become the Princess, and it is always with dire consequences, such as the untimely death of the last Princess, Daryl the Badger."*

A low little rumble emanated from deep within the mug, harmonizing with the other small dragons' slow rhythmic breathing, offered a hushed wash of soft sound through the chamber. The larger dragon watched the small head of the future Patron as she thought only to herself, *"Such a small Patron for such a large challenge. I sincerely hope you're up to the job, little one, I dearly do."* And with that she silently rose and stepping over to the pool that lead to the ocean, slid into a more familiar form as the water closed quietly over the descending shape, flying down and out to the open sea in full hunt. Fish balls can only vanquish so much hunger.

# # #

Tink rolled over on the floor, and realized that he was not in a mug anymore. The chamber was silent except for the soft breathing of Skth beside him. He watched her face in the low light of the chamber as she slept and wondered if she was dreaming. She was smiling in her sleep. Tink had not met a young dragon that he was so drawn too, even if she was barely out of the egg, she seemed to have so much wisdom and playfulness all mixed up in a small package. Of course, he did not have much experience with dragons of the opposite sex per se, other than those at work, and they did not really count. Twill, at five or ten times his size and old enough to be his grandmother. M'Ree at a hundred times his weight, maybe more, and if she ever thought his mud-green body resembled a chocolate confection, he would be gone in a lip smack. Then there was Pu - Tink never could figure out if he was a she, or maybe she was a he?

The pool exploded and a fountain of water erupted up and was replaced as M'Løree the sea dragon settled down on the warm stone of the floor. *"Yes!"* Her mental enthusiasm exploded in his mind along with a memory of a deadly chase that had ended only minutes before. Tink was not sure he would be eating salmon again for at least a while.

"Well, young children. I hope you are well rested, for it's time that you must leave." Skth rose rubbing the sleep from her eyes and scrubbing her face to bring back stimulation in her nose. Tink was still blinking and wondering about the strange dreams he was remembering, or he thought he was remembering.

"Is the storm past?" Skth asked bending forward and scratching her lower scales as a small patch of molting was fogging the scales.

"Not enough; you'll have to take the passage. I'll open the portal and send a wind to clear the air, and blow you along with a good tail wind." It is almost mid-meal in Kinnarodden and I'm sure Ki is at least wondering where you have gotten off to. Which reminds me …" As she strolled to the food storage, "Give him this." Handing Skth a small package she could carry in her hands. "Just place it on the ground and pat it three times when he is watching." Her smile did nothing to hide the fact that she was full of playful devilment at that moment. "And give him a kiss on both cheeks and tell him he looks so cute up on that official rock I built for him."

A final embrace of the two females as M'Løree took Skth in like a cute little puppy and nuzzled her in her cradling arms, and the older turned to Tink, "And you, young man, you need to listen a bit more to Guff, he will mentor you from here. Now the two of you need to go." As she shooed them down a long lit cavern. But as they started down, M'Løree appeared in a panic at the top of the slope, "Tink!" she screamed, "I almost forgot the most important thing to tell you! When you need it most, follow the warm breath or breeze; it will guide you." Then she waved like a doting grandmother at her children.

The children flew down the tunnel that never seemed to stop descending, a gentle turn here and a curve there, but always down, down, down. Tink was beginning to wonder if they were headed for the center of the Earth like the children's story he had read so long ago. And as they flew, he started to take note of the candles flames that were on a little out-cropping or in a niche in the wall set about every three or four large dragon strokes apart.

"Skth", Tink asked, his curiosity getting the better of their need to hurry. "What are those flame lights on the wall?" Flying then looping and tumbling through the air was not getting him a better view to figure them out.

"They are frozen flame that a relative put there a long time ago when they discovered that this tunnel connected the Shrine to Kinnarodden. At first, they used to carry torches, but fast flight is not conducive to a live flame. So, some were frozen and placed along the walls. The air is thin in the caves, and doesn't replenish often and a grouping of live torches could and probably did cause some to suffocate before they figured out the frozen flame."

"Is it an actual flame that is frozen? I mean, why doesn't it melt itself with the flame heat?" Now his confusion was slowing him down.

"The air is getting thinner, so if you don't hurry, we could be the next to not make it under the sea." As she increased her speed, Tink hurried to keep up. "I'll tell you and even show you when we get to Kinnarodden."

The two continued their breakneck pace through the long tunnel, now flattening out and then slowly gently sloping upwards. The walls began to be less of the blacker basalt, and turning to the greyer tones of granite and finally the granite with the lighted quartz inclusions that was the mark of Kinnarodden and Skth's home. As Tink had that thought, they took a last sweeping turn and exploded out into the grand cavern and they were home.

"Come," Skth beckoned to Tink "We must check in at the portal with Uncle Ki." She arched her wings in a climb and made for the upper shelf. Pulling harder on the now thicker dense sea air Tink began to understand the scope of the city in the mountain and wondered who had created this obviously ancient structure, and how long ago had that been? As the two shot up and over the edge of the great shelf, two guardsmen reached the same edge. The two small dragons, flipping up in a sidewise flying maneuver, missed colliding with the much larger rock- hard guardsmen who were startled to a point of a bad take off that resulted in an embarrassing loss of altitude for the protectors.

The guards cried out, "Hey!" but then as they identified the tiny blue missile, the two little ones heard a light-hearted threat drifting off into the echoing chamber, "We'll get you for that Skth." She just laughed. It was good to see the hard ones get a little feather ruffling now and then. As they let down in front of the Master Ki, they were still snickering at their unintended stunt.

"Hmmmm," Ki rumbled as he dismissed another guard that he had been talking to about guard business. "I hear you're still up to your childhood shenanigans as usual my little Skth. And, teaching our guest how to get in hot water as well."

"Hot water; yes, my most favored uncle." She bowed in a very over exaggerated courtly pass. Tink did not know whether to bow or just go find a chopping block to rest his neck. Looking up at the giant, he added the possibility that the large black could just pluck Tink up and pop him in his mouth after a dip in some plum sauce. Tink settled for crouching on his haunches and rolling his eyes.

"Most gracious and worshipful Master Ki," Skth continued in a most mocking and yet formal ingratiating manner of courtly theatre, "The Grand Dame of the Nord Ocean sends you greetings, salutations and a gift."

As she set the small packet upon the stone, Ki backed up commanding, "STOP! Do not tap that package in here." He dismounted his place of command and purview and slowly oozed down and around the stone. Coming close to the box, his ear wings pinned back in agitation and apprehension, "What do you think is in it?" he asked.

"I'm not sure," Skth whispered. "But, she also sent this," As she flicked over the two sides of his cheeks and gave them a hearty buzz. "She did bring it to me from the larder, so I would hazard a guess of possibly food." Skth was now having fun at her uncle's expense and unease with not knowing if it was something tasty or a plague of floating smelt to jam his busy cavern entrance. The tiny silver fish were tasty, but the sight of them floating and swimming around in air was unnerving at the least, and catching the last few was damnable at the worst. Some days you just cannot trust a playful Princess who has a streak of prankster in her nature.

"I appreciate the kisses, but please take it outside to open it."

Skth picked up the package and proceeded toward the opening while uttering under her breath enough for Tink to hear, "Big baby . . . afraid of his own shadow, that one".

"I heard that, little one." The black giant muttered back as he regained his post.

The storm was lessening but the weather was still not what anyone would call nice. So in the lee of the one boulder out cropping Skth set down the packet hoping it would not just blow away, and tapped it three times.

Tink was not sure what he was expecting it to do, but just sitting there doing nothing was not exactly in his list of possibilities - but there it sat. A tidy little package wrapped in gold gauze and tied with a deep blue ribbon. The package did not move, did not make a sound, and did not do anything that one might or might not expect. Tink looked to Skth for answers and got a big shrug. About the same thing Tink thought too. Tink reached to pull the end on the bow and a small voice that sounded a lot like M'Løree issued forth from the box, "You are not Ki."

Tink found his hand behind his back as he jumped then giggled along with Skth. "Well, I guess that settles it. Only Ki can open it." Scooping it up, he gave it back to Skth. "You do it." There was no way the little mud-brown dragon was getting between a talking box and the rightful recipient of the gift. And so they marched back into the cave.

"Well?" asked Ki.

"We have no idea," sounded the two in harmony, and then laughed at their dual answer.

"Tink tried to open it, but it told him that he wasn't you, so we brought it back to you."

Handing it up to Ki, Skth relinquished control and the box once again scolded. "STOP! I wasn't properly presented." Making even Ki start and almost drop the precious tiny package.

Ki cocked his head and gave the closely scrutinized the irascible box. Then stretching down he placed it in front of Skth. "I guess you had better do it," as he drew farther back on his rock pedestal. "We wouldn't want to get it angry, would we?" Tink saw him crouch a bit lower behind the pedestal, for more protection than his usual over-bearing posture. Tink almost said something to Skth, but then thought better of it, but if her uncle intended to sacrifice his niece, then Tink would stand right there beside her (hoping it would not explode or anything), and sort of hoping she would notice his protective stance too.

He had no idea that she had been devoting her side fovea to watch him and his every move for almost a full day. His every move and reaction was in her memory. As he moved even closer, she reached out and delicately tapped the top of the box three times.

At first, there was nothing. And then as if far, far away a little voice said quietly, "Very good Skth, now you can please leave and take Tink with you." With wide eyes, the two tiny dragons backed away and headed for the great cavern. But around the first turn, they stopped and snuck back to peek between the rocks and wall. Tink lay on the floor of the cave with his left eye just able to see around and under the edge of one of the larger rocks.

As they observed, the ribbon unwound itself and the package opened. A ray of light oozed and swelled straight up and then fanned out and down to create a dome of radiant light, and in that light was a night of the north. The Aurora Borealis snaked in the dome where Ki, now down on the floor, could reach up and touch or at least run his claw through. The green draping was scintillating with blues and yellows, reds and purples, snaking, sparkling, and drifting in an exploding riot of silence except to the eyes. As Tink watched, Ki marveled at the aurora, and then started recognizing the points of light that made up the constellations in the night sky, depicted in the cavern. It was a true wonder to behold, and Tink felt a little guilty and withdrew to find Skth doing the same.

Quietly they walked to the edge of the shelf, each brooding on their own private dialogs about what they had seen. Add in a little bit of self-chastisement to spice up the feelings of guilt - first, for having invaded an obviously private communication, and second, for having observed Ki in a highly private unguarded moment. Yet, Tink had to know.

"It would have been the night of his birth." Where the stars were, the placement of the constellations and what the Aurora Borealis looked like that very night. It is the art of M'Løree, and if we had been standing there too, it would have tried to blend all three of the night skies into one. It is very personal and only M'Løree can make them and she only makes them for special people on special occasions.

Skth turned to Tink, "That must mean it is his birthday." She clapped her hands over her mouth and turned a lovely shade of pink around her jowls and out along her ear fins.

"Is that important?"

She looked at him silently for a moment. "Do you know your brother's birthday?"

"Sure; it's the same as mine. We're twins."

"Do you tell anyone your birthdate?"

"Sure, a few. Why not?"

"Because then they would know . . . how old you really are."

Completely not understanding this foolishness, Tink mustered his best argument and replied, "So?"

Skth only rolled her eyes and did a mock death fall off the edge of the shelf, then flaring her wings glided to the commissary with Tink right behind shaking his head at such a silly little girl this Skth was. Also knowing that he really liked being around her.

The commissary was a very lively place as many dragons were preparing for their long flights back home, so food was fuel and everyone was fueling up. Tink spied Boomer already shouldered his harness as he stood around a tall table talking, laughing and eating with his new and old friends in the Guard. Soon it would be just the two of them winging their way back home at an amazing speed for any dragon.

"What's it like?"

"What?" Tink turned to looking to those blue eyes and crisp sky blue nose below a truly cloudless head jewel of clear deep blue sky. "What is what like?"

"Flying. Flying with Boomer; flying faster than the speed of sound?"

"I don't know," he stumbled, "I'm so used to it now, but I guess it's kind of amazing. The colors change with the different speeds. But I think that is an effect from the two eyelids getting pressed together. The cold, the cold is not any fun. It gets in your bones and it takes a lot of heat to get warm again."

"But it doesn't seem to bother Boomer. Doesn't he react to the extreme cold?"

"He would, but when he flies at speed and altitude, his nostrils close over, his mouth locks together and turns rock hard and he breaths in through his ears, which are open, but only to breathing in. The air super heats in his lungs, and then when he breaths out, he breaths out through his hollow bones and then the heat and air bleeds out through the wing membranes, keeping him warm and still able to fly.

"That's amazing."

"Nah, that's just my brother." Feeling just a little jealous that his brother had a cool talent or ability and his . . . well, he could fit in a coffee mug. Tink turned away to the food holds to see what might look tasty, even though he had just eaten a couple of hours ago. He looked over at his brother to see that he was fueling up with high-octane rice balls filled with fish livers dipped in honey. He looked for similar fare to pull his share of the burden even though he was just the passenger on the top. The baked puffballs would make him a little sleepy, but the high winds should keep him plenty awake. So he treated himself to what his mother only baked during the rare moon cycle. After all, what could happen?

Chapter 8

The Sands of Time

The sands along the strand tumbled in the wind. Eddies of smoky earth pooled and oozed like schools of fish in the ocean currents, scurrying first this way then slithering back from whence they had come. Footprints, claw marks, and dog tracks alike disappeared. The winds were never ending as the night crept towards dawn and the awakening of the world to start a new day, but for now the sea winds and loose sand ruled the surface; all hail the sand and wind. Overhead, the lone cormorant glided on what was left of the day's thermals as it stood watch over the three creatures leaving the beach and walking down the hard path to the little thatched cottage nearby.

The cormorant glided effortlessly down the length of the beach lane and twisted at the end as a warm patch provided a much-sought lift in the night's still air. In the distance and as yet unseen, came the short cry of a Leach's petrel that was the cormorant's relief. The first bird rose peacefully in the thermal as the other slid in beside and rode that slightly warmer air. Each was enjoying the lift with no effort, the true mark of a bird that is aloft two thirds of its life. Birds that live at sea are a different bird than land birds, and therefore make the better watchers; but land birds are more plentiful and therefore are more efficient to cast a net when looking for a small item on land, such as a very tiny dragon.

The two birds did not talk to each other; but there was enough communication through body language of feather placement and body attitude. As the cormorant released the watch to the second and smaller night bird, he twisted up his inner pitch and slid at an angle out of the updraft, pushed back out over the beach, and was lost in the dark night sky. The petrel swooped down and fluttered over the little cottage to see if she could glimpse the little dragon while the lights still burned.

On the third pass, the night bird spotted the dragon asleep on a pillow by the fireplace. There appeared to be a small patch of gauze on one of his wings. The dog was lying very close by and looked capable of protection if the need arose. So the Leach's petrel figured rightly that they were in for the night and he could go do a little fishing and be back long before dawn with a belly full of smelt or anchovies.

The flutter of the wings just outside the cottage window got Scout's attention and he looked at the window only to see black glass looking back. "Qu'est-ce que , Scout? What do you see, boy?" The old man asked as he patted his constant companion's head. "The night air, maybe?" "Ack; the time," he thought, as he looked at the clock on the mantle and pushed on the arms of his chair. "Our little dragon friend has the right idea. I'm off to bed too; good night, boy." He blew out the two oil lamps in his living area, then leaving them to smoke and smolder, the old man tottered down the smooth plastered hallway to the single bedroom. The little coal fireplace was putting out a warm cheery glow. A small eye open half way then closed in resolve that the situation was safe and warm. Perhaps this had something to do with the large patch of fur next to him that was starting to snore. A huge chunk of coal burned in half, split yet again and clinked as it fell apart in the field of the other bright red cinders. The dragon rumbled delicately, the dog snored; the old man's bones creaked as he slowly got undressed and donned his nightshirt, blew out the last candle and rolled into the tall bed and rubbed his feet back and forth to warm up the cold sheets under the thick down comforter. Out over the ocean, where the English Channel becomes the Northern Sea and the turbot rules the ocean floor, the lone petrel glides over the night's short waves in search of its dinner. A gibbous moon delicately silvers the occasional white cap, raised by the petulant sea breeze.

Hours later as the trio slept snugly in the cottage, the petrel returned with a happy tummy full of what had been bright shiny anchovies schooling in the luminescent sea, which did nothing to hide them but more to light them up like a neon sign pointing to a free meal at the downtown mission of a Saturday night. The night wraith swung down from a higher trajectory and cruised by the cottage for signs of an uneven night. Four passes she made as she had a bit of fun flying between the clothes still hanging on a line in the neighbor's yard, under the wire, then sharp sweep up and over the fence very much resembling the line of attack in a few of the streams with tasty trout in the spring. Finally bored with the game, she punted down the lane in search of the thermal that was there during the evening, unaware of another dragon still a few hundred miles away but coming at a swift pace.

The landscape all looked alike to Boomer, had he flown over this last night, or was it a flight from a month, a year or a decade ago? He had crisscrossed the landscapes of much of the planet in the last sixty years so that it all looked familiar. He never even set courses anymore; he just knew where he was going and went the same as you and I walking to the market, the post office, and the cleaners to pick up the dry cleaning; we, as he, just go; or so he thought.

Unbeknownst to Boomer, there was a tiny little fleck of genetic trace from his obsidian father, a fleck of magnetite – a natural compass always leading him on his way. You might even say, that Boomer always "nose" where he is going; but that does not always make it exciting.

The monotony of the landscape was also tiring and becoming just a little mind numbing as well. The black cold sea was a void in his search sight, and the sand of the shoreline little more than the same black void. The occasional sand rat scurrying through the sea grasses would register warmth but not the right one and the homes radiated random heat zones that triggered his sight, but none that came in the 110F-120F range. The search was grinding him down, but the fact that he was not finding his brother was making it even worse.

Flying northeast, along the sands and closing on the dunes of Dunkirk, Boomer noted the thin line of gold rimming of the planet many hundreds of miles to the east. He knew as the day warmed and as people began to move about, his search would be complicated. Automobiles could easily warm into the heat range he was seeking, stove pipes on house roofs could catch his attention, as would many hundreds of other items move or be heated into the range that would make his heat seeking useless; sort of like the bird that was now shadowing him so closely.

Boomer gave a burst of speed to go almost supersonic as he pulled up into a back rolled flip that left him flying above and slight behind the Leach's petrel. "Why are you shadowing me?"

The petrel startled but only fluttered a bit and then flared to rise up alongside of Boomer. Eyeing him for a few breaths, "You are searching, no?"

"Yes" Boomer acknowledged.

"Is it a small immature dragon, the color of peat in the northern bogs of the big island?"

Boomer had to think about what island before he realized that this was an English bird so the "island" would be England and Scotland. This bird was not one who cared or understood about countries and borders; she would only be talking landmasses - not countries. And the peat? Of course, it would be the brownish green of Tink! "Yes, that would be my brother. Do you know where he is?"

"We were asked to watch for him, He is secure in the walking peoples' cave near the hard river that flows from the twin lumps of tufted sea grass that smells of cinder bark." The petrel rattled off as she searched for a new thermal to regain altitude. The on-coming sun was disturbing her because she was not safely out to sea.

"Can you show me which house, er, I mean which cave he is in?"

The petrel rolled off, dove down one of the lanes, and then circled up and over the little cottage. "This one," she indicated. "If you look through the hole there; you will see him. I will leave you in charge now."

As Boomer slowed his flight to a stationary float, something she had said struck him. "Wait. Before you go; who exactly asked you to watch for him?"

"The Princess in the cold waters."

"When?" He did not understand what he was hearing.

"Two, maybe three full moons ago. Enough, I must go now." And she was gone out over the ocean where she lived at sea, floating by day, asleep, flying and hunting at night.

Boomer returned to the window of the little cottage, but could not see enough into the dark interior. He switch back into his infrared search vision, and there was the glow he had been looking for, near the brighter, hotter glow of the dyeing embers of coal in the stove and the less warm mass of a dog lying close and protective. Having found his brother, he decided he did not need to awaken anybody, so instead he rose above the thatched roof and searched for the warm spot that would be where the roof met the chimney. Snuggling into that cleft between the rough plaster and the prickles of the thatching of the roof, he wondered at the dark speckles that he saw on the red heat signature glow of his little brother. What could have caused this speckling? What would be cold enough to resist the 118° temperature his brother was radiating? Boomer's total exhaustion mercifully overcame his inquisitive mind before he began to think about the large patch on Tink's unnaturally extended left wing and the muffled glow from a large wrapping. He slept.

Far out to sea, the Leach's petrel floated in the dawn light. The golden tendrils of high cirrus clouds overhead bode for a clear day of calm seas and a good sleep. The bobbing bird rested in the middle of an almost glass smooth sea as she and the dolphin had a calm conversation about what had transpired as predicted, and what had not been foreseen. As always, there are those outside influences in any event that change things like extra spice or salt in a soup, or an expected guest who may become the evening's high point or not.

The school of anchovies swam unmolested beneath the two who were some of their biggest threats, and deeper still the turbot skated along the bottom of the great channel looking for some breakfast of their own in the dark waters. A small waterspout rose and finished to the north and the sea was calm again, all unnoticed by the two bobbing in the early light. Life continued undisturbed in the cycles of all beings. The dolphin rolled over slowly and sank beneath the calm waters, already shimmering as the dorsal fin reduced and the pectoral fins enlarged into the wings that would let her fly faster through the water than any common dolphin (or even an uncommon dolphin, as the case may be).

As the dawn turned the curtains in the small cottage from a dim gray to a warm tan, the old man started to stir. Slowly as the muscles and age-damaged joints began to move again, the body collected its use again, the need to move a little faster again called the morning to full wakefulness. The dog rolled over as the noises of morning rustled through his dreams of puppyhood and running without pain. The hand-braided rag rug felt good to rub against and slowly he twisted back and forth in a morning ritual that matched his master's and aroused the interest of Tink as he lay on the pillow that supported his wing.

"Does it hurt?" Tink asked, unabashed.

"What; the rug? No, it feels good; like a soft scratching."

"I meant your leg."

Scout, thinking, now rolled over and sat up so they would be closer to eye-to-eye, "Not really. But it does ache a bit when it's really cold and damp."

"Was it always that way or did you lose it?"

"I lost it. I think I was hit by an automobile, but I don't really remember." Sitting on his rump, Scout scratched at one side of his neck then the other. "I'm just glad it wasn't one of my hind legs," shifting to scratch the original side again, "Could you imagine being able to scratch only one side of you? Ce serait terrible! It would be terrible."

Tink did not really understand the French, but he got the gist and agreed with a small shudder. Unconsciously his tail flange stiffened as it reached around and gently rubbed some of the tender spots. "Hmmmmm."

"A very handy tail you have there."

"Hmmmmm?" Realizing what was happening in his sleepy awakened state. "Yes, I guess it is. But then, I can't reach around and chew at an itchy back like you."

"Fair said." Scout was looking down the hall at the approaching figure, "It's time to go out for a walk; ready?" Sidling over beside the pillow so Tink could climb aboard his back, Scout wagged his tail at the approach of the old man. The morning walk was always the best and longest as the old man needed to move and stretch the joints and old scar tissue, which also allowed Scout enough movement to do his business that took longer as the years compiled.

"Ma parole, Scout; you are quite the gentleman this morning." The man chuckled as he reached for his cap and walking stick. "Allons-nous? Shall we?" as he opened the door and swept his cap in a deep bow as the duo hobbled out the door, then drawing it quietly closed behind the trio. As he looked at what was turning out to be a beautiful blue-sky day, he quietly thanked whomever for another day of life. "Sacré bleu, is a magnificent morning." The three slowly made their way down the lane toward the sound of the low quiet surf as the small waves washed against the sand.

Catching up to them was a shadow that came alongside the trio and then paced them. Slowly, almost imperceptibly, the shadow got smaller and less fuzzy around the edges. Tink, used to watching for just such a shadow from a hunting killer about to stoop on his prey and tickle him without mercy, cleared his throat. "It would seem that we are either about to be attacked, or we have company."

Scout stopped and looked about; but seeing no threat, asked "From where?"

"Qu'est ce que c'est, Scout."

"From above!" Tink patted his benefactor for assurance, "Good morning, brother." He called, as he cocked his head to see Boomer floating about twenty feet above.

"You're getting too good at this little brother," Boomer admitted with a chuckle as rotated to his upright posture of static flight and descended to meet Tink's benefactors. "And to think our parents and I were worried about you." He eyed the large wrapping on his brother's wing, but decided to keep the meeting light.

He hovered at eye height with the old man, "Bonjour, I am Tink's brother Boomer." He came to float slightly about head level with the dog, and managed a closer look at the wrapping and Tink's scuffed up condition, "I see he has been in good kind hands, thank you."

"Bonjour to you, too, my name is Jon and this is my companion, Scout." The man absently grabbed his cap from his head and held it in both his hands as he sort of bowed. "I must say, I never thought to see a dragon up close, much less two that I could talk to." Then he realized that he did not know what else to say or do; but followed Scout's lead as the dog began to act just a bit in need.

113

"Please join us as, um, we have business in the sea grasses on the sand dunes" He finished with a slight blush of having to explain the obvious. The three turned toward the sea once again, with now a forth tracking alongside.

"What happened last night?" Boomer asked Tink.

"I don't know. We left Kinnarodden, and I remember Oslo, I think it was . . . a castle and fireworks?" Boomer nodded. "And then . . . well, I was waking up half buried in the sand with Scout barking at me." Tink shrugged. "I guess maybe I fell asleep or something."

"I guess I was more tired than I thought, too; I never even noticed you not on my back." If it had been possible to see a red dragon blush, this would have been the time. "I should have noticed that I had to fly harder without the aerodynamics of your set of wings on the top for the extra lift, but I didn't. It was when I got home and mom asked where I had left you."

Tink thought about what that must have been like, "Eeuw. Sorry about that."

The larger dragon rolled his eyes in a dramatic wide-open humor-ous way, "Yeah, it wasn't exactly pretty last night." A shudder rippled through his body, "At least she let me take a couple of hours nap before sending me back." He rose a bit to look at the large bandage, "How's the wing?"

"Hurts, I . . . um punctured it on with a piece of wood during my," he cleared his throat, "landing?" He matched the rolled eyes the two have shared as a brotherly joke for many decades. There are no words to convey the depth of meaning that flashed between the two brothers in the split second taken to make the gesture.

"Um, sorry to interrupt . . ." Scout looked back as he stood next to a large clump of sea grass.

"Oh," Tink injected as he jumped down, now embarrassed. "Sorry, we'll . . . um, be over here." As all of the males separated to take care of morning duties, the water washing back and forth on the rough sands of the ocean's perimeter enforced the silence.

Small gulls lifted into the morning thermals as they stretched into the day of blue skies and few clouds. They would be the accent points in the patchwork of the overhead quilt. Sand crabs, sensing the warming sands after lying buried beneath all night, crawled out of their burrows and scuttled up and down the stretch of beach, most eventually reaching the safety of the water. A few unfortunate crabs ended up in the gullets of sea birds. A sand dollar burrowed even deeper as the water retreated and the tide left exposed beach instead of protective water or seaweed. Other clams reached up to taste foam for tiny phytoplankton as breakfast. The circle continued as in days past, and as in days forward.

Strewn about the table in the sunny windows were the remains of a meal of scrambled eggs, kippered herring and biscuits. The twins were kept busy telling Jon of different aspects of a dragon's life, even though Boomer could not really tell much about his life as a confidential courier; but it did not seem to make much of a difference.

"So, you get to still be in the coffee mug anyway," Jon roared merrily. "Here, let me see if there is any more of the frozen glue on your culot." He feigned reaching for Tink's tail and the three roared with laughter again.

Scout lay seemingly bored by the fire, but was privately happy to hear his master having a happy time, something that was so rare in their lives; and he thought was probably as rare in his master's life as a whole. The warmth of the banter matched the warmth of the heat from the coal and soon, as with any dog, Scout was fast asleep, but with a smile.

Getting more serious, Boomer looked at his brother, "How soon do you think you could fly again?" He asked the most important question that had been avoided over such a congenial breakfast.

"I don't know. How long do you think it takes to heal a punctured web?" Tink asked in a worried tone. "I've never heard of anyone poking or even tearing a web."

"There was that fishing dragon a few years back that broke a wing -"

"Yes, but that was a real break in the bones."

"But I think he was flying again in a couple of months."

"If, I may be so bold . . ." injected Jon. They relinquished the conversation, "Why don't we go visit Scout's doctor and see what she might have in the way of a suggestion?"

The twins looked at each other. A doctor - one that was not a dragon? Well, why not? They both shrugged and nodded, as Boomer reached out and took another little piece of biscuit from the plate. Not good for his flight figure, but something that could become a weakness with him. A small claw came gently came to rest on his arm, but before he could make a statement of contrition about the biscuits, a trembling Tink had swung up and onto his back in the usual fashion; they had flown like this since childhood. Snickering, Boomer turned his head and muttered out of the side of his mouth, "Good thing it's not me that needs the ride, eh, tiny brother?" The fact that Tink just shrugged and slowly blinked that, "In pain" worried Boomer and they flew out the door.

"She says that the stitches need to stay in for two weeks, and you will need to not fly for those weeks." Jon interpreted for the young female doctor with jet-black hair, twinkling eyes, a lilting honey-like voice and taking every advantage to keep petting Tink as if to make sure he was real. "I zink she would like to keep you here or take you home too." Chuckling at the fawning doctor's expense, "She may even want to adopt you as her child, if you were willing."

They all had a laugh as Jon translated back into French and the good doctor blushed and admitted that it was just that she had never before had the privilege to touch a dragon. She did enforce that she would probably need to stop by the cottage and change the bandage every couple of days too; to which everyone with faces like actors playing their serious parts, nodded and agreed, as Jon added that about dinnertime would be the most convenient.

As they were readying to leave the veterinarian's office a loud boom overhead startled Jon, who quickly collapsed to kneel close to the ground and started to shake. Tink did not know what to do. Having never seen such a reaction before, he felt helpless. The doctor rushed over to comfort the old man and she helped him up into a chair. "It's only my brother returning," Tink tried to comfort; "He didn't mean to scare you."

"It's the loud noise," the dog commented quietly, but he was still concerned, "He has always been this way as long as I have been with him. I think it has something to do with the bad places on his face and arms, but I don't know. I only understand so much." As Jon became calmer, Boomer appeared at the glass door.

"See, I told you it was Boomer. That boom is when he breaks the sound barrier; that is why they called him Boomer." Scout barked at the door, and the doctor and Jon saw that it truly was the other dragon. With the help of the doctor, Jon slowly regained his feet. He thanked her and said that she was welcome to come to dinner any or every evening. She patted his arm and assured him that she would be there for dinner the next night. The doctor looked at Boomer closer as they went out and it was obvious she would like to examine him just a little bit more than he was prepared for.

Softly she said more to herself than the others or Boomer, "Vous pouvez voler plus vite que le son? You can truly fly faster than sound?"

Softly reassuring, Boomer, the world traveler replied, "Oui, certainement."

Over lunch, much was explained about the massive burn marks Jon had acquired during the battle at Dunkirk as a small boy running messages as a courier for the underground, which gave him a bond with Boomer, who opened up a bit about the danger to be a courier, even in peacetime. Tink quietly translated to Scout the nature of Jon's frailties which gave the dog and dragon a bond that would serve them well over the next few weeks of Tink'S convalescing. The cheese and bread were wonderful but what Boomer and Tink needed was protein, and Jon obliged with a scramble of egg and herring.

"Where did you take off to while we were with the doctor?" Tink asked as they relaxed after the meal; nobody wanting, needing or even able to move from the feast for the stomach as well as healing of souls.

"I went home to tell mom that I had found you and you were in good hands, being fed rich fattening food and had grown almost double your girth and that dad would have to widen the door when you came home." Boomer delivered this with almost a total stone calm face, until the part about the door. The three laughing did wake Scout from his dream, but it was one he did not need to continue and the laughter was good to hear, so he groaned, and rolled over on the rug by the coal stove so that the radiating heat could wash over more of his tummy.

"So when did the good doctor think you could fly again?" Suddenly serious as flight was his life and a hole in the web was nothing really to make light of, even with his brother.

"At least four to five weeks, was her guess. She really didn't know anything about how dragons heal and I had nothing to go on beyond the occasional burnt fingers when Dvark's flames get a little wild as I hold a frame, and she did look at the burn from last week, but it still was not the same as a puncture of the web." Tink screwed up his face in his trademark "Tink no know" face that would usually have gotten a laugh for his sibling, but this was serious. "She's going to be watching it very closely . . . almost nightly." As Tink and Jon shared a smile, "So maybe you can check in a few weeks or when you're over the area; just slow down a bit when you are in the area. Would you?" He shot Boomer his best imitation of the "one-eyed, raised-brow stink eye" that both had learned from their mother. That finally brought a laugh.

"I'll slow down. No more booms in Northern France, eh, Jon?" As he reached out and patted the man's hand, the man smiled a wane soft smile.

"But, maybe if you do, I will get to know a loud boom is my friend, not an old enemy."

The three of them thought about that as the warm afternoon sun flowed over the comrades around the small table amongst the scattering of a meeting of cultures, creatures, old times and good times to come. As they thought, a small squeak and rumble came out of the tiny battered and scraped up dragon lying on a pillow.

Very quietly, his brother, always looking out for his small special sibling, leaned toward Jon and whispered, "He's actually more comfortable in a coffee mug, but I don't think I'd wake him to move him... he tends to be dangerous when you wake him." Even Jon's unfamiliarity with dragons could tell the larger red was smiling and the sparkle in the eyes seemed to make that interesting jewel on his forehead actually glow.

"He needs sleep, and I need to get home. Jon, it has been an honor to meet you." Boomer extended his right claw in respect for the human custom of handshakes that he had become so accustomed to in his job.

And in taking that extension, "Non, S'il vous plait, the honor is mine."

They shook and the smaller dragon, a more world traveled, and almost ambassador replied, "D'Accord, both of us are favored." As he nodded his head at the now snoring ground-up dragon, "Because of a little brother."

"Agreed," Jon waved his wrinkled hand at the door, which signaled to Scout that there could be a short walk in the offing, too. "Let me walk you out. And, I think I would like to see that fast flight so that I can recognize it when you fly over and I will know there is a courier that is about important duties in the world, and he is my friend." As he slowly closed the door quietly as not to wake Tink, Scout hobbled out the gate and turned toward the beach.

Several minutes later, the man and dragon shook again as dog and dragon said goodbye, then the rcd shot slowly down the beach to the North and out to sea about a half mile then turning pushed 850 miles per hour as he crossed in front of his two new friends standing atop the low dunes in the sea grass. His shock wave at the low altitude left a rooster tail in the water that was almost one hundred feet in the air. Boomer knew that otherwise they would be unable to see him. Then he was gone. The two shook their heads and slowly returned to their new little friend.

Chapter 9

Back Home and a Request

"She said that it could be as long as two months or more before the membrane of the web would be strong enough to fly. She wasn't very specific, because she had never worked on dragons, nobody does; it seems we dragons don't really get sick or injured very much."

"But, how is he doing? And I am not asking about the hole she stitched closed." Duff was worried as she and Boomer lay under the cool shade of the hostas. It had been five weeks since the accident and she was worried to the point of finally allowing Boomer to see her.

"Well, personally I think the biscuits are going to slow him down a bit when he starts flying again. But his French is improving, and he now has Jon cooking dragon food and liking it." He snickered at the last time he visited; Jon had not tightened his belt enough and in walking along the beach his pants had dropped. "I think the change in food has actually been good for him. He seems to have lost a bit of weight."

Duff, who could not imagine losing any weight or even being anything but, well, Duff, looked at Boomer with a raised eyebrow. A new trick she had learned from the grey squirrel in the second tallest tree, and she was having fun with it, and really wanted to try it out on Tink. Overhead, two blue birds chased each other around the branches of the trees until they broke through the canopy of leaves and out into the crisp cloudless summer sky. The bright, light green new spring foliage had finally turned to the darker summer color creating the patchwork quilt of the darker evergreens and the lighter patches of the various deciduous hard woods that made up the ancient forest.

"Did your mother make any more fish rice balls to be dipped in that yummy sauce?" Duff, ever bashful, had always amused Tink at her capacity to eat at least four of his mother's rice balls dipped in plum sauce. Now she was turning her voracious appetite upon his unsuspecting brother, who in fact had been wondering why his mother had given him so much food when he was working so hard to keep his shape for fast flight. He also fought with his *own* appetite for Jon's fresh French sourdough biscuits drizzled in wild honey and soaked with fresh butter made from sheep's milk.

"Mmm, I think these were all for you," suggested Boomer pushing the last three balls towards a very delighted set of enlarged eyes above a now slightly drooling smiling mouth. Well, OK, maybe not so "*slightly* drooling"; after all, these were the best fish balls Duff had ever known. Boomer's mind was on the fact that he would be visiting Jon, Tink, Scout and those weighty biscuits soon enough as he was leaving after lunch, and would be swinging by the leather monger to pick up his re-rigged harness. If he timed everything just right, he would be landing at the northern French coast just in time for breakfast.

"So just how big is this doctor, who has taken a fancy toward Tink?" A slow drool of plum sauce traced its track down the pixie's chin. Unthinking, the much larger red dragon reached over and wiped it clean with his claw which he licked clean, tasting the strange mix of forest duff, plum sauce and Duff's unique tasting salt from her skin; a mix that Boomer found to be curiously appealing with its savory mixture of flavors.

"She's a human," as if that would explain everything; but then he thought it through. "She's smaller than most humans I have met, but maybe a regular size for French females." Pointing to a small three or four year old reproduction pine tree, hc weighed in on the size, "About as tall as that little pine tree, but without the straight top growth, or maybe even the top sprigs." He shrugged, "I don't know; she's bigger than me. " Then as he looked at the concern on Duff's face, finally understood the underlying conversation that was happening. "Certainly too big and the wrong species for Tink, if that is what you're concerned about . . ." He tried to sound reassuring.

"Huh?" Duff looked up at Boomer with total confusion. "What has species . . ." Then part of the "facts of life" began to settle in. "Oh no, I wasn't thinking about her as a potential mate. I was just . . . well, kind of thinking . . . he might, sort of . . . well, find her more interesting and never come home." Having voiced her real concern, she slumped in on herself, and her self-pity was so strong that even a whole bowl of fish balls floating in plum sauce would have a hard time even distracting, much less curing.

Boomer put out his wing tip, left arm, and gathered the small pixie in to comfort her. "I miss the little guy too."

They sat that way, quietly in their own forms of missing the little mud-green dragon who they had come to realize was such a big part of each of their lives. A soft summer breeze blew gently across and rustled the leathery leaves of the many hosta plants covering the multitudes of tracks that ran through the forest floor. A warm flow of air rose up through a fumarole in a great mountain labyrinth many thousands of miles away; as two blue dragons sat on a ledge and also thought of that same small mud-green dragon who had come to mean so much in their lives as well.

"There is so much he needs to really know." The much larger, almost transparent dragon sighed. "She didn't tell him everything, because she doesn't know everything. She was never a Patron; she was always just the Princess."

"But if you can't go to him, how can you tell him?" asked a concerned Skth, as her claw found a small pebble which she sent it pinging down the tunnel until it might hit another dragon far down the way. Nobody knew if it was just other dragons above flicking little pebbles down the tubes, or if it was a natural occurrence; but everyone absent-mindedly flicked pebbles and they just accepted being struck by the occasional falling pebbles as a part of daily life in the Kinnarodden.

"I'm sending you instead." The gold and green eyes pulsed with the meaning as they scanned the small blue dragon beside her.

"I can't fly that far, and I certainly don't know the way."

"You will neither need to fly nor know the way, my dear. You will be carried." The larger dragon noted the fear arising in the eyes of the smaller dragon whose farthest sojourn had been to the great gooseberry fields only half a day's flight to the south. The large blue reached out with her left wing tip and arm, and gathered the small blue in for comfort against what was, at least for now, her corporeal haunch. "I have requested his brother come to get you, to carry you to him. By this time tomorrow, you will be sharing a wonderful thing called biscuits with Tink and his new friends." She patted the small blue wing and shoulder as the head lay in the crease between thigh and body, and she noticed the eyes were drooping in the heat. "You must trust me about this; the life of the princess depends on you and Tink, my dear. Just trust me, and everything will be fine." She too slumped, suddenly overcome with the afternoon, and the heat in the tunnel. She thought about the challenge ahead, how small the champion truly was, and thought to herself a small supplication, "*I hope the heart of a warrior beats within that tiny chest.*"

Several hours later a red streak entered the mountain and came to a rest, bowing low with respect, "Master Ki, once again we are well met."

"So good to see you again, young Boomer," The giant black nodded in acknowledgement of the respect paid. "I believe that little scamp Skth is hovering around here within hearing, or gobbling one last herring square down on the floor."

"I'm here," the tiny blue chimed as she dabbed one last time at her chin, hoping she did not have some embarrassing bit of food hanging on a chin scale. "I'm all ready to go."

Boomer eyed the small fish leather bag hanging from a thong about the blues neck. "OK, you will have to crouch along the pad on my back with the leading edges of your wings as well as your fore-arms inside the shield. We don't have time to train you how to create the canard wings that Tink's wings provide, so the leather monger added a strap to hold you and your wings down and out of the slip-stream. You'll have to tuck your tail back under your leg and arm pits to keep it from drifting into the air stream too."

The little blue climbed into the rig as Master Ki assisted in the strap and made sure everything was ready. Since Tink was not much larger than Skth, she fit inside the rig as if her own. She settled in for the long flight.

"This first hop is almost four and a half hours, and we can't stop. So it would probably be best if you just try to sleep most of the way." Boomer looked back at a familiar sight, except the face was now blue instead of his brother's brown green. "You did think to . . . ummm . . ."

"Yes!" Skth snapped haughtily, almost turning as red as her chauffeur.

Boomer smiled with a conspiratorial grin, saluted the black giant one more time, and disappeared into the dark of the night. They slid past and were almost unseen by the incoming patrol, missing by a bare inch his friend the outrider Sekar, who only felt the air movement, but knowing what it was, said nothing. The courier's travels were never a topic of report or conversation.

Night was actually Boomer's favorite time to fly. The air was cooler (which never bothered him) and thicker because of the congealing effect; which allowed him to fly higher in the thinner and faster air, but because it was "fatter", he got the same oxygen mixture in through his ears. Tonight though, because of Skth, as with Tink, he had to keep down in the lower air, and therefore fly even slower because of the fat thicker air. He did not really mind it, though, tonight. He had allowed about five hours for a flight he could have made by himself in three or three and a half hours. However, arriving to a sleeping household and having to wait around for hours for one of Jon's biscuits would be a little bit nerve-wracking. The last five weeks of "just dropping by because I was in the neighborhood" had made Boomer an expert in his timing, even up from Sydney, Australia last week. He had to go sleep on a hillside after the breakfast because he was so tired, but it was well worth it. He did not know what the secret really was, but he knew that if his mother ever learned how to make biscuits like Jon, he would look like Guff by the end of the month. Therefore, he had made the effort to fly faster and pick up a couple of extra thousand miles a day just to burn off the extra calories in those biscuits, butter and honey. Jon's coffee was fairly good too, but not as good as the "mud" at the White House.

Off to the west Boomer spotted an airliner at about the same altitude, so he poured on a bit more speed and lifted a couple of thousand feet to go over the path instead of risking turbulence by going lower. He knew the plane would probably be the over-night, long haul out of Chicago heading to Oslo because it was so low. Most airliners fly at assigned altitudes, well into the mid to high 30,000 feet above sea level, and that was where a fanjet operated at its peak efficiency. Military planes traveled better in the even higher altitudes. Boomer actually liked to keep between 18,000 feet and 22,000 feet; high enough to be efficient, but low enough to still have enough oxygen in the air for him to breath and provide the burn to fly at the speeds and distance Boomer was capable of; a secret that he actually never shared with anyone, except his brother.

The burn in his muscles from the almost all day and all night flying was telling him that he was dropping down the final slot and lined up with the upper mouth of the English Channel. Out of his left center fovea, he could tell that he had made a little better time than he had expected. He re-tasked his right eye as well and went into full search mode. Soon he had what he wanted, a little peace, a rest, and a tiny bit of time killing travel, and just before he turned belly up to convert into a 3,000 mph stoop and a lot of fun, he remembered that he had a passenger. He continued his scheduled flight and avoided the sonic boom, which would have wakened all aboard the unsuspecting oil tanker slowly making its way south out of the North Sea. Today, he had to act his age. As he re-tasked his homing toward the small cottage, he wondered for the umpteenth time if Skth even knew that she was being delivered at the request of the oldest living Fairy Princess: someone even Boomer had never knowingly met or even seen. He wondered if such a tiny young dragonet had ever seen or met a Princess.

Although he was the focus of seemingly everyone else's thoughts, Tink was focusing on his own thoughts in the early predawn light. The window over the eating nook faced east and the crest of the dawn glowed through a set of several old chandelier crystals that Jon had hung there with fishing line from the curtain rod. The facets of the crystals cast many dots of miniature rainbows about the small rooms, and one in particular had fallen on a patch where a scab had fallen off the scuffed bumps on his skin. Instead of pink or some variation of his usual mud-green, the little bump reflecting the rainbow into his eyes, was gold. Not a tan skin that looked gold with part of the rainbow, but gold. Not a skin tone of gold, but . . . gold. Tink tapped it with one of his claws; it was him, but gold. It was just a healed sanded off nob of a bump, but gold. It felt like skin, but it was gold. Tink lay there in the grey of the morning, wishing it were an hour later when the light would be streaming more fully through the window. Then he would be able to see even better. This tiny dot of a refracted rainbow from the preverbal crack of dawn held Tink captive and he decided that some days, it just was not worth waking up. He drifted back to sleep, unaware that a pair of dragons had just slid into the front yard of the little cottage.

"Shhh," Boomer warned Skth quietly. "If we are silent enough, we can sneak in the dog's door and be inside when everyone wakes up." He crouched on the flagstones that led up to the front door, as he worked at the front buckles of the harness. He could not reach back to remove the strap on Skth, so he would have to undo the entire harness and remove it, to release her. Undoing the last buckle he gently let the harness slide back off him and down onto the flagstones.

Unstrapping Skth, he nodded toward the south end of the cottage, "I'll go this way and check the windows to see if they are up yet, and you can go that way around, and I'll meet you at the back door."

Nodding, she tried to fly off but her wings did not seem to know what she wanted. "You'd better . . . umm, walk." Boomer advised trying not to laugh at the tiny blue dragon stumbling off towards her side of the house and some privacy. He placed his tongue between his teeth and bit down hard, until there was a tear in his left eye. He rounded the cottage's white stucco plastered corner, then he gently braced himself with one arm and leaned back just enough to watch the little drunken sailor totter this way and that and finally fall over into a hedge bush at the corner. At the other end of the cottage, he became a red streak flashing into the sky; and at a safe enough distance to laugh unheard, and not offend.

Minutes later, he returned and hovered at the windows that were showing no signs of early morning life so he walked around the corner into the prim little garden in the rear. Sitting on the low stoop was the little blue who had that look of "What have you been up to?" that he was used to seeing on his mother's snout and eye with a raised eyebrow. As he walked closer, and hopped up on the stoop, he gave her back his best challenging look of "What?" Both knew what the topic was; neither was going to start the conversation. Boomer gently pushed on the little swinging door, hoping he would not startle and wake Scout.

Tink was still back in the Shrine cave, and things were coming back from that long talk about being the Princess's Patron. It seemed to him that neither the Princess nor the Patron had a choice in the matter of being what they were. They just were. The gold of the eyes floated in front of him, and it reminded him of something, but he could not remember what. Although it remained hidden from him, he knew *whatever it was*, it was important. Her eyes were so close, and the gold was floating and she was saying something about warm and breeze, or was it breath. "Follow the warm breath or breeze; it will lead you to where you need to go." But what breeze, what breath? Where did he need to go? What was the . . .

The warmth in his left ear felt like a summer breeze out in the meadow where the gooseberries wou . . . "Tink." But why wou . . . "Tink?" Who was calling . . .?

Skth gave up and just blew in his ear, the warm breath turned to a roaring airflow as she ended it with a gentle poke at his shoulder and a quiet, "Tink".

A mud green eyelid raised and before he could focus, she caught a glimpse of what she could swear was a gold eyeball, but as he blinked, she saw that it was only his usual brownish green eyes with those little flecks of gold; not what she had thought she saw. He looked at her as if she had six eyes and three heads. "Skth?" he tried.

"Wow! Those knocks on your head do that much damage, little brother?"

Tink whipped his head around to the other side as if he was under attack from both sides, and in a way, he was. Looked at Boomer, looked back at Skth, back at Boomer, back at Skth, "What are you two . . . I mean, umm," back at Boomer, then Skth, "Oh man, it is soooo good to see you." He smiled that the comment had also made her smile, settle down on the edge of the pillow, and stroke his head.

"How are you doing?" she asked, concerned as she looked him over and noticed the large scab on his left wing web, and the peppering of tiny scabs all over him as well as the entire left shoulder and various paintbrush strokes along his face and neck.

"I'm doing fine, now," Tink leaned his head into the soft claw strokes. "But why did you have to bring him?" He rolled his eyes toward his sibling standing on his other side, who struck an exaggerated face of mock offence.

"Hey," started the offended, "I'm standing right here for goodness sakes. I'm so offended; I might not even stick around for breakfast or anything."

"Yeah, right," muttered the warm deep rumbling voice of Scout. "And leave all those biscuits for me to finish up I suppose." He got up slowly and slurped a big wet lick on Boomer's face as he headed for the door.

"Oh, YUCK!" Boomer "stage" wiped at the friendly lick splash on his face. "Dog slobber from a three legged dog! Yuck - what will become of my face?" He howled in mock horror, fell over, and rolled on the floor in "stage" agony.

Scout nosed the swinging door, eyed the theatrics and decided to help the noise level a bit to stir Jon towards breakfast and knowledge that they had guests invading the front room. "Woof!" "And, it's so good to see you too, Boomer." "Woof, Woof." As he dove through the little door and it clacked in swinging back. Clack, clack-clack-clack, the morning had started as the dragons could hear the groans of the old man rousing in the bedroom. Boomer's stomach growled and Skth felt Tink start to rise as Tink realized that he needed to follow Scout outside.

The smell of bacon frying was something that Skth had never smelt, and it was enticing. She perched on the counter, hiding behind a coffee pot stuffed in a cozy. She had tasted the strange hot brown liquid but preferred a couple of sips of what Tink was drinking, not knowing that it was just coffee with cream and sugar. Maybe she liked it because it was what Tink was drinking. The bacon was definitely a point of fascination with her. The cooking of the fat was nothing like the rending of blubber when big fish were cooked or partitioned into the meat that is smoked or dried and the blubber that was rendered down into a solid that would keep for future mixing into foods. In the diet of a dragon that flies all day or night in the subzero weather above the Arctic Circle, fat becomes a very important fuel in every meal. Unfortunately, blubber does not smell like bacon, or as Jon said, "It is sad for the pig that he smells so good when cooked." Then, just when she had thought she had smelled the most wonderful smells in Jon's kitchen, he opened the oven and took out the large pan of biscuits.

Boomer laughed over the remains of yet another great breakfast. "I thought you were going to pass out and fall into the pan." She had stood perched, teetered on the edge of the baking pan, looking over at what Jon was doing and had stood weaving around as she was trying to catch every scent of what seemed to be "heaven on earth". She had heard the term, but had never understood the concept. When Boomer had noticed Jon putting on the large hand coverings and opening the hot chamber called an oven, he said, "Here comes heaven," and she was sure that was what he meant. Now they were all teasing her for not having known these things before.

She looked for help from the seemingly only friend she had at the moment, but he was concentrating on picking at his scabs. He was working on each of the tiny little scabs covering the bumps of his skin that had been sanded off by the coarse sand of the beach when he had carved a mighty trench into the wet shoreline. She noticed the bumps that he had already removed the scabbing from, and they looked every bit like gold in this light by the windows. Boomer stopped laughing as he noticed Skth concentrating on Tink who was concentrating on littering Jon's house with his tiny little scabs. At first Boomer was offended for Jon, but when he noticed the freshly uncovered skin, he switched to his hunt fovea and zeroed in on the small area. Sure enough, there was what looked like tiny dots of gold.

"Is that *real* gold Tink?"

"I don't know," his brother muttered as he peeled another and larger dot of scab. "I really haven't figured out what it is." He looked up at the other three, and turned to his sibling. "Do you ever remember me ever having a cut or wound where I had a scab?"

They thought, and slowly Boomer offered, "I really don't think so." Reaching for the large scab that ran down Tink's left arm and onto his shoulder, he hooked a couple of sharp claws into the layer and pulled almost all of the scab away, exposing not the pink flesh he was expecting but a fresh patch of Tink's skin that just happened to be gold.

The seven eyes marveled as the four persons sitting about the table sat dumbfounded. Finally the fifth person in the room, hobbled over and joined them saying, "Big deal, let's go to the beach and . . . um," looking at the only female, adjusted his intent, "exercise a bit."

Tink translated, and they all laughed as Jon grabbed for his hat, quipping, "Mon due, Scout; always the gentleman." Rising he finished, "Well, rise if we must, to move and remove." He chuckled at his own joke that skirted, only slightly the male naughty.

"Oh no, move?" Skth had just realized how deadly a half piece of bacon, almost a whole egg, almost two ounces of kippered herring and two biscuits fully dripping with butter and honey could really be. "Why didn't anybody warn me?" As the males all laughed and prepared to depart. Scout, taking pity, came close and told her, "Here, you can ride down." Once saddled up, they were off.

The strange group made a curious parade as they wandered and poked along the edge of sand and dune grass in the light breeze that filled the air with salty sea smells. The sawing sounds of the swaying grass was a soothing symphony to cover for the lack of marching in the parade as they did more poking than wandering. Joyful teasing and stories in the sharing of two brothers growing up so differently, and Jon sharing a bit more of the less painful parts of his childhood and later years working on a fishing boat in the North Sea.

Tink flew some hard laps out and around the last buoy, back and over the town and around the four steeples and back around the circuit at least five times with his brother carefully watching each and every wing stroke, every turn, every dip in the altitude, rise with an effort or facial expression that could betray pain or distress. As they returned on the last lap, Boomer confided that he thought the life of sun and sea with Jon and Scout was good for Tink, but maybe this should be his last week, and then he would come and get him.

Tink was quiet as they slowly winged back towards the tiny dots on the beach. He turned to his brother, "These days have been good. I'm recovering, but I think Jon is finally recovering too." He looked out to sea, and spotted a tiny blue speck turning rolls and flips in the air. "The good doctor, as young as she is, has also been very good for him. Even with the great age difference, he is beginning to talk to her, and not about me. I think she may be the daughter he never had, and that will be good." As they got closer to the beach, he watched the tiny blue. "And what is the story about bringing Skth away from everything she knows?"

"It was a request. Not from her, it came from elsewhere. I'm supposed to deliver her by tomorrow morning to Twill at the Paws & Claws." Tink's eyebrow shot up as he looked at his brother using his side fovea. "That is all I can tell you, and you probably shouldn't even know that. We will spend the evening, and leave around four in the morning if that is OK with Jon. I'll need his help with the harness, and I know I can't fit me, the harness, and Skth in it through Scout's little door."

"So, you didn't bring her to torment me."

"Hah! If I had thought of that, I would have brought her four weeks ago." He shot ahead, as Tink swiped at him with outstretched claws.

"You're getting sloooooooooooow," he called back as he went into an inverted spiral auguring toward the earth. "Too many biscuits!" Tink's laughter echoed his as Tink acknowledged the truth within his expanded self.

The two shot over the man and dog and were then joined in the air by a tiny blue streak who tapped each on the head in a nod to counting coup. Below, a third figure with loose flowing dark hair joined the two below and hugged each in turn, and entwined her arm through the older man's, they walked slowly following the leader, a now much happier and tired dog. Yvet thought it was just a trick of the eye that she saw a third dragon flying overhead, so she ignored it for the time being.

"You've caused quite a stir here in the village." Yvet shared with her bare feet up on the ottoman, her right index finger absently winding and unwinding a lock of her thick flowing dark hair. "To anybody's knowledge, there has never been a dragon, not even passing through."

"Through, or over?" asked Boomer from his post lunch repose snuggled into Scout's side and stomach where he could massage the sore muscle in the dogs arthritic shoulder he had diagnosed four weeks before and the good doctor had confirmed with an X-ray.

"Well," she nodded to the wisdom of that qualifier, "now I know the difference. But a dragon that the people had *known* was here or passing through."

"But there had to have been dragons coming through here all the time during the Fairy Wars," offered Skth, as she now tried to resist picking at the last scabs on Tink. Although they had established that the healed flesh was indeed gold, they just did not know why, and she kept forgetting to ask about the gilt flecks in his eyes.

"What wars?" ask the lounging doctor as she looked over to see if Jon knew, but he had long surrendered in his battle to keep his eyes open, and so she returned her focus on the porcelain doll-like tiny blue dragon. She still found it amazing that she could talk to this and the other dragons. It was just such a surreal experience. The day Tink came to the clinic to get his stitches removed; there had been no less than 30 people and pets. When he left, suddenly all seemed cured of whatever had been ailing them.

"The great wars of the Fairies; that happened all over the world; in fact, it was the widespread destruction from the Fairy Wars that caused the creation of the Fairy Princess." The offhand recitation as if she was talking about commonly known events did nothing to stop Yvet from sitting up and coming fully awake; that and a vague childhood recollection of fairytales from her grandmother. In fact, her grandmother had even stressed that they were *Fairy Tales*, not fairytales.

"When did these wars happen?"

"Hmm, now that you ask, I don't know. I'm sure that they were at least over a thousand years ago, maybe two or three thousand years; there are a lot of niches in the shrine, and they are all assigned. One for each Princess and a Princess every one hundred years . . ." Skth had not looked up and seen the intense interest on the doctor's face.

"I think I counted about seventy or more in just the main chamber of the shrine," Tink slurred sleepily. The tender ministrations of the little blue had certainly mesmerized him.

"But that would mean they predated . . . predated King Tut and that was only 2,500 BC." Yvet crushed herself back into the overstuffed couch and pillows, staring up at the ceiling. Her mind reeled. If this had been a subject of conversation even two months ago, she would have dismissed it as fantasy science fiction. But now that she knew three dragons, and knew that they were part of a much larger community of everything she had thought was real as a little girl, but had dismissed as she "grew up." The concept was just slightly jarring, not disturbing *per se*, but just unsettling.

"Well, how old is . . ." then she noticed that she had missed her chance as all three winged creatures, the fuzzy one and the older one had all departed on the sleepy-bye train. Yvet standing alone at the station, with a head buzzing with too many questions . . . and then there were six on the train as it chugged and snored its way into the drowsy lazy afternoon. The questions on the good doctor's mind would have to wait for another day. Scout rolled and groaned. Boomer snuggled deeper and grunted. Skth sighed with a smile. Jon snored, and Tink squeaked as he snored. Somewhere on a very deep level, the little Yvet in the grown-up doctor smiled as she snuggled happily into one of the big soft pillows. She felt safe, secure, and home - a strange mix for a family, but home, nonetheless.

"Just a couple of fish balls, and we have to be off," Boomer stated. He had transformed back into the official courier that was delivering a package, a very special package indeed. He knew HE was already a couple of hours late and would have to make up the lost time at top speed over open water, and he was worried. She did not know how to hold her wings the way Tink would have. Just then he glanced out into the yard where Tink had been talking to Skth, no, not talking - *training* her to hold her wings in the correct stall formation to provide the needed lift.

As he dragged the harness outside, Tink filled him in, "I think she has it, but we won't know for sure until you hit Mach 2. I think you should take a run over to about Amsterdam or Brussels real quick and see if she gives you the right amount of lift." He had turned a little official himself as he strapped his brother into the harness and checked the fit. Pulling a little at the bellyband and commenting with a raised eyebrow, "Hmm, biscuits," Tink smiled with the joke they shared a part of.

"She's got the strength, it will just need to be the right form and holding it," he continued as Skth climbed into the cockpit of the harness. Tink gently took hold of the leading edges of her wings and rubbed them against the edge of the cone and a couple of nubs caused by round head nails Tink had driven in there. "Can you feel these nubs? That is exactly where your wings have to stay." She nodded; there was no time for talk. "And if you feel him getting the speed for Mach 3, his muscles here will be getting real hot. If that happens, you have to jam your wings against those nubs very hard and keep them there! Then hold on tight, because it feels like your guts are trying to go sideways and your head and tail are trying to switch places. Don't worry about Mach 4, he can't do it over the warmer water. Just hold on tight, try to become part of his body and it will be all over before you even get to have fun." Tink without thinking leaned over and kissed the clear Perspex cone that separated him from her. What he did not notice was the trace of gold he left.

Boomer saluted, and erupted into the air, circled once and then swooshed by like a speeding bullet. Much was on his mind as his internal compass zeroed towards the ocean and then Brussels as he cracked the initial sound barrier just at the water's edge. Water, sand, crabs and bits of seaweed spewed into the air. He had never heard how riding on his back affected his brother in all the years they had been, he thought, having fun. Now he wondered why Tink would even volunteer to do something that made him so uncomfortable. He would have to ask next week when he returned for Tink. However, for now - Mach 2 in three, two - and BANG!

Everything Tink had told her was true, but it was the most amazing thing in her entire life. Her wings could feel the stress and pounding as the airfoil evolved and changed. She braced harder as she realized that the handholds were becoming more than comfortably warm. They were becoming as hot as the steam tunnels, and her wings found the nubs as she braced herself and thought of iron, her body becoming iron. They slid through into the next level of the speeds of sound as the courier began a wide arcing turn and a climb to a higher smoother altitude. He reset his compass to their final destination. The reverberation of the sonic path they were laying down blew a little more dust off the chimney of a little white cottage, and Jon looked up with a smile. His heart was fluttering, but he now knew it was only a good friend, saying "Hello." He patted the hand that now seemed so natural on the inside of his arm as he looked at the good doctor's concern and mouthed, "Je vais bien, I'm OK." They looked back at the other two as they came up the walk, a three-legged dog, and a battered but getting better little mud green . . . and gold dragon talking a mile a minute in their own language.

Jon chuckled as he opened the door, "Who knew Scout had so much to talk about?"

The day was grim and a reminder that fall was rapidly approaching with the summer little more than half over. The marine layer hung thick and heavy on the water and around the dangerous rocks that edged the shoreline. The cormorant paid no attention to any of the conditions; it was as if she was on a guide wire or could see right through the thick fog and dark day as she continued on her path. To her the day was neither a sunny summer or a wintery fall or anything in between, it was just air, wet air; and it stood between her and where she needed to go and so she just kept flapping her wings. Up and down, up and down. No elegance, no grace, no beauty - just purpose and reason. The green fire in her eyes danced around the rim that embraced the boiling gold that saw nothing but her destination. Under the bird, the sea gave way and she pitched in a slope that glided her down the lane to her mission's goal and a small white cottage with a thatched roof.

Gliding around the little cottage, she scanned the windows for her quest. Bedroom, something she could not see into, back door, curtains drawn, table. Yes, this would be the window, and she fluttered to the grass. Hopping up onto the windowsill, she looked deep into the depths of the cottage. There was a dog. Where was the dragon? Where? She searched … there, on the pillow, the color almost blending in the dim light.

She tapped the window with her beak. Again. Again. What would it take to awaken this lazy sleeping group? She tapped. Then she spied the small rock. Hopping down and bouncing over to the rock, she took it in her mouth and lifted up off the ground headed for the top of the chimney where she would drop the stone down into the fireplace. Her landing on the top of the chimney confronted her with a stovepipe and draft hat. "Damn," she thought, "coal stove." She dropped down to return to her tapping on the window.

As she flared her great wings at the windowsill, she was startled with the visage of a large man standing directly at the window in his underclothes. Both cried out and fell back, the cormorant spewing feathers about the yard and Jon, falling through a chair and upon the floor. The crashing scared Scout to duty and Tink almost wet the pillow before he remembered himself and rushed to the window and Jon.

"What happened? Are you alright?" Scout and Tink both asked.

Jon, recovering but trying to get his voice, kept flapping his arm and hand towards the window. He finally managed, "In . . . in the yard." The concept just left him stranded between what he used to know and his life as it was now. Scout and Tink both looked at the window, and then back at Jon, up to the window and his hand fanning at the window and then his face, where he was beginning to laugh at the whole idea of where his life had taken him. Laughing, he rolled over to his knees and hands and began to get up. As he came face to face with Tink, he stopped, laughed and chuckled, "I think there is a friend of yours out in the garden," he whispered. Chuckling, he heaved himself upright and sat in one of the chairs, and pointed at the cormorant that had returned and perched in the window. "Friend . . . of yours?" as he caught his breath.

The cormorant with the golden eyes stared at Tink. "I think so," he whispered in return.

Tink passed through the dog door and was around the corner of the cottage to the window like a shot.

"M'Loree?" he asked softly as he skidded to a hover in the air.

"Well, more or less. Not completely, and well, that is not what I need to talk to you about anyway." She hopped down and bounced over to a rock that would make a better perch. "Damn inconvenient way to travel bouncing along the ground, why don't they learn to walk." She muttered rhetorically, more to herself than to Tink.

Turning her attention back to Tink she looked him all over with a critical appraising eye. "Hmm, gold," she muttered, "I would have thought yellow or red myself, interesting." Then as if she was seeing Tink for the first time, she asked in a perky off handed way. "So my boy, how are you feeling now?" She bobbed and waved her head and then tried her wing, "Considering the rough landing you had looking for a place to sleep and all." Tink was trying his best to follow the large bird's bobbing and gyrations. It caused him to wonder how to fit a thousand pound sea dragon into a fourteen-pound bird, and he was almost starting to laugh. Then he realized that she was having a hard time talking and making gestures with the body of the unfamiliar bird.

"Yes, well," he started, until she actually rolled her head around and along with her upper body, almost fell over from what Tink interpreted as an arm winding along as in "get with it." So he did his best to explain where he was in his recovery.

"Forget it. Go home. Now!" She dismissed him.

"But it would take me at least two days to fly home on my own."

"Good - because you don't have three," she hopped down and got very close to Tink's nose. "You need to leave now. This minute. Right now! You have no time to spare," she demanded.

Tink turned back toward the cottage just as Jon and Scout were coming out the back door. "I need to say good bye and have breakfast," he pleaded, "I can't travel on an empty stomach . . ."

"Two pieces of fish, and say good bye now; you have no time to waste. The life of the Princess hangs in the balance and only you can tip the scales in her favor. You are the Patron; you must face the challenge." She flicked her beak at Jon, "Ask him for two pieces of fish, and then you must go; but you must hurry!" Spreading her large wings she pushed off and beat the ground with the first three beats of her wings and she slowly made air way, ascended into the fog and was gone.

After the strange strained breakfast of two pieces of fish, that proved oddly enough, Tink promised to come back some time, and he too flapped into the fog as if it was not there. He could clearly see what was hidden to others. As he flew farther, he thought perhaps his injuries would control his capabilities, he found they drove him harder. Not that he was anywhere near capable of the 2,000 miles per hour needed to break the third sound barrier, but he could feel the muscles in his upper trapezius that drove the wings begin to become a lot warmer than they ever had before. With that heat, he felt there seemed strength in his rowing with the wings and the speed with which he was continuing to row the air. He remained focused although he kept hearing M'Loree's words, "You are the Patron!" The life of the new Princess depended on him! He was the very smallest dragon in a small picture frame shop on the edge of a forest – yet he was the one. Who could have guessed such a thing?

As the night crept up on the little flying dragon, and the short shadows that had grown long became nothing more than just inky blackness, his muscles ached, but felt strangely good; the tear, scrapes, scuffs, and insults to his body and skin, were not as tender as he would have thought. In fact, they felt pretty good considering; *"Considering what?"* he thought, his focus was getting back, not even a "back to," but just "back". He was drawn, and with that draw, were half remembered, half thought, half stated questions, answers and just things. Things like *"If he was the Patron, who was the Princess?"* and his wings pushed, his tail guided, his body continued and through the night, the little dragon flew.

# # #

"What do you mean he just flew off, Jon? He was injured, I was sent to bring him back." Boomer was worried and confused. His mother had sent him to bring Tink home and now Jon was saying that he had already taken wing and was flying himself home. The red dragon did not think his little brother was capable of such a feat, and the good doctor agreed with him. Yet it was only the day before, right after a strange breakfast of two pieces of fish eaten in the front yard, and a couple of quick hugs that Tink had disappeared into the thick fog.

"The bird had scared the holy saints out of me at the window with those flaming gold eyes and all that flapping around and then Tink said he had to leave and couldn't even come in and have breakfast."

"Wait. What bird?"

"A cormorant; and it banged on the window that morning and woke us all up."

"Cormorant? With flaming eyes?" Boomer felt himself losing track of the conversation very quickly.

"Oui, certimon! Strange gold eyes, with a green flame in them. Scared me half to death."

"And Tink came out and talked to the bird?"

"Oui."

"And then he left."

"Non."

"No?" Boomer was bobbing up and down as he was having trouble controlling the conversation as much as his hover flight.

"Non, he ate two pieces of fish, hugged Scout and me, said he would come visit some time, and then he left." Jon was proud of getting everything straight.

Boomer thought for a whole claw full of seconds, grabbed Jon by the shoulder and confided, "I've got to go, my friend."

"Of course," Jon said to the empty swirling air, as he then heard the now familiar sonic boom from a mile or more away. "Of course, why should anything be different," he puttered down to the front gate. "Everybody has got to go." Turning to Scout he asked, "Well, do you have to go too?"

Scout bobbled out the gate as the two old friends traversed a well-worn track on the way to the sea grass. Hundreds of miles out to sea in the north, a cormorant finally let down and landed, tired but rewarded. The floating shape next to her began to move, and finally rolled over and thanked her for the use of a faster shape. Around her were more fish than she would need, or want. As the sea dragon with the gold and green eyes rolled over into the water and flew down into the liquid world, the sea bird was already asleep.

Chapter 10

Under the Hostas

With Chang and Tink both gone, Twill tied up teaching Skth what she needed done and the twins having free run of the shop unhindered, it had been a very long day. As Guff walked slowly between the tables, his paws slid along the edges and memories popped like little bubbles here and there; the trouble with so many years is, after a while, they all seem like this last year.

So many memories: Twill's first day spent covered in hide glue, Danny the Giant Hedge Hog (all three pounds of him), and Chang learning that just because your assistant is slow you still cannot eat him. Dvark learning that not every employer beats his workers, and wanting to nail two small tails down to a bench but settling for ten minutes quality time outside with their great-great-grand aunt. The great shoulders bounced around in the Hawaiian shirt as the palm trees swayed and the hula girls blushed. Guff reached over and turned off the glue pot, but stayed for just an extra moment taking in the smell that had been his friend for almost two hundred years. Who would have guessed that day when he wandered in to talk to the great framer Macklin the Merciless, the last of the man-fairy bloodline, that the framer would woo the bear to carry on his traditions.

Guff ran the smooth back of a claw along the equally smooth coolness of a water gilded gold leaf frame Chang had been working on. The bear could feel the cool of the stone powders that made up the gesso and red clay leafing bole that lay hidden under the gold leaf. First were the secret layers of wood, then stone powders mixed with glue made from hides of animals and finally the different clays, mixed with the same glue, smoothed on and over and then leafed. The gold applied by first brushing on a secret liquid called gilder's liquor and finally the laying of the gold pounded so thin as to be a whisper of its former self; and yet, once combined with the stone and burnished it is made to look as if the whole is solid gold. *"Kind of like some people,"* Guff thought as he reached over and turned off the last four lights, *"Not what they appear to be."*

The front door opened as he approached it, and Guff always enjoyed that little touch of mystery about the shop - it was one of Macklin's finest and most endearing touches. Looking about the front room to make sure everything was as need be for the morning; Guff nodded and strolled out the now closing front door. The satisfying click, ka-chink, and the soft sound of steel sliding into several places were reassuring sounds to the big bear.

The soft last light filtering through the trees of the forest gave an ethereal feel that in Guff's mind matched the smell of the forest that he loved; from the last vestiges of rotting leaves, twigs, and needles that made up the forest floor duff to the heated pine needles that gave off the pungent turpentine odor. Every part of the forest contributed to feel, smell and sound that Guff felt in his entire being every hour of every day of every year of every century of his life. Guff was the forest; and that made him smile.

Just as he started on his daily stroll into the forest, and errant patch of a wrong color was where it should not be. He slowly walked over to the edge of the flagstones and softly lifted the large leaf of a giant hosta to reveal the patch of gold he had spotted there at the edge of a certain coffee mug.

"Tink?" It was not that he did not recognize his smallest framer; it was that he did not expect him back until at least early the next morning.

The little head lifted, but the eyes did not open. He was hearing, maybe; but not really responding.

"Go back to sleep, Tink," the bear calmed, "And come see me when you finally wake up tomorrow." Slowly he replaced the hosta leaf, but moved it aside a bit to study the wing with the large golden patch on the web. Wondering, he was trying to figure out what kind of poultice it could be when he also noticed all of the other flecks and stripes. He stared for another few minutes, and then let the leaf swing back into place. The time for answers would be tomorrow.

The forest night settled softly down upon the ferns and hostas, kissing the duff and flowing into every nook and cranny as the large bear in the bright Hawaiian shirt and colorful footwear disappeared quietly into the forest. The mealy bugs rolled into little balls to retain heat, a stinkbug moved cautiously from a moldy leaf to a chunk of old bark decaying on the forest floor. A large rotting hosta leaf long having fallen brown upon the floor slowly curled up as a tiny dirty pinkish brown hand slowly reached out and carefully hooked a finger and thumb around a tip of mud green wingtip. The warmth of the two in perfect match, as the squeaks and rumble quietly started a common order among the hostas. On the other side of the dirty cracked mug, a small blue claw reached out and mirrored the same gesture with the other wing tip.

The quiet of the forest was deafening as the little frogs seared the night air, bullfrogs thumped the universe with a slow bass drum, and the crickets kept time as they marked off the temperature on their legs. Bats flittered through the night air voraciously straining the air of tiny living dust motes and larger insects. In the distance, the sound of a successful owl hunt reverberated through the trees, and a cool white blue dragon on silent wings whispered through the velvet night sliding as she searched, and seeing what she sought and expected, flapped once and then once again and was gone as if she was never there. Morning would be coming soon enough and for now, many needed rest.

# # #

The door stood open.

The morning dew dripped fresh from the washing of the forest, providing drink for flora and fauna alike, and the flowers began their day uncurling and opening, refreshed from the night's sleep and radiating the promises of a new day. The pill bug finished with the night scavenging, curled into the tiny ball amongst the rotting leaves, ants, moth eggs, aphids, pine needles from several seasons past and a small dirty foot sticking out of the warm cover of a comforting vibrantly alive quilt. A matching tiny hand, even dirtier, still hung near the smudgy streaks on a white porcelain coffee mug, all hiding under the variegated and deep green giant leaves of the hosta carpet which covered the smaller secret world of the forest floor.

The red clogs appeared through the large leaves as the tiny foot retracted safely back under the forest duff. Guff would normally continue towards the front door that would then open for him. Today, however, the clogs just stayed by the hostas. The large bear in the flashy black Hawaiian shirt depicting the nightlife of Waikiki beach including a full moon over Diamond Head and surfers filling the ocean night as the great waves rolled toward the sand that stood as static as the wearer stood. His deep brown eyes held a burning fire deep within as he scanned the building and a door that should open only for him when he stepped out into the entry patio. He knelt slowly and moved one of the leaves aside to make sure a small dragon was still in the mug where he should be. He was.

Guff's brow furrowed as he bent even closer to examine the gold flecks that the night before he had thought were just a trick of the light. In the light of the morning, he could now see that there truly were patches and specks of gold where mud green should be. Guff's brown eyes were glowing even redder as he rose, taking in this new information in addition to the necessity of trying to figure out the original matter still before him; and all before anyone else showed up.

As he cautiously stepped out onto the flagstones towards the thatched roof atelier, his eyes took in every window, the door, the forest around; the smells were filtered through his great nose with each and every scent registered, cataloged and identified except one. That one was the single scent that gave Guff pause. He knew he should know this scent; one of damp feathers, mixed with wet fur and stirring of cinnamon and turmeric steeped in sweat like a locker room for exotic animals; but the identity was eluding him as he stood there. Then, there was the matter of what should be a locked door, standing wide open.

144

"Down!" And Guff dropped reflexively to the flagstones as the large blue dragon streaked through the air he had occupied barely a split second before.

Only a few times had Guff seen Twill spread to her full attack size, then contracting for the door, resume her launched attack. The visual still left him wondering if she had just passed through the walls as a specter instead of a dragon in full combat mode. The white-hot blue dragon flared to protectively fill the front door then was gone as she moved to the workroom.

Picking himself up, Guff slowly made his way to the door, and entered the design room. The scent was stronger, but still only a latent lingering of a passage instead of a presence. The brown eyes missed nothing as they scanned the room and found almost everything as it had been the night before, except the frame and mat samples resting on the design table. As he moved with trepidation toward the table, he could see a small picture there also.

Still eyeing the arch that lead to the workroom, Guff moved sideways toward the design table and the tiny tableau that lay there. Taking a long look back into the darker area of the workroom, and still hearing nothing from his protector, he glanced down at the image for which the framing was being designed. Puzzled, he looked back out the front door, and then back at the same scene mirrored in the picture. He stood staring at the picture, and finally, carefully with two claws, lifted it and held it up as he faced the door, to find that it was not exactly a stereo view, but just slightly altered by a season or so. The picture was of late fall.

Guff looked again back in the silent workroom and with one last glance at the picture and outside, noted a couple of other changes as he replaced it on the desk. He now knew the identity of his unseen customer, or at least he suspected he knew. It was the nature, or rather the uncertain nature, of the visit that bothered him as he walked quietly into the workroom.

The great blue was at his office door, flared in full battle stance, ever the protector; even after all these years. Guff smiled at his very oldest and dearest friend. "Twill," she turned only slightly towards him, but he knew that she could see everything around her, including the persona in his office. He could now even smell the fresh coffee, as he glanced over at the still cold coffee pot; he smiled at the knowledge and confirmation of who was now sitting in his chair. "It's OK, Twill," he nodded, "I'll take it from here."

There was a moment of hesitation, before she stood down and became the grandmotherly Twill who ran his workshop with a soft iron claw, and a quick-to-comfort tongue. The Twill he would lay down his life for, but he was very aware that their lives were dealt the other way around; it was she who was the Patron, not he.

She relinquished the door and he laid his paw gently on the crest of her wings. He felt the steel soften to just hard iron, and asked her, "Could you start the dragon fuel please; the crew will be showing up and you know how those sleepy heads are without their morning rocket fuel." He smirked and they both chuckled at the old joke about dragons only surviving for coffee.

"Coffee coming right up, sir," as she turned toward the coffee station, the heart and maybe soul of the shop's crew; and most certainly morning life's blood, she had another thought. "Oh, and speaking of coffee, how . . ." but she found herself looking at a thick oaken door that had not been there a mere second ago.

"Well," she thought, *"I guess my concern for Tink can wait."* However, her real thoughts were on the mass of white feathers, flowing from a large head of the person that sat in Guff's chair. It had not turned around to face her but its lion's tail, hanging from the seat, had twitched as she flared in the door, though for some reason she found herself unable to enter the office.

Twill, looking back over her shoulder, she started measuring out the coffee as she strained her fine hearing to try to overhear the conversation in the office. She heard only the flap of two pair of wings coming through the forest - Trouble and his twin Trouble. She groaned and rolled her eyes. Great - the start of another perfect day!

Guff felt the very thick door materialize behind his tail, and it felt it might have even caught a hair or two. He really did not know whether to be happy or worried and decided to take an off-hand approach.

"Well Macklin, or should I say M'Loree now; I hope you got me some of that Sumatran coffee too," he began. The tail twitched and a white-feathered arm slowly swung out from the side of the chair presenting a large mug of steaming brown nectar tempered with cream and honey.

". . . With two dollops of cream, and a 'wish' of honey for the bear in your morning?"

Taking the proffered mug, Guff sipped with his eyes closed as he also breathed in the aroma of the rare coffee, sea cow's cream and honey from the bees on a high Alpine valley. Slowly savoring the mouthful of a memory over a hundred years old, he eased his girth down on the corner of the large desk, much as he had when he first came to Paws & Claws. His eyes, battling luxurious torpidity, opened and the dark brown danced with a certain joy as he looked over the large old gryphon filling his chair.

"A gryphon - now that's reaching back a few years."

"Yes, well, I was feeling . . . hmm, shall we say, historical."

Guff raised his left eyebrow, something unusual for a bear. "Hmm, that's reaching back a very long time." He sipped at the coffee and thought about the spans of time. "So, that would make this more of an official visit?"

"It is time, and she will start feeling the pull soon, but I'm not so sure he will be ready for what he needs to do to overcome the challenge." The eagle head of the gryphon nodded at windows overlooking the front entrance. "When he gets back he will . . ."

"He's back already."

The eyes of the bird flashed open with surprise. "What? Are you sure?"

"He was home last night."

"Impossible!" the gryphon snapped, and then gazed out at the lush carpet of hostas. "He would have to have flown straight through non-stop," the gryphon looked back at Guff, "and in his condition that just.... he had a hole in his wing."

"There is another development, too." Guff slid off the desk and walked to the many windowed corner of the office. "It appears that his injuries all healed over as gold."

The golden eyes of the gryphon sparkled and boiled as the green sea grass around the edges wavered in the pattern. "The Kell," she whispered. "Yes, I noticed that, but hadn't been really paying attention; I was cohabiting with a cormorant at the time.

The large bear stood looking out of the windows, sipped from the mug, and slowly nodded. The silence of their combined thoughts was deafening. He turned back to look at the gryphon now slumped with resolve, back into the soft receptive chair.

"It won't happen. He can't fly that high." The gryphon looked up at the bear and fellow Princess with knowledge of the full implication of their conversation. "I don't even think his brother can fly that high, do you?" The look between the two was intense, heartfelt, and full of so much left unsaid. Between these two old souls much never needed saying. The pendulum in the clock on the wall swung in a great glacial arc as if the time that it ticked off echoed their heartbeats. The implication of a Princess never revealed! It had never happened before. But there was always that deeply buried thought, *"What if?"*

Guff looked up at the door as it became a vapor like yesterday's fog. He started to say something, but stopped; a dam of emotions and varied thoughts froze the words in his throat. He was unsure of where to take all of this. A vast chasm yawned forth in his mind that he was unsure of the crossing or even if he wanted to.

The gryphon turned the chair slightly towards the door and as he watched the bear, parroting him in Guff's voice, "Twill, could you come in here, please, and bring some more coffee?" The left eyebrows of each, furred and feathered, mirrored each other. The smiles were quick to follow as the blue and a pot of coffee were floating between them as she looked back and forth at the two as if they were the pair of errant dragons now working diligently at their assigned tasks.

"Twill, we'd like to ask you some questions," the gryphon started in Guff's voice, until the imitated ursine rumbled a throat clearing that put the other in place. The gryphon sheepishly smiled and offered to the bear a quiet, "Sorry."

"What we would like to know," Guff continued as Twill shot the gryphon one of those famous grandmotherly "I've got my eyes on you" looks that even on this large persona still had the desired effect. "Your mentor - did they have any doubts about your performing your challenge?"

"My mentor?"

"As a Patron. Your Patron mentor."

Finally realizing that she was still stuck on who was lounging in the chair that was Guff's and Guff's alone, while the bear was made to stand in an office accessorized specifically to that end, Guff broke down, "Twill, this is M'Loree. You would know her as Nord M'Loree, Shrine protectorate on . . ."

"Bjørnøya, Bear Island; welcome Mistress err Master - sorry for the reception." She gave a curt bow, still not relinquishing her protector position. The gender difference was confusing, even after 200 hundred of getting used to the possibilities of Princesses, it was still perplexing.

"Twill, my dear, you had no way of knowing I was coming. Even Guff could not have known. As you may guess, I am not even here; officially. No harm, no foul; but good to see the old skills are still sharp and devoted after two hundred years." The kinder grandmotherly side oozed out as easy as a flare could have brought a claw. The boundaries now marked, the return was necessary.

"We are worried about the upcoming challenge and the condition of the future Patron. And we figured who better to know, then a past Patron . . . and as mine has been dead these past millennia . . . we thought to burden you." The eyes drooped in deference to the blue as M'Loree raised the mug of fresh, although pedestrian coffee to her beak.

Twill rocked her weight from hind claw to hind claw, unconsciously sinking her claws into the rock hard oak floor. Evaluating the spoken question, weighing the unspoken, this was not as simple as gold or silver, the linen mat or do we carry a more refined tone with some raw silk on the mat? This crossed borders between knowledge and propriety between Princesses and Patrons and the information shared or not shared. She was now in a position that she had not been in even with the last reveal a hundred years before; even though she had been close to all involved.

With all that weighed, she asked, "Do we know who the new Patron is?"

Guff put down his mug and with a hurt look, turned to the window and focused thousands of miles away as his heart lurched and broke. It was just all too close.

"Yes," M'Loree intoned quietly, "We believe it is Tink."

Almost anyone else could have kept Twill composed and in a dispassionate discussion, but this was too close to home, too soon, too, well, close to the heart.

Each of the three struggled with their own feelings and demons, as the pendulum swung left and then crept right. Time was almost meaningless for them, and yet time had slowed to a crawl. Nevertheless, as meaningless as time becomes, friends and family become even more meaningful and sometimes size has no meaning at all.

In a whisper that she never wanted to utter, Twill asked the most important question of all, "Do we know his challenge?" She looked to the fur at the back of the one she had protected all these years, and then to the golden boiling eyes of the oldest living Princess. Neither could voice what to expect, nor the nature of the challenge, but as the only one with the personal knowledge, M'Loree projected the image into Twill's mind.

Twill stepped back and reached out for the wall. She needed something to hold onto as she found herself flying high over the Himalayan Mountains. The lack of oxygen was tearing gashes in her lungs as her muscles screamed in agony. She looked at the point on the mountaintop that she knew to be almost two thousand feet higher than where she was now. She knew she would have to be there before the sun hid behind the world and all would be plunged into darkness once again. The sun reflected off the snowcapped mountains but only one called her like a siren, beckoned her to flap her wings harder, push longer, rise up and become the Patron she would need to be and she saw that it was her, and yet the color of her wings and along her nose were mud green with flecks of gold. All of that was only a distraction as she pushed at the thin air, feeling for anything that she could push against in a sky full of nothing.

"Enough!" Guff growled as Twill staggered against the wall. A large warm fuzzy paw steadied her as he turned on the gryphon and growled, "It wasn't her challenge. You pushed her too far."

The beak snapped with the steel of war, "She had to know."

"Why? Because he is so special to her? So you are allowed to thrust instead of just show?" Guff was chuffing now; defending his longest dearest friend, who sagged against him, drained.

"No!" The gryphon now up and pacing, with the claws of the feet, uncontrolled in the heat of the argument unfurled and leaving gouge marks in the floor. "Because, she will have to fill in!" Spinning at the end of the desk and burying an index claw half way into the top of the rock hard, solid oak desktop. "Why do you think I came here? For my health? For fun?" She was leaning into the argument with her wings half-flared and pointing a clawed hand at Twill. "She has to become

Tink's savior, because Tink's mentor is dead." Wrenching the claw out of the desktop sending a chunk of wood the size of a walnut against the distant wall, the gryphon's voice took on even more steel as it lowered to almost a whisper, "He was killed three days ago as he was leaving to come here." Her voice softened, as the circumstance affected her, because she understood the most how it affected all of them. "It was an auto accident on the A-1 Autostrada, between Florence and Milan. It was nobody's fault, it was the fog and many were injured along with the few that . . ." The gryphon melted back into the chair, broken. "He was an aerospace engineer that had a foundation of knowledge specific to dragons. He had even met Tink's brother a few times. The council had felt that he would be the best mentor to guide Tink in how to fly to those altitudes and in oxygen deprivation."

Guff recoiled from the news that he had feared would come of this meeting. That they had danced around, and he had hoped they had danced past; but that was not to be.

Guff had thought for some time that Tink was to be the new Patron. He knew that there was always a challenge to be overcome, for the Patron to become the one they needed to become, to move beyond them-selves, with no more personal considerations and to become focused on the needs of that other half of what would become their existence. The "challenge" was always one that put their life at risk, but only the Patrons knew what the challenges really were, and how much of a risk; even the Patron's own Princess never knew the true extent of what challenge they overcame. It was something a Princess, even a bear, never asked.

To know, beforehand, the enormity for this little dragon was just too much. It made Guff just want to walk back into the forest, and never return. Moreover, he would not be the first, of that he was sure. Little did he know that there was a shrine of past Princesses, or of the urns that lined the walls in the cave of the far north where few, if any, ever saw or even knew of outside a select few of the Northern Clan.

"Are you sure?" The small voice came out of the frailest part of the ice dragon's soul as she still leaned against her friend, recovering. She had asked the gryphon, but Guff confirmed.

"Yes," he nodded, "you will see, when he wakes up, what I have noticed in his eyes for these several months. The Kell is calling, and in his case, will take over his entirety."

"What does that mean?" She looked up at him with a furrowed brow of worry.

M'Loree sat back down heavily in the protesting chair, "We don't know, Twill. No dragon has ever completely been consumed by the Kell." She slowly rocked back and as the chair softly squealed, she looked at Guff... "Really Guff, you need to get a better chair. It was fine for Martin as a large human, but really..."

The big fuzzy bear rolled his shoulders and looked out the window, embarrassed. The lead surfer on the left side of the shirt wiped out and the sun sparkled across the beach and waves of Waikiki as a hot air balloon lifted off over Diamond Head. "It suits me."

Twill, now fully engaged drew the conversation back like the shop master she was, "What do you mean 'consumed' by the Kell?" As her left eye shifted to the central fovea to watch the bear's very active shirt, as distracting as it was, it was in unguarded moments a very good meter of where Guff's mind was, or in an uncomfortable situation, where it wanted to be.

"For those dragons that have ever been called to the Kell; sometimes referred to as the soul of the dragons, it is always for a purpose or reason. The golden eye and head jewel are the marks the great jewel leaves on us. It is the most direct link any dragon ever has to the entire collective of all dragons." As she spoke, the jewel surfaced on the forehead of the gryphon.

"Link?"

"Do you remember when you lived in the Kinnarodden and you could feel the whole of the clan? When one dragon died, the whole clan knew right away?"

Twill nodded.

"That is the way that we who have been to the Kell are connected to every dragon." She ran her off hand, with the backs of the claw smoothing the feathers as it went, down her body. "It is that connection, along with being a Princess, which allows me to shape shift as I need."

"But the connection is only, shall we say, temporal, and not corporeal as it will be in Tink's case." The bear added as he sipped at the coffee now cold in his mug, so he passed it to Twill to blow on.

She gave him "the eye," but acquiesced and with one blow the mug was hot and the coffee steaming. Inwardly she chuckled as she watched her friend quickly put the mug down on the desk, as it had become a little too hot to be comfortable. Her fine sense of smell picked up the singed fur smell as he calmly licked an imaginary drop off his paw.

M'Loree picked up the explanation and ignored the antics of two longtime friends that shared a bond that she could only try to remember. "As where we have all only gone and seen the Kell and stood in its radiance, for some reason, Tink has been called, and I believe he will actually touch the Kell; and we have no knowledge as to what effect that will have on him; and that is worrisome."

"But more importantly at this point, is the question of how a dragon the size of less than the size of a fist, can fly in that rarified air to an altitude of nearly 27,000 feet, and survive."

Twill was still leaning against the wall with the vision vivid in her mind. "I don't know," she shrugged herself off the wall as she noticed outside the window some activity among the foliage. "But I can tell you two things. First is that when a Patron starts on their challenge, there is no other thought in their mind; so there is no option for failing." As she moved toward the workroom, she added at the doorway, "Second, your Patron is coming through the front door right now," and she was gone.

Guff opened the window as the barred owl with boiling golden eyes hopped to the sill, and was gone as the voice in his head mentioned sharing a conversation and dinner that evening in a certain clearing a few miles to the North under what would become a full moon. Guff decided that the day would be pleasant enough to leave the windows open, as he carefully stuck a claw in the coffee to see if it had cooled sufficiently enough to drink. As he sat down at his desk, in his own chair at last, he thought about putting his feet up, and then looked at the doorway where his next conversation waited. "Come in, Tink."

Twill walked up behind Tink with a small cup of coffee with honey and milk in it, just the way the diminutive dragon liked it. "Come along dear, we need to talk to you," as she shooed the rum punchy little tyke into the office and the door materialized behind her catching her tail which slid easily through the seemingly solid oak door, which was OK with Twill, but still a bit unnerving to have happen to your tail. Tink flittered to the top of the desk.

"How are you feeling, other than tired?" Guff asked the cross-eyed, red-eyed, weaving as if he was a drunken dragon. "Don't you think you might need a little more sleep?"

"Coffee," the tiny dragon slurred. "I just need some rocket fuel, and I'll be right with you."

Twill and Guff both worked hard at not laughing, as well as resisted the urge to reach over and pull the little head out of the coffee in which he seemed to be drowning. True to dragon form, the level of coffee lowered at an alarming rate. The shop coffee had taken Guff such a long time to become accustomed to but seemed like mother's milk to the shop dragons.

Finally, the little guy slowed down and Guff leaned over to look at his tummy, which was amazingly not bloated. For the thousandth time, Guff wondered where dragons stored all that coffee. Then the mud green head with the bloodshot eyes rose up out of the bottom of the cup, as the little pink tongue cleaned the lips, nose and everywhere else that had been submerged so happily in the brown elixir…. Then it hit Guff, that is exactly why Tink was the color that he was… he was supposed to be a green, but for all the coffee. The only two dragons that consumed more coffee were Pu and Chang, and they both outweighed him by at least forty to fifty times. The thought was too much for him and Guff started laughing, Tink was confused, and Twill just threw up her claws, said something about boys never could behave and stormed out.

Guff was almost crying as he patted Tink on the foot and the desk as if to say, wait around this is too good not to share. Tink fell back on the base of his tail with his hind legs splayed out, wavered a bit and fell over dead asleep. Of course, this just set Guff off even worse. But he still felt awful for the little guy, so he gently picked him up and took him back out to the hostas and placed him properly back into his mug.

A dirty little head appeared out of the rotting musky leaves, a pine needle draped over on pointed ear, and bits of leaves matted in her hair. "Hello," she squeaked.

"Hello, Duff." The great bear seemed to get a little smaller, as he sat down on the last flagstone. "We haven't met yet, but I know all about you. My name is Guff."

"You're Tink's boss," she thought a moment and finished, "and friend."

"That's right."

"You make picture frames."

"My crew does most of the work these days; but yes, that is what we do."

"Does Tink make the picture frames too?" She peeled back some more layers of leaves and some other stuff that Guff could not even begin to identify.

"Ooh!" She lightly squealed and quickly reached behind herself, apparently in her leggings and her right hand brought back a pill bug. Duff blushed, kissed it on the nose and as it rolled up, said, "That was not a good place for you", and bowled it away back under the darker areas of the forest floor.

In an effort to conceal his embarrassment, try not to laugh and be gracious, Guff continued the conversation. "Tink is part of the whole team. He is a very important part and that part is helping others to do their job as well."

"Can he make things gold?"

"I don't understand the question." Guff feared he was about to step out on some very thin ice in this conversation with this very interesting small creature.

"I had a dream last night that Tink made me a picture frame with hard water with gold floating around in it. It glowed, and it was for one of the forest pictures I make."

"Forest pictures?" Guff had truly become completely confused. "What kind of pictures of the forest do you make? Wait - how do you make them?"

"Just pictures of the forest." She said now becoming shy, as she did not know how else to explain what she did.

"I can show you," she offered.

"Please, I would love to see them." As he looked to see if they were disturbing the small dragon, he realized that the fact that Tink had even woken up and come into his office was probably the most amazing thing he could expect to see this day; but he was about to find out how wrong he could be.

"I'll be right back," Duff cautioned as she drove back into the deep layer of leaves and bugs, pine needles and droppings, moss and mold, smells and . . ..

"Over here," she stood waving from about twenty feet away. Guff got up and carefully picked his way through the lush undergrowth, until he reached Duff standing next to a tiny puddle of water about a fifth the size of Guff's shoe print, if they left a print.

Duff looked about with the eye of an artist. She weighed the light streaming down through the deep part of the forest, the field of hostas, the small thatched cottage of the atelier, and looking back through the break toward the city. Then deciding, she shared her intent with Guff.

Pointing toward the front door of the atelier, she said, "This morning was very unusual. Like every morning, I heard the door unlock, but I hadn't felt you coming from the forest. I had never heard the front door open when you were not there, so I looked. And when I looked, there was a person like I had never seen before walking toward the door." She placed her right hand over the tiny puddle, continuing, "And this is what I saw," and she laid her hand gently on the water, and as it rippled, there occurred shimmers of color on the water. A certain luminescence spread through the tiny bit of water, and as the surface stilled, there was the image of the door opening and a gryphon walking into the atelier, then the door just standing open; and then the scene repeated. Guff was watching what had happened over two hours before.

"How long does it keep repeating that scene?" He blinked, trying to comprehend.

"Oh, I've left a pretty one to repeat over and over for days before, or until the puddle dries up." She was unimpressed with her own talent, because she just "did it" and did not know any better. "Oh course, if I stick my hand back in and swish it around," as she demonstrated, "it just returns to being water." She looked up at Guff, as if to ask if she had done good, like a small child. "Can Tink help?" she asked.

"How can he frame water, and wouldn't it change or go away?"

"Oh, that is where my dream solved that problem. Tink had water that was hard and didn't move; just like the water that is in the windows of your office."

Guff looked back at his office where she was pointing, and saw the glass in the windows that was reflecting the activities of the forest, same as the water of Duff's pictures.

"That is called glass, Duff, and it's very hard."

Guff got up and started toward the shop, "Wait here a minute, I will be right back."

When he returned, he held a small piece of glass in his paw. "This is glass, Duff." He tapped on the glass with one of his claws. "Do you think you can make one of your pictures on this?" He put it down on the forest floor. Duff looked it over.

She looked around at the different thing and views she could picture, and then she looked up at Guff and a smile washed across her dirty face.

She stood silent with her hands clasped together, and then she knelt. Timidly she reached her hand out and placed it on the cool surface of the glass. Guff watched as the surface shimmered and then colors washed across the surface, or was it from within. As the colors slowed, they sank and the glass was dark, dark as the forest floor layer of rotting leaves.

Gruff started to ask something, but Duff raised her hand, and then pointed to the speck of light that grew into a larger area that became a bear in a Hawaiian shirt coming out of the forest. It kept coming until at last, a foot broke through the undisturbed plants and the red clogs were still forming. "I like that picture," Duff said, "You make it every morning and always have a smile. Seeing you that way makes my heart sing."

Gruff realized just what it was that he was seeing. He realized that Duff saw only the dark before he appeared, whereas he saw himself, appearing out of the darkness that *was* the forest. More importantly, she had put it on the hardest liquid known - glass. Her dream must come true.

"Can I keep this Duff?"

"Of course," she tinkled, "it's your piece of water."

# # #

The moon had risen a few hours before. As promised, it was large, bright and full. The owls were having a wonderful time teaching the young ones about the finer points of night hunting, as they could see every little nuance of the flight, stoop and attack. The bats had fed well, as the full moon always brought out more of the flying feast for the fangless. The chorus of the frog trio: grass, tree and bull, was an opera to match anything by any creature. The instrumentals of the cricket, cicada and snap beetle added the needed backbeat that would keep any party lively, even a large bear and a gryphon sharing a picnic of famous fish balls dipped in plum sauce, along with some other tasty tidbits that the chef knew at least one attendee was partial to.

"Tink was right you know," the gryphon mushed out around the fifteenth fish ball, "his mother does make the best fish balls."

"It's a long way to fly just for a few fish balls." Guff burped, long past sated with his limit of twenty, along with the occasional fried fiddlehead. His eyes rolled as he savored the repeat scent of the burp, and then slowly lay back on the grassy side of the hill.

Turning the small piece of glass over in her claw, M'Loree marveled for the hundredth time at the beauty and simplicity of the talent; "and she just put her hand on the glass, and it changed for her?" The bear walked out of the dark of the forest as she held it up to the moon, she could see the moon through the image for the hundredth time with the backlight.

"Her body seemed to generate a bunch of heat when she did it, but other than that, yes."

"And she wanted to know if Tink could gold leaf?"

"No," Guff sat up, thinking, recalling and making sure he got it right. "She wanted to know if he could 'make' gold; very specific on the 'make' part." He rubbed the back of his neck as he thought, "But it was the other part, 'the glass that was lit from within.' That is the part that I don't get." Shaking his big head back and forth, the upper lips waggling back and forth with a touch of the ursine froth just peeking out betraying his frustration with a problem, he sat in his problem under the full moon with the oldest person he knew, and still without answers.

"You know; there is something Skth does with freezing a flame . . . I wonder . . ."

"Freezing a flame?" His face almost screwed up in a snarl, except for the lost look of not understanding mixed the message, "How can you freeze something that is burning?"

"I know," popping the last fish ball in her beak, smearing a bit of the plum sauce happily about on white feathers. "That's what I keep asking. I asked her for a little flame, for by my bed, so I could watch our sisters when I wanted, so she froze the flame in five fingers that reach up and touch at the tips. It is a ball that I can hold, but a light that represents the five worlds of the animal kingdom. There are nights I just lay there staring at the flames, and they never move."

"Have you ever asked Skth?"

"Humpf! Plenty of times," she chuffed, lying back into the grass, and then rolling over on her side to face the bear. She pulled at some bits of grass, and petted the growth that was so alien to her world of sea and stone. "She really doesn't know how she does it. She says, she just asks the flame to burn in a certain shape, then stay that way; and it does." She pulled a few stems of the grass, threw them in the air and blew them even higher, just to watch them flutter back to earth, lightly, delicate and green.

"But, what about the heat from the flame?"

"There is no heat. Nor is it cold like ice. It is just the light of the flame, and the quiet of the freeze. No cold, no heat; just the frozen flame for light."

The bear looked long down the hill as he sensed movement that was intermittent just inside the tree line. Maybe it was a rabbit or some other small creature of the night, searching for food, yet hoping not to become food; turning back to confront the white face of the eagle that was watching the tree line with the intensity of a hunter.

"How long does the flame last?"

Breaking the hunter urge the gryphon turned, "We don't know. She lined the long tunnel that runs from Bear Island to Kinnarodden about 70-75 years ago, and none have stopped burning yet, nor have they dimmed." She shrugged at the information she lived with every day.

"Hmm," now Guff was in the blade of grass tossing and gazing about the pastureland. Then it hit him, and he turned back to his old friend with "one of those looks" that a kid gets into mischief from having.

"70-75 years, eh? So how old is the little dear?" The look of devilment mirrored in white feathers.

"Why, old friend?" The gryphon gave him a hard look then wiggled both eye ridges up and down in a suggestive fashion.

"Stop," Guff rolled his eyes. "It's not what you're thinking, and you of all people should know that we can't no matter what, so get your dirty mind back out of that muddy swamp," he laughed.

Then easing in and lowering his voice to conspiracy level, he whispered in his deep growl of sharing a little fun, "Because, in some of my conversations with Boomer, he was under the impression that Skth was an immature dragon; adolescent at best. And if he thought that, I know his little brother probably believes it too."

The gryphon laughed a hacking laugh, "Hah! She's been chased by every freshening arms dragon who thought Master Ki wasn't watching for at least, hmm, forty years, maybe fifty!" She extended her left wing and stretched it into the night, feeling the breeze. Feathers and breeze were such a difference from rubbery webs and cold dark water.

"Why would it matter how old she is anyway?"

"Because Tink is convinced that there is no other dragon as small as he is; and from what I see, there is a little more room in a coffee mug of Skth, than of Tink."

His face softened and he bit at his left lip, "I also think he's kind of sweet on her, but just doesn't know it or want to admit it."

"Would it make any difference that she is about 87?"

The big bear slowly grew his grin into a large smile as he lay back into the grass, and folded his arms very un-bear like behind his head as he looked up at his favorite star formation, Ursa Major, as the smile reached maximum proportions, his voice oozed "Oh, yeah."

"Tink Toss!"... —©L. REYNOLDS 2010

Chapter 11

Playing Tink Toss

It all happened very fast. The witnesses could have sworn nobody could survive such an event; but there it was, directly in front of them, exploding in all of its potential for destruction and mayhem brought about by the two dragons meeting, both traveling at close to 350 miles per hour. They collided, resulting in the smaller ricocheting off into the sky with the combined necessary 670 miles per hour to break the sound barrier with a resounding "Bang!" The locals were used to the "BOOM!" which accompanied their familiar red streak as he launched himself skyward. This "Bang!" was different; it was unique and perfectly suited for a very proud mother on her 150th birthday. For almost a year the two boys had been practicing the maneuver for just this special day. This training exercise had been one of their most closely guarded secrets ever. Actually, they had only recently started hitting the right speed and had perfected what they called the "sling-shot" grip that was necessary to perform such an amazing aerobatic display. They called it the Tink

Toss. With its signature sonic "boom-lite" as Boomer called it, the sound was like something the size of a hardball breaking the sound barrier.

The small gathering on the grassy pasture, spread among colorful picnic blankets for the festive flare, all cheered and clapped as the two aeronauts returned for their bows. Tink at the last minute, due to a stuck protective eyelid came swooping in distractedly, flying upside down, and an inverted mirror to his brothers perfect kill dive. At the last second, realizing his errant posture, Tink flipped in what looked very much-rehearsed maneuver and garnered some extra hard clapping from his mother, and a certain tiny blue dragon that missed nothing.

A large furry mouth hung still open in total amazement that the little shop helper would even be able to come to work on the next day. In his over long years, Guff had seen many things that were amazing, but none were so . . . well, amazing; and awe inspiring. Sitting next to him and as equally stunned was Twill, with her blue glass feathers sparkling with full fluffy beauty in the delightful end of summer sunlight. Guff leaned ever so slightly to his constant companion, "Did you see how they did that?"

"No," she muttered back still stunned. "But, obviously, it wasn't something they just thought up last weekend." As they looked at each other, they knew that neither of them was thinking about an entertaining trick for a birthday party; both were thinking about a mountain, very high and very far away.

"How high do you think he went?" Guff asked, conceding, "He was well beyond the distance I could track with my eyesight being what it is these days."

"Hmm, I'm going to have to join you on that bench, coach; it was out of my range also." Twill rolled her eyes, inserting her new favorite sports jargon of being "benched" and having to "sit this one out."

"I wonder how high up they could do that same trick, or something like it

They watched as a tiny blue streak had joined in on the fun in the air, which was now a game of tag. The three had a wide sky in which to swoop, twist and spin, but held it in easy watching distance for those on the ground. Skth was proving to be a very adversary player, as she held her own with the roughhousing shenanigans of the two brothers. Between Tink's ability to do a back flip in the air in just over the length of his body and resulting in flying in the opposite direction, Skth's penchant for her much practiced feint high and right and drop left, the two smaller ones were proving that they could hold their own in close quarter flight attacks.

Skth tapped the top of the much larger red's head, with a flirtatious tug on his right ear wing. Guff leaned toward Twill, but commented in a loud enough whisper for the entire party to hear, "He's going sonic," he laughed as the red wings blazed orange and then the whole seemed to disappear. "I'll bet he will be right back with a double tap." As the whip crack of Boomer's tail breaking the sound barrier resounded less than a mile away, the red streak blew right between the two smaller dragons as they hovered in confusion and were now both tapped, and bowled over in the sky by the shock wave of the larger dragon, garnering a round of applause from below.

Ever the worry-prone mother, and "Queen of the Day" Q'Nt, nudged her husband who was enjoying the contest without the "maternal" hindrances. She returned his expression of wide-eyed innocence with the lowered eyebrow of warning and a nod toward the picnic basket.

"Hmm, yes, well there is that," he smiled as he gave her a little smooch on her now red cheek winglets. "After all, we do have guests who might be hungry also." He rubbed his tummy in anticipation of the contents of the bundle.

H'n let out his most fatherly dragon whistle that probably had many ears perking up and many children dropping whatever mischief they were up to, and then called out, "Boys! Fish balls!"

From about a mile down range, three dragons turned instantly into ballistic missiles, homing in on a particular basket woven from the river reeds in Peru during a long and interesting honeymoon about a hundred years before.

H'n laughed, "Look honey, it seems as if the littlest can now fly supersonic as well." The party all laughed as the three approached in perfect formation, and ready for the eating to begin.

The sun was lazy and moved grudgingly as the laughter laced with dribbles of errant plum sauce, or Q'Nt's new recipe of gingered fish sauce (which proved to be an instant hit), landed where a quick paw or claw could scoop it up and reward an open mouth. It seemed as though the contents of the basket should have been more than enough, but once set upon by the hungry gathering, as almost anyone that sat at Q'Nt's table could attest, nothing would remain but bowls licked clean.

"So the grip is first loose in order to pivot, and the arm is limp to become elastic?"

"Not elastic like a rubber band," Boomer explained to Guff and Twill, who seemed extremely interested in the details of the Tink Toss. "But elastic as in limp enough to stretch entirely out, because it is the full extension of the arms that bring the wing muscle group into play." Boomer seemed a tiny bit uncomfortable being the teacher, trying to explain things that came to him more as physical knowledge than as explainable "book knowledge." "When the wing muscle is pulled hard, it retracts and bunches up; it is the natural occurrence that happens in a conversion from search mode to kill stoop. The last sculling by the wing is a full extension, with a stall spread to stop the forward motion. When the wing makes the final snap up into that stall, the body is pushed down into the dive with maximum effort; that is caused by the large wing muscles in the back twitching into a bunch, very fast and very powerful."

"It is actually part of how my muscles work to get so much push thrust to fly as fast as I do for so many hours." He leaned over and elbowed Guff in the outer reef, causing two surfers to wipe out. "Actually," he confided in a stage whisper, "I cheat and fly down to the airport and hop onto the back of a domestic flight with the airline that's going my way." The two shared a wink and discrete smile about a certain flight Boomer and Tink had flown past on their way to Norway and the bonding of Thor and Chil.

"But the snap at what, 700 miles per hour must be painful, if not damaging to the shoulder socket. Maybe not so much to yours, but definitely Tink's," Twill worried.

"Oh, about a year ago, he was quiet sore until we had the grip down right, and started flying faster and faster."

Guff turned to Twill with a flash of gestalt mirrored in his eyes, "Remember that big order with all of those engraved edgings we did for that company up north, and we just thought it was Tink having to hold all of those frames?" The two nodded in understanding. "He never complained, or said a word about his shoulders or back; he must have been in excruciating pain."

The three looked over at the subject of their discussion three blankets away, talking quietly with the smaller blue. "It doesn't seem to be bothering him now," Twill chuckled, as inside she was tickled that the two little dragons had really become close friends.

"So, you two have been working on this for a year now?" Guff pawed around in the little blankets to see if there was maybe one more fish ball hiding from a fuzzy bear.

"Actually, it was almost two years ago when Tink was moping about not being able to fly fast and would never know what it was like to fly supersonic. That was when we first came up with the idea of the flight harness." Boomer stretched out his wings in a lazy arch and lounged along the blanket. "We liked traveling places together, but we were at first restricted by his flight; then he started flying tandem on my back, but we still couldn't really travel very far, so the harness would facilitate us to fly supersonic and widen the range of where we could go see things in the world." Adjusting himself, he continued, "I mean, I have flown all over the world, but Tink only heard me talk about places; places he would never be able to fly to."

"But that was pretty fast flying today," Twill pointed out.

"That was the most amazing thing," Boomer marveled. "Everyone was watching the Toss; but that was just the "trick". The amazing part was that a year ago, Tink could barely fly faster than 200, much less the critical 350 we needed for the sonic break. He had to learn how to fly all over again; and for something that comes natural for someone, that is not an easy thing to do."

"Wait," Twill put up her hand in a stop motion, then thinking about it with a smile, made the football sign for time-out. "About six months ago, Tink came crashing through the trees right above me one morning. Did that have anything to do with this?" Her left eyebrow had automatically arched up in the shop manager-on-duty mode.

"Does that eyebrow thing work on Tink?" Boomer laughed.

"Yes."

"Oh, then he's more of a . . ." Boomer stopped laughing as Twill's eyes flared brilliant red. "Sorry. Um, where were we . . . oh yes, the famous morning crashing through the trees at three hundred miles per hour." Boomer rolled his eyes as he felt the heat rise in his cheeks, "He slipped off of my back during a turn and I didn't catch his leg as we had planned."

"So he couldn't fly that fast; so he was on your back?" Guff rumbled, "I'm confused."

"Oh he could fly that fast, but we were experimenting with me bringing him up to a certain speed, and then throwing him in a tight arc turn so it would be kind of like a sling or catapult that would throw him through the barrier. That day it just happened to go wrong."

"But you have successfully thrown him?" Twill thought a second about what she had just actually said, "Oh; that sounded horrible."

Boomer shrugged, "But that is exactly what it is - a Tink Toss." He reassured her with a smile as he picked at the bits of grass on the blanket, "Well, it's one kind of Tink Toss."

"Hmm" the bear rumbled in thought, "Let me ask you from a different perspective. How far up do you think you could throw, umm, toss Tink?" Thinking, he rephrased the question, "Or more specifically - how high can you fly, and throw him to get him how high?"

Looking at Twill he asked, "Did that sound right?"

From old friendship, she patted his knee, "No." Turning to Boomer, "Let's just start with this, how high can you fly?"

Boomer just stared at her. The silence was deafening. It took a moment for her to realize she had just crossed a barrier and it was not about sound.

Guff, realizing that the conversation had stalled, laid his paw on Twill's knee and addressed Boomer. "We have a problem that is rapidly approaching, Boomer, and we are desperately seeking solutions." Looking at and nodding towards Twill, he continued, "She didn't mean to ask you for information that is probably a closely guarded secret; and we apologize."

Boomer nodded, as Guff continued, "We need to bring you into some different secrets; ones that have nothing to do with your job, but as it appears, will affect you directly - you and especially Tink."

The young dragon sat up and nodded his acquiescence slowly.

"Very soon, Tink will be the recipient of a request, one he cannot refuse, yet one that will require him to get close to 27,000 feet; and I doubt he can even fly to 15,000." Boomer noticed a warm cherry color heating the bottom of the deep brown eyes. "I personally have no problem getting to around 37,000 feet, but the big silver plane isn't what we are talking about."

"Anything over 25,000 and you're talking about the Himalayas." The globe-savvy courier started, "and if you're talking a dragon and Himalayas in the same breath, you're talking the Kell specifically. Why would Tink go to the Kell?"

"He won't have a choice," Twill injected. "That is what the gold on his skin and in his eyes is all about. He is being called."

Boomer sat in silence and turned to look out across the late evening countryside in the last light. In the distance he could see a barn owl out for an early daylight hunt, crossing over the tree tops and headed down to the 300 acres in what last week was deep alfalfa and was now a couple of inches of small animal-exposing scrub. The long fingers of shadow reached tenuously across the pasture as he thought about how just out of curiosity he had tried to fly to the Kell. He had only made it to about 24,500 feet. He knew that the void of 1,500 feet would be enormous for one the size of Tink, especially when there is no air to fly in. In addition, that was only if he could avoid the other even more dangerous elements such as super cooled liquid in the clouds. There was a lot to weigh.

Turning slowly, still considering what he could tell, and what he would even want to share of his highly private life and capabilities, "Can you tell me why he has to go?"

The two elders looked at each other sharing that moment of stepping out into space together; there was no precedent for them even consulting as far as they knew. They had no guidance about sharing so that the future Patron could have a chance at success. This was uncharted territory for them, as it would have been probably any of the past teams.

"Would it suffice for now," started the bear softly, "If we just acknowledged that we have information that to reach the Kell, Tink's life and another's hangs in the balance?"

"Does he know?"

"Not yet, but we have reason to believe the trigger event may happen this week."

"He will receive a request," Twill injected. "He will be mentally or physically unable to deny this request. It will take over his being until he performs the duty or fails."

"Failure," the bear continued in an even lower voice, "in this case, he will not survive failure."

Twill flared her cheek feathers and lifted her wings in a stretch by appearance, but displayed more of her former self, and Boomer was attentive. "We have personal knowledge and experience from which we speak."

Boomer's eyes flared with an inner heat of battle as he engaged Twill's flare of Patron armor and strength. Joining the two elders out in that space of new uncertainty, he confided, "22,000 feet. I can fly at 22,000 feet with Tink and the harness on board, probably less. In the Himalayas, I can only get to probably around 1,200 miles per hour, then go ballistic which would take us to maybe about 23,500 or hopefully 24,000. The snap toss would only give him maybe another thousand or so feet, unless we can come up with some different flight configurations. But even then, the energy of the toss probably could never get him any closer than maybe 500 feet; then he would have to climb the rest of the way."

Guff processed the information, and looked askance as he turned to Twill. "How is the work load right now?"

"We'll survive. Skth is picking up some of the slack, but soon she will have to work closer with me on the other part."

The large shaggy head took it all in and nodded. The palm trees around his collar waved in unison to his nodding as the large waves crashed on the shore along the famous Banzai Pipeline. The only peace was a long distance away with a peek of Waimea Falls filling the pocket as a diver sought to dive through the lei of Plumeria flowers that floated there.

"Tink is off work duty until he returns from the Kell; so you two can practice."

"But I have to work."

The former Princess looked to his Patron, "I'll take care of that," she stated.

If things had not been just a little strange before, that mere statement of certainty just pushed the envelope for Boomer, "When do we start?"

"About a year ago," smiled Guff. "Now, it's just enough time to hone all that effort into the skill that will save his life; as well as another."

"And maybe all," muttered Twill at Guff's knowing eye.

The sun of a perfect late summer day touched the distant mountains, as the birthday girl snuggled under the arm of her partner. The march of twilight sparkled in her eyes as she watched the "children" tearing across the pasture in a game of ball as the lead would hook the ball and spin in a spiral effectively flipping the ball (a walnut wrapped in rags and string), high into the air while the other two raced to snatch it. The successful hunter became the new lead and dropped the ball to start the circling anew. Boomer had invented the game back when he was help-ing teach Tink to fly faster and compete with the other local kids. The result was a neighborhood of very fast dragons, faster than anyone had ever seen before.

Q'Nt snuggled her head onto H'n's chest plates to listen to his mas-sive heart. "Happy, my little one?" he asked, stroking the favorite spot on back of her neck.

"A perfect day," she replied. "Two great happy kids, the best partner, and no worries; what more could I ask for on my 150th?" She sighed and leaned deeper into his embrace as Tink grabbed the ball for the fourth straight time. "I think Skth is going to have to learn to fly faster if she's going to keep up with Tink."

The larger dark green with black edges rumbled his wisdom, "Or Tink needs to learn that if he doesn't slow down a bit, he won't get to catch her."

His bond partner pulled away and looked at him seriously a moment, then at the kids. After several seconds, she slapped his belly and leaned back into him. "You're just a dirty old dragon. She's much too young for Tink; she's barely out of her adolescence." She mumbled into his chest, "He needs to find a girl that is at least 60 or 70; not a child."

"I think he's found her."

Q'Nt now sat up looking at H'n, then at the kids. Especially watch-ing the way the little blue flew and twisted expertly in the air.

"Don't let the size fool you too," he chuckled, "You, of all people should know better." Then he added an even larger truth, "And Tink should have recognized that too, but he hasn't."

The sun rolled backward and faded behind the ridge, casting the final long shadows of the day, exploding in rays of yellow against the graying blue sky and the tiny clouds laced the light into a stereoscopic display. Fanning from horizon to horizon, forest to city and mirrored in a now somewhat worried mother's eyes, the last light winked out, soon to be filled with a billion other lights. Tomorrow would be another day.

# # #

"Ready," the ripple of Boomer's back muscles signaled; as speaking at this close to the speed of sound was impossible. Boomer's drafting right hand searched for Tink's hind leg. They were experimenting with what they were coming to call the Hammer Throw where Tink would curl himself in the tightest ball he could with his right leg just sticking out enough for Boomer to grab it. The larger brother would surge from active flight into a snap turn and stoop that would bring his wing out of the way, as he snatched Tink from the enlarged harness hood and with the assistance of centrifugal force would with any luck pitch him another 1,500 feet higher. Skth, a couple of miles away, was tracking and estimating the trajectory.

Tink didn't know what to think of the Paws & Claws door refusing him entrance, and Twill telling him that he needed to spend more time with his brother, but as the muscles heated to almost red hot, by dragon standards, Tink was ready for the ride of his life. The sore muscles were long gone under the ministrations of some wonderful tiny claws and hot stinky water his brother had known about, but had never needed to share until now.

The first throws had been, they felt, pretty good, about seven and eight hundred feet high, but now the "ride" was consistently well over the thousand-foot mark, as they shot for two. Boomer doubted hitting the two, but Tink and Skth just asked, "Why not?" A few short years ago, nobody would have thought that what they were doing was possible, but now they did just that, daily.

Tink felt the bunch in the right wing cluster, directly followed by the snap roll. He loosened his right hip in preparation of taking the decompression from the pull of the snap, and in a blink, he was flying straight up as a ball flies. Pulling the ends of his wings in around his fetal body, he made a close approximation of a ball. His leg had not paused as before, but had started the retraction as soon as he had felt the pressure of his brother's grip release. This flight even sounded different; the whistle of the moving air was higher, brighter and shriller as the projectile rocketed through it faster than ever before. The mud green ball arched ever higher into the late morning sky, and the eyes of the tiny blue so far away, got larger and wider as she witnessed what they had been working and hoping for.

The expected red blur did not distract her focus as she continued to track the tiny ball to its conclusion as it slowed to the final apogee and exploded into a dragon in full flare. "How high?" Boomer asked. Not having been tracking, he could not locate the tiny ball in the sky.

"By my estimates, he was very close to an additional 1,600 feet before he burst."

"It felt really good at release, I could feel his leg starting to pull in just as I let go."

"One more Toss before lunch."

The tiny mud green dragon flashed in, back sliding into a flared hover, "Well?"

"One more and we'll know for sure," as Boomer presented his back.

# # #

"It was the most amazing feeling; hurtling up through the air, and having no control, just hold the ball shape and listen to the air." Tink popped another nettle and rice ball into his mouth.

"I still think it sounds scary." Duff traced the dribble of sauce on her chin as she ran the back of a finger up and into her mouth. She looked over at Skth, "Would you do it?"

Skth just laughed. "Do I look that crazy? I may be blue, but I'm not that bad."

Leaning in to share a private whisper with Duff, the little blue confided, "I think it's a boy thing." The two just giggled, as Tink and Boomer both pretended to ignore them.

The sun was warm on the small patch of hostas at the edge of the clearing. The deep trees provided the over shade, but the slanting light reached in just enough to warm the late summer's giant leaves as their edges browned and foretold of the coming fall and winter. Duff watched a very fuzzy caterpillar make its way along the underside of the one leaf and onto another, as she thought about the coming fall and possible winter. She leaned closer to Skth and pointing to the well bundled up crawling denizen of the forest, she remarked, "Maybe we will get some snow in the forest this year".

Skth, who had never seen a winter without snow, thought about how strange that would seem, no blanket of white cold to create the winter. That thought brought a pang of something she had never felt before: homesickness. You have to be away from home to miss it enough to have that gut wrenching feeling of not seeing everyone and everything you love. It was a very strange feeling for Skth, as she had never been away from Kinnarodden for more than a few days.

"What is it?" Duff asked as she stroked Skth's sad cheek. "Why are you sad?"

"I'm just missing my home and family, that's all." Skth spoke softly. "I have never been away for this long. I miss everyone, but it's not seeing Uncle Ki that I miss the most."

"Would it help if you could see him?" Duff asked brightly.

"How do you mean?"

"A picture; A picture you could look at any time you feel sad or just want to see him." Duff put her arm around the shoulders of her little blue friend. She felt sad just because Skth was feeling sad, and she wanted to help.

Skth slowly turned to her, "I guess; but how would I get a picture of my Uncle Ki, he's all the way up in the northern-most point of Norway?"

Duff took her left hand and laid it on Skth's chest. "No, he's not; he's right here in your heart. I can feel him in you."

Skth stared at Duff and saw that she was not making fun of her, and that she truly meant what she was saying.

"But . . . how would you . . .?"

"I can make a picture," Duff assured her. "He's the big black dragon on the pointy rock isn't he?" As her friend nodded, she continued, "He's somewhere kind of dark . . ."

"He's in a cave." Skth shared as Boomer and Tink turned to pay attention.

Duff turned to look at Boomer, "You too," she paused and placed her hand on Boomer's chest, sending shivers through his entire body and wings like an electric shock. "You carry Ki in your heart too; but it's different. It's more like how you feel about . . ." She stopped and wide eyed, the two stared at each other, as Boomer also knew who the people were that she had just glimpsed; people he worked with or dealt with, people that he trusted explicitly and respected.

"I'm sorry," she said quietly, "I didn't mean to intrude."

He placed his claw on her shoulder and with his other, raised her chin until he was looking into the deepest reaches of her eyes. "I feel that it will be OK. I think there is a trust there."

Duff thought about it for a second then rose up and on her tippy toes, gave Boomer a hug around his neck. He hesitated at the strange feelings inside of him, and the strange circumstance, then slowly, gently, and deeply hugged her back.

Duff finally let go, and as her right hand slid from around his neck, tracing down along his arm and took his claw in her tiny dirty pink hand and gave it a soft but firm squeeze, a very special conversation between just the two of them.

Turning, she asked Tink if he could get her a small piece of the hard water. Since that request drew a blank, she described the windows until he finally understood that she was talking about a piece of glass; and he was gone. Even Boomer was surprise at how fast he had transitioned from static sitting to full flight. Three pair of eyes sat blinking above three gaping mouths.

Finally the tiny northern blue dragon marveled softly to herself, "That was fast," as she continued to blink trying to comprehend the change in the little mud green dragon, "Very fast."

Two other heads slowly nodded and blinked in unison, "Very, very fast."

Suddenly there was a small mud green dragon with gold spots here and there, hovering in front of them, holding out a small oval of glass, not much larger than a field mouse's body. "Like this?" he asked.

"That will be perfect, Tink, thank you." Duff took the offered glass, laid it on the ground, and closed her eyes. A low hum started from seemingly far away, and then it was with them all. Boomer and Skth thought it was nice that Tink was able to hum along with Duff.

Without looking up, or opening her eyes, she reached out with her left hand, laid it on Skth's chest once again, and continued to hum, but deeper. Her right hand hovered over the glass, and then slow lowered it to rest on the glass itself. From the side, Tink could see the glass start to glow in many different colors; sparkling as she slowly touched the surface.

Finally, her left hand dropped, and she looked at the glass in her right hand. "Yes, he is a very handsome dragon; very official." She turned to Skth and held out the piece of glass, "I like the little rock he stands on."

Skth looked with amazement at Duff, and then glanced at what she expected to see as a clear piece of glass, but was not. She looked up, but her bottom jaw was hanging loose. She looked down again as Tink on her right and Boomer on her left, looked over her shoulders and saw the same image of Master Ki, thousands of miles away greeting and checking dragons as they entered and left Kinnarodden. The image did not repeat, it just kept moving as Master Ki's day kept going.

Boomer pointed with his claw and exclaimed, "There is S'kar and D'Lth!" He looked up at Duff, "How did you know about them?"

Giggling, Duff just waved it off, "I didn't." She took hold of Skth's wrist, "Skth was missing her Uncle Ki, so I made the image to show him as he serves at his station. When he is not there, it will repeat the previous day." She looked the tiny dragon in the eyes, "Is this OK? I'm sorry; I don't know how to make voices."

Skth reached out, flung her arms around Duff's neck, and hugged her like a long lost sister. "Thank you, it's perfect," she whispered in Duff's ear. "It's absolutely perfect."

"But, how do you do that?" asked Tink.

Turning to him, "I don't know; I just make the picture that is in my mind." She hugged Skth more against her side. Turning she smiled, "I think I'm going to really like this hug thing."

They all laughed and continued to watch the perpetually official Master Ki, even though Boomer felt a twinge of guilt for watching someone who did not know he was being watched.

"Why haven't you made a picture like this before?" asked Boomer.

"I didn't know I could until I had the dream."

"Dream?" Skth asked.

"Yes," the pixie shared, "It was about me making a picture, but it needed a frame and you and Tink and someone else had to make the frame together." Now a bit distracted she rifled the box in search of more tasty morsels. "Tink made the gold that was in the hard water, and you made it glow so the Fairy Princess could see the picture, even in the dark of night." Duff laid her tiny grubby hand on Skth's shoulder, "I know how scary it can be in the dark sometimes. A little light from a frame would be perfect, and I can make a picture of the forest which is a very nice place to watch."

"I made it glow?"

"I made the gold?"

"I'm confused," added Boomer, "what is hard water?"

"Glass," the two small dragons said in unison, as Skth held up her tiny picture.

The two tiny dragons looked at each other with snaps of their heads. "Twill!" They both shot off in a swirl of leaves.

Boomer looked after the two tiny dots speeding away, and turning to Duff asked, "Care for a ride back to the frame shop, Duff?" The forest edge was empty as far as Boomer could see. He looked under the hostas and rifled through the forest floor. "Duff?" There was no small pixie, just forest floor and forest. Hmmm, he thought, as he lifted off and lazily winged his way back toward the meeting of the minds as it were, while he quietly wondered just how long it would take for a small pixie to make it the mile back to the Paws & Claws Atelier. He had a feeling that there was more to that little pixie then met the eye.

Guff was trying to nap, but the noise of two small dragons yammering at Twill was just too much. After all, it was naptime! Grudgingly he extracted himself from his chair, shuffled back into his red clogs and moseyed out into the workroom and over to the bench where Twill did her special work. The children were both trying to talk to Twill at the same time, and Guff noticed the leaf on her tail ticking up and toward the left; from years of association, he knew that she, despite the frown on her face and look of deep concentration, was having a lot of fun humoring the two children. Playing along, he quietly stepped up beside her, tapped his right clog on her left foot twice as their secret signal that he was up to speed, and would follow her lead wherever that would go.

" . . . and if you could blow some glass," Tink continued as Skth overflowed with, "I don't know if it would work with just the glow, but . . ." Guff knew instantly what was being discussed, and that if he really had to let Skth wind down, he would end up with a headache. His right foot felt pressure applied from above, and then he felt a bump on his paw. He turned his paw up to catch whatever it was that Twill was passing him, and he immediately recognized the familiar feel of the small piece of glass with his image trapped to repeat every fifteen or so seconds, coming in to work from the forest. As his paw closed around the glass, Twill's thumb claw raked his hand in a forward motion. He counted three, and then stepped slowly down on her foot. He had transferred the lead.

" . . . but the only problem is," prattled Skth, "Oh, there's always more than one problem with picture framing," finished Tink, "but I don't know how to 'make' gold, it is a metal; and I can't even blow a flame." As he screwed his face up and tried hard to do something, a wisp of steam that smelled a whole lot like peppermint, drizzled out of his left nostril. "See, just steam, and not even a very nice steam at that." Tink was not a very big fan of any kind of mint, but peppermint was his least favorite.

Guff reached forward quietly and placed the piece of glass on the workbench. The two had not noticed until Tink took a step forward and his toes touched the glass. Glancing down he saw the image at its final stage and started to glance back up at Guff, but caught the shift back to the forest dark and then the bits of the forest coming together to form a bear with a shirt. Tink bent down to look closer, but the third time through he was positive of what he was watching.

He looked up at Guff with new understanding. The words of M'Loree wafted through his head, " . . . anything they want to be at any moment, any minute, any day or for years . . ." The questions he could never ask pounded down tunnels of his mind that were dark and forever closed; but still . . .

"Could I see you for a moment in my office, Tink?" Turning, he preceded the small dragon that he now knew had no choice. Or at least, would soon have no choice. The large thundercloud over Haleakala raged as the large storm-driven wave curled up and five riders caught the crest and began their descent down the face of the wave. The blond with the long ponytail shimmied her right foot forward and hung five on the point just before the backwash caught her and she was gone. Tink always wondered how at times, it was just a shirt, and would be the same print all day, then suddenly, it would come alive and be the most entertaining thing a person could watch; but he always wondered why there was never a bear surfing, always humans and the occasional dog with their human companion. It never entered his mind that a dragon might look kind of cool on an old long board; but then, there was always that "water" thing too.

Lowering down into his chair and reaching for his coffee cup that was rapidly filling itself as he reached for it, Guff thought about how he needed to proceed in quizzing Tink about exactly what Duff had asked. She obviously had not asked directly for his help, or all of this would be a moot exercise. Motioning towards his desk, "Sorry I don't have an extra mug for you to use"

"I'm fine, Sir." He picked a spot, and then moved and dragon squatted with the base of his tail providing the third leg of his shortened stance. Guff knew that dragons say that it is comfortable, but still . . . it was not his chair.

"What exactly happened out there with Duff?"

"Sir?"

"You were out at the pasture and Duff made the picture in the glass; what I want to know is what exactly did she say about it?" The one claw extended out of the sheathing and he scratched behind his right fuzzy ear, no itch, just a nervous habit that he had not been able to break himself of for almost two hundred years.

"Well, it all started with Skth feeling kind of sad and missing Kinnarodden and her uncle Ki; well, Master Ki to me I guess." Guff smiled at one of Tink's enduring, but irritating habits of self-deprecation. "So, Duff asked her if a picture of home would help her feel better." Tink looked up into Guff's eyes. "It all happened so fast, I'm not really sure what was happening, but I came and got a piece of glass and she made the picture and then was saying something about making a frame on a picture but it would be gold but glowing and we thought of shaped glass and Skth and I knew she was talking about Twill." Tink's arms were pumping the air and swinging about, as his wings were folding into shapes that Guff had never seen or knew was possible before, "And of course Twill would be the right person to also know about how to make the gold in the glass and make it glow so it would be like a night light . . .."

Guff was holding his paw up in the universal form of stop.

"Take a breath, Tink" as he sipped his coffee.

"But, you . . ." Guff's paw went back up; backed up with a hiss of "Shhh."

"I just wanted to know if she had asked you to do something specific or not; that's all."

Tink thought, his face screwed up in his "Tink thinking seriously" mode. "No, nothing specific . . . but she did say that I would be making gold." He screwed up the one side of his face and lips as well as shrugged with his hands out and up in supplication. "Blowing gold? Not even Dvark truly blows gold; not really." Guff's frown of not understanding spurred Tink on. "He can't really produce gold when he blows it, he starts the same way every time, he bends over to fill his glass with water; but it's a magician's trick, misdirection. He's really stuffing a wad of leaf in each of his cheeks. The water he sips is to make the leaf stick to the bole clay on the frame. Water reactivates the hide glue in the clay and the leaf sticks."

Guff was amazed that this little dragon had discovered the secret that had remained hidden from the bear for over 150 years; and yet, it was everyday stuff for the little dragon. Everyday stuff that was about to turn his world upside down the bear thought, as he looked once again at the spots and patches of pure shiny gold on the mud green dragon; Completely upside down.

"Ok," he said as he noticed a certain leaf move out in the forest. "Thanks for your time Tink, Duff is back and probably wants to talk to you." Tink followed his gaze out the window.

As Guff felt the flow of air across his leg, he called out, "Oh Tink," as he turned to the dragon now hovering mid doorway. "You will let me know when she asks you to do something specific won't you?"

"Yes Sir, right away Sir." Then he was gone out through the back door, over the roof and into the hostas to share with his best friend.

Guff thought about the future and the possibilities. Could a tiny clearing hold a world court, under the protective shade of a field of hostas? Maybe the change would do the world some good. The change of power from the Fairy Wars did the world a lot of good; maybe it was time for more changes.

Chapter 12

In a Word: Quest

The red and mud green gold dragon missile shot across the sky at 980 miles per hour then rotated and went almost ballistic or straight up. At about 24,824 feet, the smaller dragon, suddenly pulled by the snap turn, streaked even higher. Inside the compact ball of flesh and bone, Tink did not even breathe, for the slightest change of form would cause a disturbance in the airflow that would prevent him from reaching his highest potential arc. He was suddenly weightless, and he stretched out his wings, found his orientation, and dug his wings into any air he could find. His lungs hurt from the lack of oxygen but he pushed his tiny body even higher as he was running out of any substance in the air from which he could gain "wing." The muscles along his shoulders burned from the exertion, the wing straps of the trapezius muscles felt almost white hot as he sought even more altitude.

The attitude of Tink's position in the air was now almost as flat as level flight. The critical point, as he sculled the air, was his head, now slightly tipped, as he heard the sonic boom beneath him. His forward claws were poised; ready for the catch they had worked on so hard this last week.

When Boomer had first released him, the larger red had flipped over and plunged straight at the ground. At Mach 3, he had pulled out of the dive and circled around at 18,000 feet, reaching for as close to Mach 4 as he could get. The great circle also brought him around to the highest flight elevation he could obtain and still be over Mach 3 or 1,024 miles per hour. As he reached a location almost directly under Tink, he rotated and was now flying as fast as he could straight at Tink who had his arms out and pointed down in the same catch configuration that the circus acts use in the high wire. Rapidly approaching, but bleeding off speed as fast as he was climbing, Boomer reached his arms out in the form of the "catcher." But unlike the circus catcher, Boomer was traveling at 425 mph when he grabbed his tiny brother, and dragged him another 630 feet up in the air, before he snap-rolled in a back flip, slinging Tink to the final height of their attempt.

Four miles away and 36,000 feet in the air, a human sitting at a desk locked on his target. In a hundredth of a dragon's blink, the data on this target raced through computers and displayed in front of him.

"Eagle Eye, target squawks 28,758, over."

"Roger, Eagle Eye. Copy 2-8-7-5-8, over."

"Confirm, Happy hunting White Goose, Eagle Eye out."

"10-4 Eagle Eye, and thanks for your assist, White Goose, out."

The smart-looking man, dressed in casual black shirt, slacks and highly polished shoes, scanned the distant sky for the AWAC (Advanced Warning and Control) airplane. Even with its distinct saucer floating on top, the only thing he could see as it turned was a small glint of sunshine reflecting off the pilot's window, and the only reason he was able to see that was because he knew where to look for the "borrowed" radar tracking group. The single star on his collar sparkled in the first fall sunlight, as he turned to the large bear in the Hawaiian shirt. His raised left eyebrow mirrored the bear's, as he asked, "You heard? Tink got to 28,758."

"I heard," Guff scratched slowly behind his right ear as he thought and looked at the Rear Admiral, "We sure appreciate your help in this matter Admiral."

"Boomer and I have been friends more than associates for over than half my life, and most of my career. It's because of him that I have the best job in the world." He looked down where he was digging with his foot in a habit that he thought he had left on the shores of a Georgia river, when he was first working on getting married right out of Officer Candidates School and had a fresh bar of gold on his collar. He looked back up at the one person he was still a little nervous around, a bear that was at least six hundred pounds his superior, and who spoke perfect English. "Look, I don't know what you people are working on; but if Boomer says you need our help for a few hours, it was the least we could do for all he does for all of us."

Guff reached out and laid his right paw on the much smaller shoulder. "Take my word for it when I say it is of global importance; we are just not at liberty to talk about it." He looked off to the distance where his superior vision picked out the red dot streaking their way. "Maybe someday Boomer can share with you the role you and that plane's crew played here today, even if it does not seem to make any sense to you now."

The single streak separated into two as they rocketed over the heads of the two bipedal observers. The formation split and they rolled out into what had become their favorite, yet most difficult aerial trick of flipping in the air where they tumble in all three axes at the same time. The airplane aerobatic fliers call it a Lomcevak which is Czechoslovakian for "cause of a headache" because it looks like the gyrations of a drunk; but the brothers call it the busted bird or the stumble; a move that was very hard to do, but even crazier to watch.

The two observers were amused and applauded loudly, and two small echoes, between them, continued after they stopped clapping. Both looked down to see they had company. The man was not going to say anything for fear that they would disappear.

"Good afternoon you two, so glad you could join us . . ."

"Hey you two," Boomer rocketed up, as Tink continued, "did you see?"

"It was glorious!" Skth swung out her arms wide to their full 7.63 inches as Duff laughed at her antics.

"You two were a dot in the sky before you even started your flight, silly boys." She giggled, as she seemingly paid the new person no mind. "It was fun to watch these two try to find you in the air… first looking this way," as she did a fair imitation of the Admiral with both hands shading his eyes while standing ram-rod straight. "Then there was one of them," she rolled her eyes dramatically as she pushed her tiny tummy out, widened her stance a bit, and did a great Guff impression, "Looking back for lunch or something."

The two butts of the joking were amused, as were the brothers, and only Guff was amazed that it was Duff, standing out in the middle of a field with no cover, who was the center of the entertainment. "Maybe," he thought, "she might just do OK at her new position." Change is coming, and it could be better than he thought.

Boomer hovered a bit closer for a dramatic look at the very shiny insignia on his friend's collar, "Hmmm, you seem to be wearing someone else's shirt there, Jake . . ." he teased the newly minted Rear Admiral.

Rear Admiral Jake Morrow beamed back at the dragon, "One of the perks of being a human, kid; somewhere to hang your busted bird or a star," he retorted in reference to the dramatically well-done flight maneuver they had just exhibited, with no need for a place to hang a tiny piece of brass or silver.

"Well, I'm proud of ya, squirt." Boomer laughed and shook his hand. "Now you will never have an excuse for bad coffee in the shack."

Boomer felt a tiny thumb and finger tug on his trailing toe. Laughing at the boldness of the gesture, he introduced the three. "Admiral; it is Admiral, correct?" He got a nod, "I'd like to introduce you to the quickest, fastest pest to the warriors of the Northern Clan of dragons in Norway at the coldest yet warmest place on earth, Skth; and too, our own pixie keeper of the forest and epicurean extraordinaire, Duff." As they bowed, "Ladies, this is my good friend Rear Admiral Jake Morrow of the United States Navy."

"I'm honored to meet you two." He also performed as formal a bow as he could muster for two very small people. "I've heard absolutely nothing about you two," he teased back at the two that seemed the most likely fit for a bit of joking.

"Well," flirted Skth, "we can tell you so much less, over lunch."

Duff slapped her tiny grubby hands to her equally grubby cheeks in mock shock as she gushed, "Oh goodness! Is it really that time already?"

Guff leaned into the Admiral to share a stage-whispered secret, "Fish balls soaked in plum sauce. Not that Duff is addicted to them or anything . . ." as he rolled his eyes and wiggled his right eyebrow. "And if that isn't enough, I'm sure we can rustle up something more to your liking, although, Boomer's mother Q'Nt makes the best fish balls that I've ever tasted."

"Well, I was due back at the salt mine," the Admiral winked, "but I guess we could chalk this one up to . . . well, diplomatic extracurricular activities?" He looked toward Boomer for a conspiratorial nod and found him on the ground with Duff clambering aboard his neck and shoulders for the ride back.

"Call it what you want, Sir, but you do have to eat some time." And he and Duff were off as Duff called out a whoop and something that sounded a lot like "Ride 'em cowboy."

Tink pulled a long face and gazed askance at Skth, his eyes huge. She just shrugged and raised her hands in a defensive posture of "what the heck do I know?" and the two exploded off like two little bottle rockets and were quickly two dots becoming one and then none.

The human turned with wide eyes toward the bear, whose shirt was changing from an overcast day to a sunny one off the North Shore as several surfers were catching mild lulling waves on a lazy Sunday afternoon. The Admiral decided he did not even want to know and looked the bear in the eyes instead, "Is it always like this?"

Guff just smiled a knowing smirk and shrugged four surfers off his chest as the surf pulled them into the washer. With a slight toss of his head, a curl of his upper lip and a roll of his eyes, he confided with a verbal shrug, "Sometimes. Other times it's more exciting."

He put out his paw in the direction of the Paws & Claws, asking, "Lunch?"

As they walked, the Admiral started on his list of things that were new to him, things Guff knew he would be curious about " . . . And Duff is . . .?"

"A pixie; they are a possible branch of the fairies, but very different."

The human nodded as if to say "of course, I should have guessed that." The bees and flies busy with their work over the last of summer meadow skittered here and there among that last of the wilting summer flowers. A vole found an unusual lunch in the noonday sun; but back under a log, he listened to the flap of wings; the most dangerous animal in the vole's world, a small kestrel, was also looking for a lunch. The last buzz of Indian summer heat across grassland is the sound of a million conversations of a hundred species all engaged in life. It is one of the most reassuring sounds in the world, and a music Guff was loath to leave; but duty called, and his stomach was growling another tune.

As the two larger diners showed up in the workroom of the Paws & Claws Atelier, the small mud green shy retiring Tink was hovering above the dining area retelling his flight, probably for the tenth time. Duff was sitting cross-legged on the workbench next to Skth, Boomer perched on a stool next to Twill and all were having a great time with a very large basket of goodies that Guff's nose confirmed were from Q'Nt and her magical hand at making the tastiest morsels in the Forest.

Admiral Morrow looked to the bear for guidance, but Guff told him, "Oh no, with this motley gang, you are on your own. Just watch your fingers and don't let anyone dip them in sauce or you may just go home shorthanded." He gently slapped him on the back and pushed him toward the workbench that was doing duty as a feast table. "Boomer, guide our new friend here in the delicate exercise of your mother's culinary talents."

As the Admiral stepped up, Boomer took him alongside, "Here, you can be my wingman," and started pointing out the different balls and cubes and rolls. "That one; or grab one of those" as he guided the man's hand about the fare. "Right, that is a fish ball. Basically it's roasted fish meat with some herbs and stuff from the forest mixed into a rice ball and pressed, those are the delicate flavored ones, so you dip those in the plum sauce, over there." Pointing and showing by example was the name of the game.

"Oh my goodness gracious, that is sweet and smoky," the Admiral approved.

"Next up the scale is the Stink Bug Cube," seeing the Admiral's face of consternation, he forged on. "Don't worry; there aren't any stink bugs in them, those taste awful, so she keeps those for Halloween. These Cubes are slightly bitter, but it's all plants, so again, you need the plum sauce to balance the salty bitter flavor with the sweet."

Chewing with renewed interest the Admiral made an attempt, "Water cress, parsley, and dill?"

"Close," Tink laughed, "flat leaf nettles, choke weed and pasture grass . . . don't worry, it's well washed then rinsed with lemon water," his tongue cleaning his chin of green semi-hot honey and cilantro Dribble sauce.

"Here is where we separate the dragons from the bears," Boomer smiled at Guff who was known for not indulging beyond the sweet fish balls and plum sauce. "These rolls are filled with pepper cured honey bees, grasshoppers, and grubs mixed with corn flour and mashed sweet potato rolled in pepper paper." Boomer was watching Jake as he rattled off the ingredients of his favorite roll. "If you want it mild, you can dip it in the plum; medium and you go for the fish sauce or Tink's favorite honey and cilantro Dribble sauce, but if you're a red dragon this here is called Lava Sauce." Demonstrating, Boomer slopped his roll through the Lava, getting lots of sauce and plopping it all into his mouth with a smile.

As the Admiral slowly reached for one of the rolls, the table turned silent as all eyes were on the man to see what mettle he was made of. His hand hesitated over the fish sauce, but noticing that nobody made any suggestion or facial comment, he progressed to the Lava. As he dipped, Tink's face contorted back in a stage version of horror, but they all watched and waited except for Guff who had wandered over to the coffee urn and poured a cup of steaming rocket fuel. As the Admiral chewed on the new food, his mouth experienced a new sensation as at first, it went numb, and then started to tingle as the heat began to build.

Guff strolled back to the workbench with the steaming cup, and while watching the man as the sweat began about the temples and the red began to creep across the orbs of his eyes, Guff knew that the vision was starting to get a slight red haze. The bear eased the mug of coffee towards Twill, who had been waiting for it and she gently blew a small cooling breath, to make the coffee ready to drink.

Offering the mug to the Admiral, he confided, "Here, for some reason the coffee stops the burn and gives it all a better flavor." Boomer interceded, grabbing the mug and sipped off half of the fuel, before giving it to his friend with a smile.

As the Admiral drank the coffee, first with trepidation, then with gusto at the nice, nutty aftertaste it gave the whole mix, Boomer offered, "Welcome to the world of Red Dragons." Then, as he looked around at all the others, he added, "We are the only ones who eat these rolls and sauce. Well, other than Tink; he's an honorary Red."

The Admiral looked at the rest for a sign of another joke, but all were nodding their heads and Tink was making the crossed claw sign as if he was a vampire, but laughing. "Boomer and I have been eating those since we were just hatchlings. I tried them once with Lava, just once; it was enough." He laughed, "I couldn't believe Boomer was lasting that long without the coffee; but our father, wow, he can plow through a whole plate and bowl of Lava sauce before he will temper it with any coffee. But then, he is an almost pure obsidian black, and obsidians really like their hot volcano food."

The man looked at the empty coffee cup and the remaining stack of rolls. "Here," offered Guff, "let me refill that while I get hot stuff a cup of his own," winking and nodding at Boomer who was reaching for a repeat on the Lava before the coffee temper wore off; Guff took the mug and returned to the coffee urn.

"So, I'm still not really clear on the color thing." Jake hesitated as he reached for another roll, but passed and went back for a fish ball and plum sauce. "And, thank you Guff. I will be needing that," as he wiggled his eyebrow and smiling a goofy smile at Skth and Duff making the two girls laugh.

"What don't you understand?" Twill assumed the position of matri- arch, understanding that color was a delicate and serious subject among humans.

"Well, you and . . ." indicating Skth.

"Skth," she assisted. "Think of it as skip, but with a 'th' for the end."

Faux offended, Skth pouted, "Why would anyone want to skip me?" Then beaming at the Admiral and waving her hand in the universal roll- ing motion for carry on or continue; which made Duff giggle as she mirrored the motion into a Duff version of a hula dance until she caught the look on the Big Kahuna himself, as all nine surfers wiped out in a sudden swell on his shirt.

"Thank you," the Admiral nodded, "and see; that's another thing, the shortening of some names, but not of others. Skth and you are both blue, and Tink said you're both from Norway, but she has scales, and you have feathery sort of whatever. But your names are also different, Skth has no vowels, but Twill does." He grabbed the two sides of his head in a comedic gesture to display his confusion and the headache it was causing him.

Chuckling, Guff started to wander off, "Go ahead Twill, try to explain that one without revealing the rabbit hole," he said in reference to Alice in Wonderland and falling down a rabbit hole into pure insanity. "You folks carry on, but I have some work to attend to." He waved farewell, "Very nice meeting you Admiral; and once again, thank you for your help."

Twill shot him one of her sideway cold looks for abandoning her. "As I was saying, you need to sometimes forget about the color thing. Most of the Northern clan are blue, but Skth's direct Uncle Ki, is a pure obsidian and black as night; most of the warriors are red with maybe some black markings. There are a couple in our clan that are even completely white, but are not what you humans call albino, in fact they are just the opposite, they are a full mix of color, and their eyes are solid black so that you can't even see where the pupil stops and the iris and orb begin."

The Admiral was now sitting.

"Tink and Boomer are clutch mates or twins; well brothers, and their parents are different colors than they are, and too, there is at the difference of their size; nobody knows "why", it just is." She rubbed her face in the magnitude of the information; "There are estimated ninety-four different types of dragons, with over 3,000 subsets of identifying configurations. If this were a workday, there would be Chang, who is a snake dragon from the Western Mongolian Steppes near Nepal. He has no wings, but flies by slapping his oversized large scales down to his body, and the compressed air is like a jet.

Dvark is a winged dragon, but does not really fly at all. He is what is called a Fire Vulcan dragon in that he has certain traits like the obsidians, like diamond hard claws, but he also can make his flame into a cold pointed tiny flame and do engraving.

M'Ree, Pu and Poul are all wingless, and flightless, but are sea chameleons and can change color. Neither one looks anything like the other. I do not know if Poul can even really emulate a color he is near, but M'Ree, on the other claw, can almost disappear she is so adept; but, that is where the similarities end, at the "kind" of dragon.

The twins, who are true twins out of the same egg; one is green and the other is blue. Skth, Boomer, Tink and I are all "right" dragons, because of our body shapes, the wings, and the tail ending in a rudder

instead of some kind of ratline. There are snakes, as you are used to seeing in Chinese parades and adorning clothing, which are a close resem-
blance to Master Chang. There are worms that are thinner, and actually
live in the ground, ball dragons that are little more than a baseball with
feet, head and wings; and then there are the flight dragons that have
large wings and four legs instead of arms and legs.

Therefore, you see, I cannot tell you everything all at once, much
less in an afternoon. Boomer in his travels may have accumulated more
in the way of dragon lore, but there are a larger variety of dragons than
most dragons realize. Does that help?"

The Admiral nodded his head in the universal motion up and down
while saying, "No." They all laughed.

As Skth interjected, "And then there are the talents, which are all
over the board for even those of us who can produce a flame, even if it
doesn't look like a flame."

The Admiral laughed, "And what would a flame look like, if it
doesn't look like a flame?" He made some goofy eyes at Duff just to see
her laugh. It was still hard for him to get used to her being so tiny and
real. The laughing helped.

"Well, you saw Aunt Twill chill your coffee," Skth pointed at the
mug, "she can also freeze it. But her real talent is a flame of glass."
As she spoke, Twill flamed a round ball of very thin iridescent glass in
midair. "Now another dragon could maybe blow a flame into that ball,
but for our purposes, I'll use this candle," as she lit up a candle and
stuck the flame up into the ball through the hole in the bottom that Twill
had left. "And now my talent, or the one I use the most." She started
blowing gently into the hole and the flame danced into several fingers
that suddenly stopped, frozen. She removed the candle, but the flames
in the glass ball continued to stand there, radiating their cheerful glow.
Twill sealed the hole in the bottom and added a small loop on the top
for hanging, as Skth carefully took the ball out of the air as if it was an
apple to pluck from a tree, and presented it to the Admiral. "There you
go Admiral, a permanent night light or tree ornament that will never go
out."

"And," Twill added, "the glass cannot be shattered. It's dragon
glass."

The Admiral marveled at the captured flame in the ball, not knowing what to say.

"We are all working on something similar, but it will only be the glow of the flame, instead of the flame itself, and it will be captured in solid glass, with gold floating so it looks like a gold frame that will glow like a night light." Skth described.

"What will you do with that?" The Admiral asked, still awed by the ball.

"It's a special frame project Duff wants," nodding at her friend who was sitting there simply beaming to be acknowledged and part of this large family. "The frame will go around one of the glass pictures she makes." Skth shared, and then turning to Tink, "We'll do it, just as soon as Tink learns how to make gold or blow gold. You will learn how to make gold for me, won't you Tink?"

"Yes, Tink," Duff chimed in, "we need you to learn how to blow gold."

"Yes, Tink," Boomer teased in Duff's tiny voice, "You will learn how to blow gold for me, won't you, Tink?"

Tink's eyes started to spiral, and the other dragons thought he was just being his usual ham of a guy; but as he stumbled a little, he then came back to himself and turned to his brother, "We need to leave."

"What? Now?" Boomer started to laugh; as he was sure it was a joke.

"Yes, now." Tink was now hovering, and Twill noticed his glowing gold eyes.

"Yes Boomer, now." Twill concurred. With that, the two were out the door.

Barely stopping to install the harness, the two were flashing past the office window, and less than five seconds later, the boom of the sound barrier being broken not once but twice confirmed that the time had come.

Guff bolted out of the office and into the workroom looking at Twill who was coming his way nodding, "What was said?"

"I'm not really sure. They were all teasing him when it hit him."

Guff stared at his Patron long and thoughtful, "So we really don't know."

"Correct."

He thought a bit more, and then turned toward his office. "So, now, we wait."

A third sonic boom sounded almost too far away to hear.

The Admiral was confused, "Did I just say something wrong?"

Twill stepped to his side and rested her claw on his shoulder, "Not unless you don't think us girls are cute and pretty," imitating May West, as she attempted to distract and lighten the air; but getting a strange look from the man.

"Madam, I hardly know you," he retorted in a poor imitation of Groucho Marx; and they both laughed.

"No, its fine Admiral, the boys just have pressing business that they have to attend to, and none of us, least of all Tink, knew when they would get the call. So what seemed like rude behavior was just something that Tink had no control over; so please forgive the rushed departure and have some more rolls." Looking at the container of Lava sauce, she added, "Now that Boomer is gone, don't be bashful, you don't have to share."

As they settled back in with the food and education, Duff curled up with her head on Skth's lap with sleepy eyes as the Admiral tried a roll with Dribble sauce. Dabbing a napkin at his chin he resumed his questions as his left hand still toyed with the frozen flame in the ball. "So do the talents have any correspondence to the colors?"

"None at all," Twill said as she stroked the little foot of the now squeaking Duff. "None at all; in fact, what we call 'talents' are just something we do, and they can't be learned or taught." She popped another soaking fish ball into her left cheek and she continued. "Some of the dragons have no talents that we know of, like Tink or the Twins; others are born with the talent such as Boomer who broke the sound barrier breaking out of his shell. Then he came back and broke his brother's shell with a sonic boom directed at the shell.

"Talent is actually a misnomer in that 'talent' can be trained, such as Dvark's engraved patterns, and Chang's carvings," as she pointed out the many examples about the shop. "These are talents they were taught and developed, and should more properly be called 'skills.' But the 'talent' that we dragons refer to is Dvark's ability to hear patterns and their harmony, or Chang's ability to see what the wood is doing and wants to do and that he can speak to the wood, my blowing glass into shapes, Skth freezing flames and Boomer flying as fast as Boomer does. We dragons refer to these as talents. It does not make a dragon any less or more, just like their color or size; it is a distinguishing mark that makes up part of our identity as to who we are. Same as you're yellow and grey hair, pink skin and that the third finger on your right hand is 5 whole millimeters shorter than the one on your left hand - it's who you are."

The Admiral looked at his hands and put them together looking for difference. The fingers were, by his eye, matched. Then he noticed the sly smile on Skth's sleepy face and looked back up to the mirrored image on her great aunt's face. He knew he had just been had, and so he laughed. He made a mental note to himself that he would always have to be on watch for pranks and jokes around dragons, because he just knew that this would not be his last time sitting in the Paws & Claws Atelier.

It was obvious by the rhythmic thunder from the office, the squeak from Duff, and the drooping eyes of Skth that it was naptime. The Admiral quietly thanked Twill for indulging his thirst for knowledge and left with an auraof amazement as he wondered if maybe he had indeed fallen down that proverbial rabbit hole.

A thousand miles away, shooting into the gloom of deep night, a red and mud green gold missile arrowed its way towards a very tall mountain, a meeting of destiny and a trial. The night was cold, and Boomer worried about what the conditions would be like when they reached Nepal. Of all the dangers this trip, it was the chance of super cooled liquid hanging un-crystallized in the clouds, which could kill his tiny brother the fastest.

Worried, but obligated, Boomer kept pushing east and the destinies of the two brothers.

Chapter 13

Uphill Battle

The boys were flying over their second Mediterranean coast of the night, the first being across the bottom of Spain, and now over the beaches of Lebanon. Drawn across their vision at about mid-point, was a golden crest of the thinnest line. Boomer wondered with the relaxed lazy part of his brain just how many dawns he had flown into in his lifetime. Thousands easily, and probably tens of thousands more likely as he thought of a day not too long ago when he had flown out of the day into sunset, and with seven stops across the United States and finally up through Canada, he had remained in the glow of sunset for almost six full hours. Not that he had timed it that way; it was just that the flexibility of his kind of delivery allowed him to reward himself with a special treat of that sort of eye candy.

For many years, it had distressed his mother that he would leave and start work in the middle of the night. She thought the demands were unusual, demeaning and harsh, but it was his own design as to the hours he worked. The flights for the first many hours in the cool of the dark were his choice. The quiet and lack of distraction allowed him to think long and hard about many things. To a dragon at night, an aircraft's blinking light is like a bonfire at a range of over a hundred miles - easy to see. Mountain ranges were no longer any problem as any of the high ranges had snow almost year round, and even starlight alone would light them up like a flare over a frat party.

To Boomer, the long flights were best made quietly in the comforting blanket of night. That comfort was the calm and the salve for the other things he saw in his days, the gives and takes of the world, the messages he delivered. He was sometimes privy to message content; so a little quiet and the cover of darkness provided the peace he needed in his life, too.

As seen from high altitude across large flat oceans and vast deserts, it is easy to understand why dawn is called a "crack," for it certainly splits the dark in two. Dawn is not just morning as in the start of the day - that comes about an hour later. Dawn is the harbinger of what is to become, what is new, potentiality.

At these speeds, a scene like the crack of dawn is a snapshot taken with the mind. The next image is the rays created by the actual sunlight finding its way through mountains and clouds, obstructions that define the rise of the great ball of burning gases that gives life to all that is on and in the planet. It is no wonder, thought Boomer, that so many cultures worshipped that rising, ordaining and setting orb. His right sight shifted subconsciously to the central fovea as it looked off towards where he knew Egypt to be and the other looked forward to the ancient areas of Mesopotamia, now known as Iran, Iraq and for turmoil and troubled times among the human tribes and nations. The brothers, undetected, flew above all of that, as theirs was a mission of peace.

Tink shifted in a telltale move and Boomer responded by dropping out of supersonic flight and thinking about where it would be safe to stop for a minute or two. He tipped and circled right, and headed to a mountaintop where he was sure nobody would disturb them, and they would disturb no other souls.

Unchanged for two thousand years, Masada rose from the desert on the edge of the Dead Sea. Once the legendary site of an amazing conflict and an engineering feat that still stands today, the former fortress was silent in the predawn as they let down.

Tink climbed down and flew off to exercise and limber up a bit, and to take care of his needs. Boomer stood with his claws digging into the earth. He thought about the steeped history of this lone outpost, about the humans of today and those in the past who had spent years in their attack on this mountaintop. He looked across the top towards the east as the crack had grown and clouds and other obstructions were splitting the light into rays. Rays of hope, Boomer thought, for more peace in the future; and at minimum, more peace than had been visited on these lands in the past.

He sensed Tink returning, and presented his back as he lifted into the last of the graying dark, as the smaller shadow dove into his pocket and they were off like a wraith in the night.

This part of the flight was where Boomer knew it would get tricky, and was glad they were crossing this section before the mountain warriors would be paying too much attention to a small flying object in the sky that those below may mistake for a small drone airplane. Even at 18,000 feet, that would still put them in visual range, as they would transition through the high mountain passes of troubles. Even though the entire crossing would be less than ten minutes, it was always something in Boomer's mind, especially as the mountain range now rose in front of him.

Already the snow had dusted the tops and down through the passes, the ground was registering a very cold morning, so Boomer knew that there would be no one up and about yet. The three or four heat signatures in the human range were probably young men, low on the tribal pecking order, paying their dues for their jihad by standing watch in the least hospitable time of the night. Yet the nighttime was the safest for neophyte warriors sleepily huddled against a rock face in a high mountain pass with only a pair of dragons passing over in the early morning sunlight.

The land fell away and then rose again higher as the two brothers continued on a course of East by Southeast. The higher passes of this range were clear of any trouble as they made up the spine of Pakistan. The hardscrabble lives of the nomadic tribes of the high mountain regions always separated from the lush fields of agriculture in the Der Valley and especially a certain orchard near the Gomal University where Boomer was now heading. He did not know if Tink would or could eat, but he suspected that his little brother would need all the energy some honey and dates could provide.

The morning buzz of bees, crickets, birds and early bird humans setting about their day's business filled the air. The lush moisture and heat rising from the perpetual rotting of vegetation in the never ending cycle of agriculture filled Boomer's nose as he let down into the lower valley, gliding for a hidden grove of trees around a small barely used or known tiny temple in a country of a million tiny temples. Tink squirmed on his back and Boomer wondered if it was nature calling, or if it was agitation for the delay; either way, Boomer splayed his full wingspan and feathered his approach as he glided the last few hundred yards toward a glowing figure in a small earthen doorway.

As they landed, the monk bowed in a rite of homage to the red dragon. The two were long friends and had discussed many concepts of the world: religions and the place of religion in the world, as well as the place of the world in religions. Although a Buddhist monk, T'Ng was first and always a red fire dragon, and he would always see the world from the vantage point of one who has lived long enough for his color to fade and the ruddiness of the clay to model his appearance. The monk's eyes sparkled as he noted the smaller dragon dismounting. His left arm extended out towards his small stand of orchard trees as a couple of ubiquitous bees hovered about his head.

"Your journey is long and arduous," the monk had intoned as the two consumed many calories of honey, dates and rice in an exercise that resembled more of a shoveling of fuel into the burn box of a train. "According to the internet, there is a storm moving down from the Gobi desert last night and today. This could be fortuitous or dangerous. The Gobi can cause large formations of clouds and storms, or it can suck the moisture out of the storms leaving little but puffy white adornment of the sky."

"No word on the humidity?" Boomer stuck another gloppy handful of the fuel mix in his mouth as his brother probably matched him calorie for calorie as the Patron challenge drove him to prepare.

"They do not report that sort of information for these remote regions, as they do for city dwellers who need to decide on a jacket for rain or dress for sun. Here, we get wet or we have sun, the day decides." The monk played to his philosophical leanings. "But in the area of the mountain the humans call Manaslu and we dragons know at K'Tng, the air can be very dangerous, even when it looks dry. There are very valid reasons why there are so few dragons with the golden eye."

Boomer nodded down his last mouthful of the high mountain nectar, "I once got caught in some super cooled liquid that formed instant ice, back when I was young and flew through clouds." He rolled his eyes, "I think I dropped over ten thousand feet in seconds before I could burn it off. I've never forgotten that lesson."

The monk nodded, "But sometimes we hear of the ice in the air, when there is no cloud. The air ice has taken the lives of many climbers who were not prepared; this small one has very little to protect him." He acknowledged Tink with a nod.

"This is one time I am not in control. He will do what he has to do, I can only deliver him as best as I can," looking at his brother, "and hope that is enough."

Tink shoveled a last wad of food into his mouth and licking his claws and lips pronounced, "Must go now," as he nodded a curt bow of thanks and acknowledgement to the monk for his help and kindness.

Boomer apologized and hoped as he retreated after his brother, "He'll be better tomorrow."

The monk bowed, "May you both be strong of wing and return for more honey."

Boomer never tired of the wind when it whistled a sharp tune at 940 miles per hour. When the brothers were just hatchlings, their father whistled this same tone arriving home each night. He had not wished to scare them by his size and color. He had no idea that they had imprinted on their parents long before the eggs had cracked, or in their case, exploded. Tink still insisted that he had just been drilling an exploratory hole to see if he wanted to come out.

Boomer turned slightly to the left and almost due east as he passed through between the two ridgelines. He could feel a pull coming from the western end of the range as he would be flipping Tink into the wind coming down from the northern steppes and he needed to put him as close to the top as possible.

In practicing the toss, they had consistently obtained altitudes higher than the needed 26, 780 feet that the mountain reached; but it was always better to err on the safe side and give Tink the most help. After all, neither dragon had any idea as to what he was facing; just that the force that was within all dragons was guiding them.

They had passed quietly over a sleeping New Delhi as Boomer recognized the landmark he was seeking; the mountain known as Dahaulagiri; only slightly taller than K'Tng, it was the seventh tallest mountain in the world and his turn point. Just short of the mountain face, he turned slightly right and shot down the long valley past Annapurna, called the Roof of the World; a hulking mass of black rock and perpetual ice and snow. The valley radiated no heat, not even an occasional dot of an animal or human glowed in his search vision.

Rounding the bend in the valley, they were greeted with a worrisome sight and Boomer veered right to the south wall of the valley and finding a perch of a rock outcropping, he landed.

Tink got off, "What's wrong?"

Boomer pointed at the lower mass of a mountain that was boiling at the top with roiling gray and white clouds. "K'Tng." He watched the clouds, nothing registered on his vision with any heat. He worried, "The storm is full of super cooled liquid."

Tink looked at the mountain and clouds, then at his brother as if there should be more to his brother's explanation as to why he stopped.

"The liquid is just humidity in the air of the cloud, searching for something to form ice on," he explained. "If I throw you into that, you will instantly be covered by a layer of ice that could be a shell as thick as paper, or several inches thick."

"If you don't throw me into there, I will have to fly myself to get to the Kell."

Admitting that he had no argument against that, Boomer pointed out, in his mind, the worst, "Because of the ice, and not being able to see you, we may not make the grip for the final toss."

His brother stared at him, and then climbed back up onto the harness. "Then, I guess we'd better not miss."

As they shot out over the vast valley, Boomer gauged the winds. The approach would have to be a sweeping arc that put them directly into the wind. He would have preferred to have a wind at their back, or even a sunny day; but the day and weather had dealt them the condition that would determine their approach and Tink's trial, whatever that held.

Boomer's job was just to get him as close as he could to the door; it was up to his brother to walk through it.

As he climbed to the top of what he could, for the running start, his wing surfaces and body became slick with a light coat of ice that would form and then slough off as his heat would melt the contact area. At just under 22,000 feet, he turned back down the valley hoping for some help from the winds to push him slightly higher; today, he would need all the help he could get. If they missed the grip, Tink could end up with a deadly thousand feet or more of a climb where he would have little oxygen, icy conditions and no flying to maintain his body heat.

The light wind pushed as the two brothers worked together to capitalize on the assist, Tink's wings flaring in a cup as a set of sails, and Boomer pushing against the movement converting to upward thrust. As the effort played out, they turned for their final assault.

Tink tucked in behind the cone shield with his wings set for lift and Boomer reconfigured into a shallow dive that would help in the drive to the needed 1,200 miles per hour or as close as they could get. The double syncopated boom that rolled off Boomer's nose and Tink's wings as they broke the barriers was separated by less than a split second. The giant mountain of black and white patterned rock and ice approached at a dizzying pace. Then the two seemed to disappear in an instant as they turned and shot straight up into the oncoming clouds roiling over the mountain and falling in towards the valley.

Light gray became dark gray as they surged upwards; a projectile of living flesh at a speed that only machines were meant to endure. Primordial flesh in a primordial battle with the rawest and basest assault that nature delivered short of hurricanes and tornados; the winds churned and buffeted the small insignificant motes of dragon flesh as they pierced the very heart of the oncoming assault.

The ice was lighter than Boomer had feared and they were progressing better than he had expected with the look of the clouds from the outside; but he still worried as he felt Tink slip out of his stance and start to ball up. Boomer's right arm drifted back as he prepared to snap roll, and his claw grabbed the tiny ankle and gave it a double squeeze as if to say, "Good hunting."

A gust of turbulent air hit as he made his snap and Tink flew; but Boomer did not know if it was straight enough. The back roll sent him crashing down through the cloud, as his only sense of direction was internal. The first sonic concussion sent out a wave that cleared the thick cloud in a ball the size of a soccer field and the second sheared away the bottom of the cloud as the small red rocket arced in a sweeping circle and aimed at a point that he could only hope was there.

Gray upon gray, light and dark blurring to a different gray as the supersonic missile shot back through the cloud, heat searching with his most fervent heart for that tiny speck of heat in the maelstrom of cold and freeze. The speed was bleeding off the rocket form as his two arms snuck along his body ready in the next second as he still scanned the gray for his tiny target.

Boomer almost missed the low heat register masked by the sheen of ice covering the now static tiny dragon. He snapped his arms out at the last possible tick of a very short clock, dragging the tiny payload the last short distance before one final snap back flip. It was then that Boomer realized with horror that he had only grabbed one claw and arm; the other dangled free in the non-aerodynamic air and now rapidly freezing liquid.

And Tink was gone.

Boomer's heart sank as he realize that he had just thrown his only brother into a pocket of super cooled liquid that was already condensing into a deadly shell as he released. The red dragon sank through the lower cloud like a shaken rag of despair with no way of knowing what would transpire from here on out. Falling in gray was a mirror of how he felt and the numbing cold of helplessness that came with now being just a spectator. With a silent pop, he transitioned out of the bottom of the storm and winged his way down into the valley floor in hopes of finding some kind of warmth and a place to wait for however long it would take.

Many thousands of miles away, Guff and Twill pushed picture frames around in front of them, as children play at eating their least favorite food by pushing it around the plate. Skth and Duff were mindless drones as Pu directed them to reroll or fold fabric. Not in a hundred years had the fabric room been cleaned and straightened as well as they were cleaning and straightening it now. Well, OK... the fastidiously fussy Pu directed the constantly in trouble twins to clean it annually. Now it was clean!

M'Ree sat at her desk staring at the same set of bills she had been looking at the hour before, and they still made no sense to the mind-numb accountant. She was seemingly oblivious to the large box of double deadly black and blacker chocolate fudge sitting untouched on the corner of her desk within easy reach. The red stone glasses hung unused from the chain about her neck as her vision focused on a place she had never known nor would ever see.

Stuffed away in his pocket hole of a library, Flith sat staring at an ancient book with a fine watercolor of a high valley surrounded by even higher mountains. Even the watercolor looked cold enough to be covered in ice as his eyes saw the picture, and his mind filled in the temperature and thoughts. The archivist and company researcher wondered at the reason that more dragons never even attempted to go see the valley below the crag rising into the blue-black sky. The altitude placed the eye so close to space that the lack of air did not diffuse the light into the lighter blue we are used to seeing in the sky. The sky in the watercolor was almost ultra-marine and reflected in a small tear at the edge of his right eye. His heart beat slowly and his mind focused numbly on nothing, for fear it could possibly wander back to a much different time, place and circumstance.

The twins sat under a hosta leaf, one each side of a mug that they had come to prank, and now had no heart to do so. They sat staring at the windows of Guff's office and the open door. Even the building seemed to be holding its breath . . . for something, anything that would not be forthcoming for who knew how long. It was as if time was holding its breath or just standing still waiting.

What was not standing still was the little growing ball of ice that was rocketing, sort of, upward in a wobbly trajectory towards an unseen, unmovable, unyieldingly hard mountain. Inside, a tiny Tink was muttering in the most pitiful form, "Ow, ow, ow," as he held the proper shape that was very painful for his now-dislocated shoulder. The ball was adding ice layers at an alarming rate, already an inch and rapidly approaching two inches thick. As Tink tried to breathe there was no air, and soon he was panicked, as the ice was now a closed fist around him, keeping him from moving, keeping him from breathing, keeping him.

The ball of ice hit the side of the mountain, gratefully a bit on snow, a bit on ice, but luckily it came to hit and bounce off several rocks as they cracked then shattered the shell. The small mud green gold ball of ice caromed about on the rocks of the modest mountain shelf, pinging from rock to rock, tinkling about on the shelf like a Pachinko ball in a crazy game of ricochet, and finally the ice was all broken and shattered off, leaving only the beaten muscle and dislocated bone of the tiny dragon to take the one last hit against a big rock. Then he was still.

Across the valley, another dragon sat staring up at the heights lost in the violent storm that engulfed the top of the mountain. For Boomer, this was the most important mountain at the most important time, and the storm had swallowed the most important dragon he could think of, that is, if his mind was allowing him to think at all at that moment.

"How did we even come to this point?'" he asked himself, and the answer was a deafening resounding crushing silence. For all the millions of miles he had flown, the thousands of messages he had carried, the go-betweens from enemies, the shuttling of pacts, the hand-offs of deals - and at this moment, he felt useless. The hollow in him compounded his sense that there was nothing he could do, no way to help, and so he sat. His vision, a patch of boiling gray on darker gray that hid probably even more gray, and then a mountain, on which he had no idea of what was happening.

"This is your job for now."

He looked about, but saw no one.

"Sitting is support, and support is helping," said the voice.

Boomer got up and looked behind the rock and all around. The cockroach on the rock moved a bit and stopped. "Senseless random seeking is still senseless," it said.

Boomer looked at him. And thought about the altitude, and sat back down and looked back at the mountaintop and the storm.

"Better to wait quietly, conserves energy; energy you will need soon enough."

Boomer nodded, resolved to ignore his hallucination.

Much higher and in a much colder spot, a small wing moved slowly, painfully, also resolute. Tink was not happy and in his bed at home, "And I wonder if I will ever be there again," he thought. The air about him was gray, but the pull inside him was stronger, and he started to move. He was a long way from where he needed to be before the sun rose in the morning, and he knew that nobody was coming to help, even when he really could use a good dog like Scout.

The wall in front of him was sheer, but there were tiny little cracks that to any larger being would be useless, although even his claws barely fit as he began to climb. The ice was building but mostly on the outcroppings. Tink stuck to the inner crevasses that ran up along the face of the upper reaches of K'Tng. Each inch was a grueling ordeal as he reached out with his better arm, and only used his dislocated shoulder arm to steady his movements; even then, his pain was like a nightmare.

The hours dragged on as the small dragon made steady progress up the mountain face. Reaching out, pulling up, a bit of wing here or there, each bit of real estate was a trial of a new idea of how to move up. As he moved, he got closer to an outcropping that was forcing him to be more hanging from the ledge than traversing the face of stone.

He reached up and back, sinking only three claws less than a third of the way in to an ice lined crack. As he swung his weight, the crack gave way and he dropped, crashing to the end of his injured arm and as the socket pulled and reset, the pain was enough that he passed out into a gray of pain.

He awoke to the sound of someone screaming in agony. The blood-curdling shriek was the high register reserved for people in serious pain. Tink soon realized that he was the person screaming in pain, and then the pain really set its claws and started to draw forth in him a new understanding of pain. Tink was rapidly becoming a well-educated expert in the subject.

As the pain settled in, Tink became numb and very much focused. He had heard of shock, but had no idea what it was, or how to deal with it. He did know that he had no time for any thought that detracted from him reaching the Kell, and so he reached out again with his good arm, and got a better claw hold, and was soon over the lip of the shelf.

Tink decided, in his numbed state, to take stock. His shoulder had reset itself, and actually felt a lot better and might even be usable again. He examined that claw and lower arm, that must have gotten wedged in the crack but he realized, not before ripping off large portions of his skin. Thankfully, with the cold, it was not bleeding, but rather attempting to ooze, and had formed a frozen scab instead. "That's going to leave a mark," he thought.

He was actually feeling a bit better, more vitalized, refreshed, and warmer. "Warmer?" he thought. He shifted his right wing out of the way and warm breath oozed from a large crack in the rock face. Tink twisted around some more and he stuck his head in the crack; yes, definitely warmer. Enough warmer that he wished he could just stay there and get warm, but the draw pulled and he was engaged to keep moving just as . . . That's when another voice replayed in his head, saying something that had made no sense, until now, "Follow the warm breeze or breath, it will safely guide you." The small dragon did not need another invitation, as he wormed his way into the crack and back into the mountain following the warm breath.

The air was warm, well warmer, but only in reference to the frozen nature of the mud green flesh that was now numb and as he wiggled and squirmed his way into the crack, the numbed frozen skin was torn and abraded from the working muscle now exposed. With each crawling inch, the little body was torn, scraped and flayed by the sharp-edged rocks in the crack of a tunnel.

Tink's thoughts were as frozen as any vegetation would be outside in the storm. There was no processing of choices or ideas, the dragon merely crawled and clawed his way toward the siren call of the Kell. The closer he got, the more power it held over him - drawing, guiding, and powering him. Around a bend, up a tube, through a crack, across and through a tumbling water fall of freezing cold water, and still he progressed uncaring, unknowing, unaffected by anything that was beyond what was in front of him and how he needed to keep going to reach his goal.

Outside the temperature dropped even lower as the storm encased the entire upper face and started sliding down towards the valley floor. Rolling, tumbling, chewing clouds of evil black slicing through dangerous gray that consumed anything and everything in its way as it swallowed the mountain whole and reached for the individuals on the other side of the valley.

"We need to seek shelter," the cockroach insisted.

Boomer continued to ignore the illusion.

"That storm will freeze you into a stone in as long as it would take you to fly across the valley. I've seen you fly, so I know you're fast."

Boomer turned and looked at the ever so small tiny monk. "At least he doesn't have to shave his head," he thought. He blinked as he scratched slowly behind his right ear winglet, a habit he had not been able to break in the 80 years he had been trying. He blinked slowly and turned back down the valley to watch the mountain.

"I know you think I'm just a high altitude hallucination, but I can assure you that I am as real as you are." The beetle continued to try to convince the dragon to seek shelter, "Imagine how I felt this morning when I see not one but two mythical beasts, and one is riding on top of the other and they are flying faster than they should be able to." He shook his head and wiggled his antenna. "What was that loud noise anyway?"

Absently Boomer replied, "Sonic boom." Turning towards the cockroach, he explained as he continued to blink in an attempt to understand, "It happens when I break the sound barrier."

"Barrier? There's no stinking barrier in the air."

"Not a barrier like a wall, but it acts like a wall when I fly faster than 700 mph. The air is expanding so fast it creates that noise."

"Like thunder."

"No, that is when the lightning burns up the air so fast the new air rushes back in and makes a very loud noise like a clap."

"Clap, what's this clap?"

Boomer looked at the legs and antenna of the beetle and thought about the old question about "What is the sound of one hand clapping?" and how it would be lost on this particular monk. "Maybe that shelter would be a good idea if we are going to continue this discussion."

The beetle looked at the dragon, and then back up at where the mountain had been earlier, but now the only sight that existed was the storm boiling down the valley. He dropped back down to all of his legs, "We need to hurry, this way," as he scurried off among the riff raff of shattered boulders.

Much higher, in a tighter more sheltered tunnel, small even for the likes of Tink, in cracks that even a small field mouse would hesitate to navigate, the little dragon doggedly followed the warm breath of the mountain. He continued to tear his way, claw pull by claw pull, shredding his wings as they were dragged through the ever closing crystal sharp crevices. Up through the interior of the mountain crag as the mountain crack of a tunnel continued to tear and scrape Tink, peeling mud green skin from every part of his body, and still he pushed or pulled on. His back muscles, normally heated from flying, were now searing hot from the strain of climbing and using his upper body and arms to move through a universe that tore at his flesh, numbed his vision by the sheer darkness, and toyed with his hearing with the howling or vibrating of the storm outside.

"Or was it that dark," he thought, "and was that sound outside . . . or in?'"

The tunnel, that had been steeply vertical for the last hundreds of feet tempered and then smoothed out as it also became larger until it emptied out into a large chamber lit by frozen flames atop torches that were stuck in slanted holes drilled into the walls. The tiny dragon stood calmly taking in the cavern; shredded skin hanging like dreadlocks from his body, wings, legs and arms, and the newly exposed under skin oozed the goo that is plasma and platelets to dragons. The scaling tendrils of skin enhanced the tiny dragon's similarity to reptiles and their shedding of skin, as he stood dazed, looking about with exhaustion-glazed eyes that did not see or understand the mosaic that was set in the floor. The walls with the torches were uninterrupted. The floor was a pattern of reds and blues, whites and blacks, emeralds and opals, obsidian, rubies, quartz, malachite and lapis lazuli. These were all of the colors of dragons represented by precious stones set in a pattern that was floral and yet geometric at the same time depicting all of the dragons, their colors, and subsets; and in the center of the chamber, stood a white statue.

The statue was pure white like the clearest Corinthian marble. No flaw colored any part of the perfect right dragon. The wings extended slightly and were translucent as Tink could see the light behind glowing through the webbing on the wings. In the statue's right hand, something metal. As Tink started to walk towards and around the statue, he could see that it was a large and very ornate golden key, as if to a very important lock that protected an important object. Tink blinked as he started to understand that he had finally reached his goal. The Kell was within his reach; he merely needed to locate the lock.

Tink reached out hesitantly and touched the key. The statue blinked.

Twill blinked again as she tried to understand what Skth was showing her. The glass she had just been blowing into a ball was glowing. It was clear; she was looking through the glass and seeing Skth, distorted, but Skth nonetheless, upside down in the ball, yet the ball was glowing. There was no flame, just the glass. Twill blinked again. The brothers had rushed out of the shop many hours since. The Admiral had called for a ride. Duff had long since fallen asleep in a pile of scrap fabric from Pu and Poul making fabric wrapped mats, and Guff, well, who could ever know where that bear would get off to, and she had stopped trying to keep track of him well over a hundred years before. "Tell me again - where is the flame?"

"There is no flame," exclaimed the exasperated small blue. She tried once more to explain, "Or not as we understand a flame." Her tiny hand reached out and lay gently on her great aunt's shoulder, "Maybe what we really need is to join Duff and get some sleep. She's a pretty sharp pencil in her own box you know." The perpetually smudged pixie snorted in her sleep and rolled over on her side, drawing an even larger pile of cloth scraps over on top of her.

Tink, on the other hand, may have thought he was tired before, pushed past the point of shear exhaustion, but the statue's blink was like an electric shock. The white hand curled tighter around the key and lifted it. Tink stepped back a few knee shaking steps as the white dragon with the solid white eyes, rose up and turned to look down on tiny dragon.

"You seek the jewel." The mountain rumbled in what Tink thought must be like being in the middle of an earthquake. Slowly the snow-white nose came closer to Tink's raw scraped and semi-frozen nose. "Hmm?" Cold air poured off the frozen stone statue's head. The white eyes that were the same stone white color of every other part of the dragon were unnerving. Slowly the stone cold statue blinked, for Tink was sure that this dragon was not one of flesh and blood, but of the mountain itself. To confirm, the little dragon watched for any flaring of the cheek or ear wings and movement in the chest of it taking a breath.

"You are a stone dragon," Tink offered.

"I am the Key Master, the keeper of the key to the inner chamber. Only with me, can you enter the chamber." Tink marveled at the sound that came from the entire mountain and was the voice of the dragon at the same time. "You have come for the jewel."

"The Kell; yes, it has called me here." Tink confirmed as he confirmed the lack of blood or any other liquid flowing through the body of the dragon before him. It was either an amazing statue that moved, or a hallucination. Either way, he was sure that to get to the Kell, this was something he had to endure: a trial, a test, something that was inside of Tink himself. More to himself as an affirmation he muttered, "I am ready," meaning that he was ready for the test.

"Good," the statue rose back up, turning to walk deeper into the cavern. "The jewel awaits your arrival." As they moved into a roughhewn passageway, they left the warmth Tink had felt from the multi-colored bejeweled mosaic floor. The deeper down the tunnel, as it was becoming a tunnel more than a passageway, the colder the air became.

Tink followed as he watched the statue's tail, and wondered at the flag twitching to the right. He felt he had watched that same sort of twitch before, and he thought of Dvark etching and talking at the same time as he was telling a good story or pulling Tink's leg in a mischievous tale the older dragon's tail would twitch to the left. The thought of his friend warmed his chest with a bond and affection he felt for and from the mentor and fellow framer.

The little dragon was falling a bit behind as he thought of Twill, cooling Guff's coffee when the big guy wasn't looking, as Guff hated cool coffee. He pictured the prank being performed not even a short year before, he noticed Twill's tail flag twitching toward the left and center, then left again. Always, her tail twitched to the left.

M'Ree walked across the stage of his memory, her tail looped up and over her left arm, twitching in anticipation of an upcoming reward of chocolate. Tink smiled as he thought how only the accountant could find chocolate at both ends of a short journey through the shop. He chuckled to himself and the head of the white dragon statue turned and looked back as it paused at a very wide and very tall pair of iron doors set into the craggy walls of the tunnel's terminus.

"Are you ready?" The statue asked as he inserted the gold key in the cast iron door's lock. Turning the key to the right, Tink was again nudged by the thought of having seen that same movement many times before. But where?

The doors swung open wide as the statue pushed. As the doors floated across the golden floor, the light flickered, sparkled and danced over, in and among the mounds of jewels, treasures, riches, and tumbles of chests open, bags spilled, bowls overflowing with jewels, gold, silver and platinum. Tink marveled, looking through the white dragon's legs as the two progressed into the amazing jewel chamber. The walls were hung with tapestries so ornate that it could take years to see all that was just in one, much less the dozens of dozens of intricate priceless weavings. But what struck Tink the most was the chill that crawled across the floor and gripped at his feet and up his legs.

As the white dragon turned, his tail flag was twitching even stronger to the right, and in Tink's mind, the color altered and he watched a green and then a blue tail twitch as the Twin's tails always twitched right, never left. The white dragon rose up and spread his arms and wings in a dramatic show of all that surrounded them in the room, as the one thing that had been nagging Tink from the first time the statue had moved. Of all the jewels - and there were rubies the size of eagle eggs and sapphires with two or even three radius stars. He saw emeralds as deep a green as the night sky and large enough to play baseball with and opals that had flames dancing across faces the size of dinner plates. He counted many sizes of diamonds from tiny to chicken eggs - there were riches the value of the world many times over. Then he noticed that one jewel was missing from this room. The most important jewel of all was at that moment missing and with that realization, Tink turned to find the giant doors silently closing, too late to run through. He was trapped. The tiny littlest dragon exploded from the floor, and was gone just before the great heavy doors thundered shut.

Across the valley, the tiny monk was not so sure being this close to a dragon was such a good idea. The dragon was hungry enough to be chewing on a small wad of grass. He thought about asking if the dragon was a vegetarian, but then, why give a dragon large enough to make a cockroach just a snack, any ideas. "Are you warm enough?" He thought if maybe the dragon could get some sleep, he might not be focused on eating.

"I'm fine, thank you." Boomer stared at the small cave into which they were jammed. Cozy for maybe someone the size of Tink, but for a dragon eight times that size, the headroom left a little to be desired. He moved about a bit in an attempt to become more comfortable. "So, you live here all the time?" He asked the cockroach in an effort to make small talk and feel more relaxed at talking to his first cockroach. He hoped it was a talking cockroach and not a hallucination, as he had feared. After all, Boomer did not think he could have found this cave on his own.

"I've never been here before," the cockroach monk replied, and was relieved as the dragon put down the small tuft of grass as if he was full. "I live down in the lower area where the heat is more conducive to my body."

"Then," Boomer's face screwed up as he tried to think, "What are you doing up here?"

The antenna swung back and forth, as the two forward legs swung in the air also, "That my friend, is a great question." He shrugged his carapace and rolled his eyes, "I have no idea what I'm doing here."

"Well, how did you get here?"

"I don't know that either."

Trying to help, Boomer became a little more investigative, "What were you doing before you got here?"

The cockroach continued to clean and wipe his face and head. "I don't know, I just remember you two streaking across the sky and then you went up into that cloud, but only you returned."

Boomer thought of what he hoped would be a trick question for a hallucination. "What were you doing yesterday?"

The monk dropped his legs from his face, "Oh that's easy; a bunch of us were headed for a small house near the log we were under. We could smell the rot of food, and it was some very heady stuff, free food."

"But, you have no idea what you're doing here now?" Boomer looked down at the unsatisfying snack of grass. His stomach was reminding him of his last meal among friends, and wondering about finding something a little more pleasant to restore his balance and energy.

"No, no I don't; but then, do any of us truly know what we are doing here?" The cockroach smiled, or at least it was what Boomer assumed passed for a smile on a cockroach.

"Well, I hate to say this, but I'm hungry." Boomer started, the cockroach's antenna stood straight up, and if he had eyes that could get larger, they would have. "No, relax. The last thing I would want to even think about eating would be a cockroach," and the roach collapsed in relief as Boomer continued. "If you can tell me more about exactly the log and house you came from, maybe I can get you back there, and then I can look for some food."

The tiny hole in the ground seemed just a little bit friendlier and not so bad after that as the monk explained as best he could for a ground bound beetle to a high flying supersonic air riding entity, just where he was from and how much he would appreciate getting back to his friends. Boomer listened, as he lifted the roach up to his shoulder and explained how he should tuck into the very point of the harness shield. Especially when he realized that the cockroach was not from Nepal at all, but from Mumbai, India, over 950 miles away. How the tiny creature had gotten so far, was beyond him, but he would do his best to get him back with his friends. "Are you holding tight?"

"Yes," came the tiny voice as they lifted into the air, and Boomer slowly ramped up to speed as he barreled down the valley, the first of two sonic booms blowing rain back up into the storm cloud, and pounding the surface of the small stream meandering down the middle of the valley.

The surface of the molten glass smoothed as the glow from the heat stayed steady. Twill had never realized that for her glass to be molten, it was hot, but that it cooled from her breath, but each new additional grain, sliver, shard or layer was still molten, and heat radiated light. Something Skth was now trapping inside the glass Twill was blowing.

The two had been practicing off and on, as they could not really sleep. Between catnaps and raiding M'Ree's many chocolate stashes, they had globes, and frames, and even a sleeping pixie draped over the back of a small dragon that were all glowing in the darkened shop.

The two blues sat back sharing the last of the triple dark raspberry stuffed fudge truffles as they stared at the lights glowing softly. The light, an eerie glow in the shop usually highly lit better to see the fine details of picture framing, cast a soft feeling that was almost like a photo that was slightly out of focus to add a mystery or a feminine quality to an image.

"Who would have thought?" Twill leaned back in the large chair she had absconded with from Guff's office.

"I know," agreed Skth, "These are the most amazing chocolate morsels I have ever eaten."

"No," Twill leaned her head over towards her great-great-grandniece and laughed, "No, this chair; it was made for a dragon."

Skth looked at her blinking; caught with one claw in her mouth as her tongue slowly swirled about seeking every last smear of fudge. "But that is Guff's chair."

"I know," Twill swiveled the seat with only on claw on the legs. "I just never sat in it before." She thought about the almost two hundred years, and how strange it was that she had always just come to roost on the corner of his desk instead.

"How can you tell?" Skth asked absently as she tried to decide among the apparently last five morsels of truffledom. Diet is not a word in the dragon dictionary. The need to refrain from eating them all, sharing with Twill, leaving one or two for Duff (if she ever woke up), vied with just flat not caring about the consequences of being a hog. If she had known that M'Ree's way of dealing with waiting for important news was to bake more chocolate, she would have long stopped worrying over something as ridiculous as when to stop, and when to share.

"I can just feel it." Twill let fly and spun all the way around several times until finally coming to rest looking into the eyes of someone much larger.

The raised eyebrow over the one dark brown eye told the whole story, but added for impact was the, "Having fun in the boss's chair?" The two stared at each other with the stone faces of two people who are used to being obeyed by others who quake as the recipient of their controlling looks.

"M'Ree!"

Skth's hand retracted from the chocolate container with the speed of Boomer on a "rush job" over open water. Her face reflecting the color of the stone glasses now directed not two feet away from Twill's nose.

"Chocolate, to calm the waiting nerves my dear?" She offered out a large box stuffed heaped with at least half a dozen kinds of tasty fudges and chocolate morsels to create many small "deaths by chocolate."

With a slightly controlled blush, Twill reached in and chose the smallest of pieces and graciously adding, "Thank you M'Ree, you are so thoughtful."

The sea chameleon dragon's one eye brow lowered as she continued to stare at the shop boss over her red stone glasses for the measured count of four, and then turning the other eyebrow raised as she spied the box she had forgotten where she had hidden it over a year before. "Oh child," she scolded Skth affectionately, "Don't eat that old stale stuff. It's probably half rotten by now; here, try this fresh chocolate I made this evening."

The small blue, now feeling almost as full as she was embarrassed, reached out with all the delicacy and decorum she could muster as she took the smallest piece she could see. The smell of fresh chocolate was almost intoxicating as she understood why and how this dragon could be the size she was. However, Skth suspected that the "made for comfort, not speed" in her younger days was just the opposite, she looked at the box and reached for one of the now imprinted raspberry truffles, "Well, maybe one more." M'Ree nodded to her good choice for a final morsel and raked off five or seven as they flew unerringly into the air in an arc to her mouth with a much-practiced move.

M'Ree laid the box on the workbench next to Chang's array of woodworking tools, and her left hand openly, lightly softly stroked the worn and well cared for chisels and mallets as she admired the talent and artistry drawn out of the amazing snake dragon. Her right hand, on the other hand, was quietly searching about the box for seemingly its favorite little morsels that disappeared in her mouth as she turned to say something to Twill, but notice the glowing glasses that were lighting this area of the shop.

Clanging shut, the great iron giant doors echoed the scream of, "Noooooooooooooooo!" The mountain reverberated, and the key in the lock retraced its own course and slowly turning, locked the doors shut. The doors sealed closed forever. The only "person" who could extract the key, was in fact, the Key Master; now standing unmoving in the middle of a solid gold floor, surrounded by jewels that could buy the world four times over. Surrounded, that was, by every kind of jewel that was ever valued, ever thought of, ever made and cherished except two.

"Except two," Tink thought as he came to rest on a floor of jewels set in a mosaic that was a pattern of the diverse dragon world. "Except the two most important jewels in the entire world to a dragon, and the dragon world; those jewels being the Kell itself and the jewel that is in every dragon's forehead that speaks to the Kell. Without it, you are no dragon."

True to Tink's words, the Key Master stood frozen for all time, a perfect statue carved in the purest of white marble. The webbing of its wings so thin as to be translucent, each scale perfectly carved, perfectly formed, lying perfect and blending into the bumpy skin that led to the feet and hand claws and even out to the tips of each and every one of the eight claws. The winglets on its cheeks looked ready to flare with each breath, its eyes white and sightless but ready to see. Its nostrils flared in a last assault and its mouth was open and frozen in its lasting scream of protest as it failed its challenge. All because of the one detail that set it aside as a pretender instead of a member of a society of creatures with a jewel set in their foreheads.

Opal is a blend of colors floating in a matrix of white and cream; pearls are not a jewel of the earth, but nacre shells of the sea. Diamond is a clear stone with colorings that shade the clarity. Marble, however, even the finest purest white, is but a stone. If the creator of the statue had carved its replica into the forehead of the Key Master, there would still be no jewel. Without the jewel, it was no dragon.

As Tink lay on the warm floor of the mosaic, he marveled at the setting of each of the millions of jewels. At this range, he could see the fine gold line threading between and around and on to the next jewel, much as the Kell threaded between all dragons. From ultra-marine sapphires, to clear and colored diamonds, to the red and pink blush of rubies, the wash of green emeralds, softened by the whiter jade, the counterpoints of obsidian or onyx, sparks of orange fire opal, and around the lulling restful purple of late night and amethyst, the gold traced a path that tied each and every one of the jewels to the next and on unbroken to every other. The pattern was that of the entire world of dragons, and through the dragons, the entire world of beings was connected.

Battered, beaten, tumbled and cheated, the tiny dragon, lying in the chamber high above the world in the soft light of dragon flame, on a mosaic floor warmed by the very world he was touching, as he reached out from his dislocated shoulder, and with his index claw began to sleepily trace the gold line. His eyelids slowly closed, and he did not see or feel as his claw slowly sank into the fine tracery of the gold line, as his claw drew up the gold of the Kell.

Boomer let down over Mumbai and into the wild edge of the poorer section of a filthy region he had never been in before. The last rays of sunlight were making it hard for him to see from very far above, so he had come within a hundred feet of the ground. The fetid smells of sixteen million humans and all the attending animals that also means, living in such a close proximity, was not exactly a pleasant experience for Boomer. Used to the clean smell of nothing at the high altitudes and purifying speeds he cruised at daily, he had no idea that people or other souls could even live in these conditions.

He searched for the building that the monk had said he could see from a distance, a unique structure that didn't fit in with the rest of the structures in the area or the city. He was looking for a structure of pure steel and glass, but a shape that was more western. They glided down along the western areas and over neighborhoods. Finally Boomer lifted back up to a couple of thousand feet as the city lights helped light up the night and would reflect off of the glass, but not in the usual way as the walls flared out, the reflections would be redirected down, and the building should become a black void that still registered with heat, maybe even warmer because of the dark glass, or cooler if the interior had been air conditioned in a city of no such amenities.

Boomer glided north, then south as he worked a grid over the whole of Mumbai. The night was pleasant as the temperature dropped to under ninety degrees Fahrenheit. For humans, Boomer knew that was a hot sticky night of discomfort and sleeplessness, but for a dragon it was pleasant; for a cockroach, he was not sure.

Switching from heat seeking, to searching for cool zones, he was finally able to find the building. He should have known that a gigantic building for a cockroach would be little more than a leaning ready to fall down house for a much larger dragon. Boomer landed flat on the top of a roof and asked if the building in front of them was the right building.

"Oh yes. That is the one I told you about. This is amazing that you could find this building." The cockroach yawned. "I am very sorry; I was sleeping so peacefully while you flew."

"I'm glad I provided such a smooth flight." Boomer replied with only a tiny bit of sarcasm. Down deep, now that they were where the tiny monk needed to go, Boomer was actually very happy to have had something to do and to feel useful. "Where to from here?"

The cockroach looked around the neighborhood from his new vantage point. "I think we are here," the monk said looking back. "I believe this is the building that we were going to when I ended up sitting next to you."

"Well climb back on," Boomer nodded, "and we'll get you down to your friends."

The gold eyes of the beetle swirled as Boomer picked him up and placed him on his shoulder for the short ride to the ground, "This is most kind of you Boomer, it really shows you are truly a compassionate person," as the monk settled into the cone of the harness; adding silently, "And very highly protective."

L. REYNOLDS 09

Chapter 14

Chang Worked Late that Evening

Chang was working late that evening; now that there was finally quiet in the shop. Whether out of sheer exhaustion or that they had given up on the return of the two brothers, Twill and her great niece had finally stopped making glass objects that glowed; although if the truth be told, Chang really liked the little statue of Duff lying asleep on top of Tink. He had never seen it happen, but he did know of their deep love for each other; and that Skth shared in that love as a latecomer to the great friendship. The two blue dragons and the pixie had left for dinner at Tink and Boomer's parents' house, to share their missing of the boys together.

The rest of the crew had long ago flown off into the evening air, at least, those that could fly. Guff had just shambled off in his usual galumphing gait, into the darkest part of the deep forest. Chang had wondered for many years where Guff headed each evening. Giant hosta plants covered the forest floor three feet deep and some of the enormous leaves were large enough to support a small dragon for use as an afternoon hammock. At nearly five feet tall, Chang was much too big for trekking into the forest. His bones and scales although hollow to allow for his unusual form of flight, were of volcanic iron glass. His static weight would crush almost any vegetation. The large bear should be leaving tracks from his red clogs in the forest floor, but there were none. Nor was there any sort of trail to mark Guff's comings and goings.

Chang never gave it a lot of thought; much as he never thought about the impossibility of his being able to fly without wings and weighing in as if he were an anvil instead of a balloon. The Asian Snake dragon was just as content with his long life as a squirrel would be, stretched out in the sunshine on a warm summer's log. He was not sure how old he had been when he first extended his large over-sized scales, and then slammed them shut causing a jet propulsion that projected him above his parents' house. Then of course, there was the delicate art of learning of how not to crash land without a pair of wings to use as a parachute. Over the years, Chang had perfected the small subtle differences in his dorsal scales to propel him right or left and the reshaping of his body and tail to rise or dive. Even when he was a small dragon child, his crossed eyes presented him great difficulty in seeing where he was going. He was heavy enough back then that when he accidentally stepped on his mother's wooden rice bowl; it shattered into a hundred pieces.

That had been his epiphany that he was heavy. With tears in his eyes, he promised his mother that he, Chang, would make her another bowl. It had never dawned on the small dragon that there was anything called money and that the family could simply buy another bowl at that Saturday's market in the village. Standing there with the offending shards of wood scattered about his small glowing red body, his mother took him in her arms and reassured him that she would enjoy his bowl above all others. That was how he had met his mentor, the village master wood carver, Su Chee the Moon Bear. Over the next fifteen years, Su Chee taught the young Chang to speak to the wood, and shape it with tools and cooperation. Chang learned also that there was a difference between *eyesight* and *vision*: he may always have crossed eyes but his *vision* would allow him to see in many different ways both the wood and world before him.

The evening gloom of the forest settled in like a warm fuzzy blanket on a cold winter night. Fireflies and dadie fairies (which were not really fairies at all, just a little beetle that glowed reddish or bluish if it was a boy or girl dadie) danced in and among the trees and patio clearing. The music of their dances and the harmonies of the trees cooling from the day were a relaxing symphony to Chang as he focused on the wood in front of him on the table.

The miters of the two legs to the picture frame were not coming together in the inside of the frame. Chang knew that he had cut the faces at the correct 45 degrees and that they should not have a small gap. However, try as he might to push the two large pieces together, there was that constant narrow gap. The two pieces refused to come together and become as one. He opened the join and examined the two almost glassy faces. As he laid the steel hand plane up to the faces, he could see that each face was flat and true. However, upon running his left thumb over the area that was the offending problem, he could feel that something was not right, almost as if there was an argument going on between the two pieces of wood. His right ear wing expanded and twitched in annoyance. There was an old memory about another couple of trees whose wood would not join. It was a problem of silly status.

Chang's was indentured to master Su Chee, who had once fought with a square hole or mortise and a square peg on the end of a furniture part called a tenon. No matter how he had cut the hole or the tenons, they would not fit one in the other. Careful measuring had not solved the problem; the woods were at war. If he cut the tenon too small, the hole would become grandly larger; if he cut the tenon perfectly, the hole would shrink.

This battle raged for days in Su Chee's shop until finally in frustration the Master had taken all of the offending wood out into the noisy bustling street in front of the shop. There he had started to pile all of the wood into what would become a bonfire. Suddenly, as the village people watched in amazement at this strange behavior, all of the pieces of wood separated and became two piles.

The Master observed the two piles for a moment. He then instructed half of his workers to re-pile the wood, while the others surrounded the woods in a tight circle while holding large torches. The woods shook and quivered as they perceived their fate. But even with the threat of fire, the wood would not mind. The Master had his workers take a piece of wood and move it to the other pile only to return to the original pile to find the same piece of wood back where it had been.

Finally, after several hours, the Master had turned to the now not-so-young dragon and simply told him, "You talk to them," and had walked back into the shop for a cup of hot tea. Chang had no idea what he was supposed to do, so he just started talking to the pieces of wood. He began by explaining how the two woods were not working together and why this behavior was upsetting the Master, which was also making Chang's life miserable. He continued by telling the two piles of wood that if they could not work things out, he would be forced to burn them. The pleadings by the young apprentice continued for some time.

In the end, the sound of Chang's voice got quieter and quieter until a whisper would have been like a large explosion. Then there was an eerie silence. The sunny street grew dark, and although hundreds of people were still wandering among the shops and vendors, it was dark enough that Chang could no longer see the people. The silence to him was almost deafening. The young dragon could hear his heart beating and the wind in his lungs. Then ever so softly, there was a little voice saying, "How can you expect me to rest myself inside of a tree that grew so far down the mountain as to not get enough sun?"

Chang was astounded and jumped back. Another voice answered in a deeper timbre, "But deeper in the valley we were closer to the river, shaded for protection and raised in the comforting shade of our parents and ancestors. What makes you think you are worthy of becoming part of us in a piece of furniture?"

Chang listened to the petty arguments as the centuries of position in a forest and snobbery of up-hill versus down-hill versus near water, not enough sun, too much sun, long needles, short stature, growing west facing, tilting left and other silly arguments unveiled themselves in his mind. He sat down slowly in the dust of the street to listen to this lumber. Finally, he had suffered enough and he stood. "Silence!" he had roared at the two piles. "I have two choices," he started as he slowly walked between the two. "I can burn you both this evening and cook my dinner from your death, or I can separate you." As he now stood between them, there was a pause.

"Separate us," crept forth the simple answer.

"And if I do, you will abide with my wisdom and forever work together in silent harmony and strength?"

"Yes," they both answered.

Therefore, Chang wrapped the tenons with a paper-thin layer of the finest birch wood, and then slid each into the proper mortise holes; they fit so perfectly that after a second there was no need for glue or fasteners. The two woods had given their word to work together and needed nothing else . . . except a few slivers of the silent wood, birch.

Remembering all of this by the glow of a single hanging light, the very much older Chang, now Master Wood carver of the Paws & Claws Frame shop slowly stepped out of his Japanese wooden sandals and climbed up onto the workbench. The heavy legs and understructure, although thankfully made to withstand both his great weight and the very large pieces of wood for carving into fine picture frames, groaned in the stress of its joints.

The great red and orange head slid sideways and looked under the tabletop, "Shhh," the Asian snake dragon warned. Silence prevailed. Chang's eyes began to whirl as the focus of his attention returned to the mitered join of the picture frame rail. Looking deeply into the thin crack that was opening wider as he watched, he thought of fire. He imagined a great roaring fire with four very special pieces of wood in the middle of that fire. While he thought, one of his eyebrow tendrils withdrew a small sliver almost paper from behind his left ear wing. The eye tendril held it out and his snout tendril took it and held the small piece of birch wood mere inches from the crack; then as the crack grew larger to accommodate the slip of separating wood, the tendril inserted it into the now closing crack. In seconds, the join was smooth and seamless. Only Chang knew that there was no need for glue, and that this join would never come apart except by fire.

As a Chang leaned back to rest on his haunches in the primitive stance of a snake dragon with the back hunched and the forearms acting as legs, a flash exploded through the open window and rocketed across the large area of the shop. A trail of gold almost like pixie dust, or what people imagined pixie dust would look like, floated in the air, mapping the missile-like projectile that had landed in the large utility sink.

With trepidation, Chang eased himself down off the worktable and slithered in an arched path to approach the porcelain receptacle of the interruption to his quiet work. Silently in his bare feet, his now less than 5 feet of stature was evident as he bent low to stay hidden until he could somehow look in the sink without being seen. The gold pixie dust fascinated him as it was not falling but rather staying in the air as if it had been glued in place.

With one eye watching the gold trail hanging in the night's air, and the other looking down into the sink, Chang raised his body up until his nostrils were even with the lip of the sink in preparation to looking over the edge as surreptitiously as he possibly could . . .

The golden head of a very small dragon popped up out of the sink at the exact same time. "WAAA...?" Chang exploded upward as his scales expanded and shut in a mighty rush resulting in his head hitting one of the ceiling beams, knocking him out cold; he fell into a red and orange tangle of dragon and tools on the floor.

The very littlest dragon shook his tiny head and a cloud of gold floated out away from his head much like dust on a dog that shakes after rolling in a dirt bath. The tiny gold beads for eyes grew wide and a silly smile grew on his face. Tink grinned in awe of this new phenomenon as he eyed the trail of gold still floating in the air, unmoving.

A wave of air crushed Tink back against the porcelain wall of the sink as the sonic wave caught up with the hot red dragon that looked like an incoming missile. ***"BOOM"!*** His brother arrived, blowing the gold dust trail everywhere into tiny little nooks and crannies where it would be found for years to come.

"Tink!" Boomer rushed over to his little brother. "How did you get back? After the storm was gone, I waited for you at the bottom of K'Tng for four more days and then I *just knew* you would be here; but how?" The dragon was almost white hot at the outer reaches of his wings but even still red hot on his hands as he grabbed the solid gold Tink.

"I don't know," Tink began, then shouted and shot straight up, "WOW! You're burning up!"

"Oh, sorry," Boomer turned on the cold water and stuck his hands into the stream which immediately became steam boiling up and around him like a cloud for a second until his hands and arms were just warm. "I must have really pushed the speed limit getting back here."

"Well, I have no idea how I got here," responded Tink. "I was lying very peacefully on the floor of the Kell. Then I started getting dizzy from the high altitude or something and the Kell told me to think of my favorite place, and that's my porcelain mug but it wouldn't believe I could fit in the mug so I guess this is the only porcelain it could find and there was a gold explosion and then BANG! I'm bashing my brains against the backsplash of this sink," his eyes got big, "Oh my gosh! Chang!"

They both turned to find the red snake dragon, more cross-eyed than usual, slowly rising above the lower carving table. A low groan emanated from the snake, "噢，我的傷害的頭!"["Oh, my hurting head!"] About his head, his tendrils still holding tools dangerously and wildly in a slow drunken wave, swept about his head like the snakes on a Gorgon. Slowly reaching into the middle of the carving table, he tried to claw his way back to the land of stability and a room that didn't swim about in a stomach lurching fashion.

The two smaller dragons rushed to help him up. One on each side they took his arms and lifted the weaving rubbery-legged dragon. "Hold him," Tink commanded and rushed to fetch Chang's one-legged stool with the crescent seat to accommodate his tail. Placing the stool under his haunches, they eased him down gently.

This is when Boomer noticed the Tink handprints on the old dragon's arm, "Uh, Tink?" he warned, "Don't touch anything else." Then for the first time he really looked at his sibling and his new gold skin. "Oh, definitely don't touch anything." Quickly Boomer glanced at the now gold claw printed leg of the stool, then happened to glance at the palms of his claws where he had grabbed his brother, and emphatically stated, "Touch absolutely nothing."

"Chang, can you sit here by yourself?" The old dragon nodded, then started to turn to the smaller red dragon but his eyes started swimming and he could feel his dinner trying to get out and fly away, so he stopped moving and just moaned in Mandarin with one claw holding the top of his head with his ear wings drooping. Slowly he just closed his eyes and leaned against the workbench in the hope that this nightmare would just go away.

Boomer pointed at the gold claw prints on the old dragon's arm and then rolled over his own claws, gold palms up, "Definitely don't touch anything or anybody while I'm gone. I've got to go find Twill or Guff!" and like that, he was gone, into the supersonic storm that was Boomer. Slowly, dejectedly, Tink sank to the floor. Absentmindedly rocking up on one haunch, he checked the floor. Sure enough, there was now a tiny pure gold dragon butt-print, printed indelibly on the concrete.

"Oh great," he sighed, "I'm never going to live this one down: a gold butt-print on the workshop floor for all eternity!" All he wanted was to just go out and get in his mug, not realizing that he may never fit in that mug again. The Kell has a vast knowledge of many things.

The little golden dragon rose into the air and slowly made his way back out through the open window he had traversed just moments before. The moonlight shone on the gold wings and reflected with golden light that showered all about the patio as he lowered to the edge and the draping withered hosta leaf. With a flick of his hand, the leaf lifted and Tink, now in routine mode, turned and lowered into a mug that he did not notice expanding to accommodate the now only slightly larger dragon; the Kell had forgotten the original owner of this coffee mug. The ever-present crack, just to the left of the handle, slowly filled with gold and healed as the entire inside transmuted into gold, covering all past transgressions. The small, but deep, now golden, rumble of Tink's snore was a familiar tone in the hostas as the night continued about the business of bats, and owls gliding through the night, a vole looking for dinner under the hostas as well as a tree peeper frog singing his fond farewell to the long days and warm nights of summer.

The deep sounds of the forest blended and washed from tree to tree, branch to limb, sky to hosta as the fresh little breeze played down among the larger leaves. A rustle and a grimy little head with dirty yellowy hair and streaks of chocolate and dirt on her face, popped up above the general forest floor duff. The rotting leaves fell from her hair unnoticed as she listened to the pulse of the forest; everything was as it should be. Everything sounded just the way it should. Everything was sounding . . . wait - that snore . . . Tink!

Bounding back under the cover of rotting leaves, needles and hosta plants Duff disappeared only to pop up next to the mug. The dragon she was looking at was not Tink. This one was a gold dragon that looked kind of like a slightly larger version of Tink.

Duff walked all around the golden dragon, as she listened to the humming snore that was also resonating in her chest. *This was not right.*

Boomer crashed through the forest, as was his custom but scared Duff back into the forest duff in hiding. Moments later, she could hear the sounds of other wings; Wings that were not so fast as Boomer, but friendly ones she recognized and she popped out again above the hostas. "Skth! Twill!" she called as the two blues wheeled through the last of the forest.

"Duff!" Skth called as she came into a landing on the edge of the flagstones, as Twill continued into the shop through the now standing open door. "Duff, Tink is back."

Duff was hesitant as she stuck one tiny fist onto her hip, as with the other she gently held the edge of the hosta leaf. "Well, maybe he is and maybe he isn't…" as she raised the edge of the hosta leaf with a smudge of gold on the underside.

Skth looked at a gold statue of Tink in his white mug; but the statue was snoring - softly, but still snoring.

"Don't touch him!" Boomer yelled into the night as he shot out of the work-room window and headed for the small tableau at the edge of the forest. "What he touches turns gold or into gold, we don't know which, but he touched Chang and left his hand print on his arm like a tattoo, and there is gold all over the sink where he hit, and there is also a butt-print on the floor so we know he's tired enough to sit down. But until we know what is going on, we don't dare touch him." Boomer wound down, flustered.

"What happened out there?" Skth asked in harmony with Duff. The girls giggled then leaned on each other.

"I don't know," Boomer started, "We got to K'Tng last week and there was a massive storm covering the mountain so we did the Toss anyway up in the clouds. I knew it was going wrong when I first tossed him, but there was no going back; Tink was so focused and driven we only stopped once the whole way over. We stopped again at the valley, but he just looked at everything and said let's go. That was the last I saw of him. I went down to Mumbai the next morning to take a cockroach home, and then went back and waited all week."

Duff looked at Boomer and sized him up, "Seriously, a cockroach?" The girls looked at each other with gaping mouths, easily falling back into their familiar routine of making fun of each other to break the tension.

Skth looked at him seriously, "Was she cute?" She smiled and batted her eyes at him in a stage flirt as she suggestively wiggled her body.

Boomer blushed, but not so you could tell, "I think it was a he; but how can you tell?" Now flustered, he tried to tell about a cockroach that just suddenly appears 980 miles from home, in the middle of nowhere Nepal. It just did not sound right to him either.

"Did he speak with an Indian or Hindi accent?" the deep rumbling voice came out of the forest, followed by a loud Hawaiian shirt with a fuzzy bear inside. Guff put up his thumb and forefinger about two inches apart and asked, "About this tall, and a monk?"

Boomer nodded. "He was there," Guff confirmed. "Did you notice the gold eyes?"

"Now that you mention it, yes; he did have gold eyes." Boomer scratched behind his right ear, as Guff scratched behind his left. "So, you know him?"

"Nope, never met him," shaking his head, "But you can ask Twill about him, she knows him." Guff leaned over and lifted the large leaf with the gold mark on the underside, and looked at the snoring golden Tink. He rubbed the gold on the leaf, but it did not rub off, and he looked at his thumb; no gold, "Well that's a relief," he mumbled to himself.

He looked at the other three as they looked to him for an answer. "You'll have to excuse me, we need some specialized help." Turning, he walked into the shop. The three looked at each other, then at the hosta leaf where the snoring was getting a little more audible. They snickered in the darkness.

From within the Paws and Claws they could hear the raised voices of Guff and Twill. Soon, very soon, the Chinese snake dragon Chang walked out the front door and over to Boomer. "The Master and Mistress need you to be inside please," he intoned and then expanded his scales and exploded into the air and with a ringing of each new explosion was soon gone.

Boomer had no idea what could be going on as he walked into the workshop. He saw Twill, bent over the utility sink, trying to remove the fresh gold stain to no avail. She had many of the chemicals that framers use in the application of gold, but none was working for the removal, or so it seemed to Boomer, "Chang said you wanted to see me?" he asked.

Twill held out a claw holding a sea sponge that was smoking from some kind of chemical that burned the inside of Boomer's nose. "In the office," she pointed.

"In here, son," the gruff sound of the bear demanded.

"Come on in," Guff sighed as the red dragon shadowed the doorway. "Grab a sit," as he indicated the corner of his desk.

"It's been a long day hasn't it?" the bear solicited.

The supersonic courier shrugged, "I've had longer and worse."

"Do you think you could fly to northern France, pick up a rider, and return before your brother wakes up?"

Boomer considered the time, and travel. "No."

Guff blinked at the answer he was not expecting.

The world traveler, with his internal global time clock jerked his thumb over his shoulder at the large grandfather clock slowly ticking in the corner. "In four chimes of that clock, biscuits will be ready, if I'm out of that meeting in under an hour, it would be amazing, and then to get back here with a package? No. It would be closer to mid-morning." He sat, staring down the bear. Boomer could tell that this was not about a test of wills. This was something else. This was about a request that was all the harder because of respect and the bear knew that he did not want to leave his brother alone right now, at least until they figured out what was going on.

The bear slowly nodded, "Fair enough; take all the time you need. We'll look after Tink and make sure that he is safe, and see if we can figure out what has happened." He started to turn to his half-opened drawer, and then thought better of it. Turning back, he continued, "I would rather not have to ask you to go, but I need you to meet someone there, and bring that someone here. I do not know if you will be able to meet up in time for biscuits, or shortly thereafter. I know this is a lot to ask of you right now, but it's for your brother," Guff reached out and laid his paw on Boomers leg, "It's in his best interest; or I wouldn't have asked you to do this right now."

"Can I get some rocket fuel?"

The bear reached for his mug with his great paw covering the top as he felt the mug fill itself, "Cream and sugar I believe?" The bear slowly passed the mug over to the dragon, "Freshly brewed."

"Mmm," sipped Boomer, draining half the mug, "I could have sworn you were a straight black kind of drinker," draining the rest and putting down the still steaming mug.

The bear just smiled that silly grin and shrugged his shoulders, as five surfers slid down the face of a now very large wave, with the full moon showing over Diamond Head. For emphasis, he rolled his eyes and chuckled, "Always had a thing for some cream and honey."

Boomer revved up and hovered off the desk, and then half pointed at the moon on the shirt, "You need to get the calendar on your shirt fixed; the full moon isn't for another 12 days." They both laughed as he flew out the door.

Guff looked down at the now half-moon; staring intently, he could have sworn there was a blush on the cheeks of the Man in the Moon. He harrumphed and leaned back in the chair with a warm smile, enjoying the extra room for his fuzzy not-so-little tail as it wagged happily and excitedly.

Chapter 15

The Frame

Boomer reached across the table for another warm biscuit. The sun on his back was not as warm as it had been this summer. It was a sun of autumn - late, low, and anemic, but the radiance of the good doctor across the table was more than enough to brighten the morning for Jon and Boomer alike. "So, what did you two decide?" as he smeared butter and honey on the fluffy delicacy.

"Don't you mean three?" she asked with sparkling eyes.

Jon quietly cleared his throat and gave her a knowing look, with a nod towards Scout. The old man was hunched over the edge of the table in obvious morning pain, but said nothing, nor gave in to the torture age was wreaking on him. "Um, we have some peu de nouvellus."

The doctor blushed and shied her head, quietly confiding, "Jon and I are going to be parents."

Boomer froze. Biscuit halfway in his mouth, his eyes grew. Slowly the biscuit lowered as he looked at Yvette, then at Jon. He knew that he did not know that much about humans and much less their anatomy, but he was certain that late thirties and late eighties probably did not produce offspring. He looked at Jon, and then slowly looked back at the good doctor, "I thought you were just talking about sharing a house? I had no idea that you two were more serious than that," as he waggled a pointed claw back and forth between the two. His right eyebrow arched as he continued his thought, "But, after all, I guess; it is France."

With horror as she now understood Boomer's misconception, her eyes grew wide in mock terror and then began giggling and blushed even redder. "Mon deu; it is not that!" as she begged a look of help from the form at the end of the table who seemed to be the last to come to her aid at that moment as he was confined to a silly grin, and the mirth at the miscommunication. She threw her napkin at him, "Oh you're no help! Vieux coquin!" He laughed even harder.

"She is calling me a sexy old man," he laughed.

She tried to recover some order, "We are adopting."

Boomer opened his mouth in the human sign of the light going on, and understanding coming to that light, "Ahh."

Jon started laughing even harder, "Ma chère, il ne comprend. He thinks you are talking about a human baby," This set the old man off laughing even harder, until he started coughing.

Boomer looked back at Yvette, eyes large with now comprehending the whole of the miscommunication and understanding. "Non! Non, non, non…. It is a child. I mean it is a baby, well two, a chat, I mean cat, and a puppy." She was still blushing as she caught her breath and still chuckled, "They were brought in together, left in a box."

She thought about the two in the box, and crumpled in on herself; crushed by the sadness of the abandoned dog and cat. "It is so sad, these things that happen," she almost whispered.

Reaching out with a comforting claw on her hand he asked, "So," then looking over at the twitching dog near the coal stove, "Scout gets to be a parent to two children. How does he feel about that?"

The doctor leaned into the table and whispered, "He doesn't know yet." Then she looked up and her eyes grew as she sat back. Her face drained of blood and as she turned ash white, she asked, "I hope this is a friend of yours, Boomer?"

Boomer looked at her, and then whipped around and looked out the window as an enormous bird the size of a city bus was slowly landing in the tiny yard. The three were stunned and just stared as the roc descended, and as the right claw touched the grass, the whole vision shimmered. In a blink there was a man standing in the yard, dressed all in black with a peacock plumage shirt under his sport coat. The hair was almost wet looking in its jet black, slicked back way.

The man looked around and then waved at the tableau in the window. As he approached the back door, Jon excused himself and went to see who it could possibly be; closely followed by Scout, Yvette and Boomer.

Opening the door, Jon asked, "Oui?"

"Pardon, but my French is lacking horribly since I last got to use it with any regularity," the man apologized. "My name is Macklin, Macklin the Merci- ... well, let's just leave it at Macklin." He bowed a little theatrically, "I'm here to meet with Boomer."

Ever the gentleman, Jon stepped back and waved him in.

"I hope I'm not being too bold when I say I hope I'm not too late for the famous biscuits I have heard so much about." His smile was infectious as he swept into the small room to face Boomer, and allow Scout to smell him.

The knot of people, dog and dragon moved as a body back into the small cottage and away from the ganging appearance at the door. "Please, come, join us at the table." Yvet offered with an extended hand as she surreptitiously leaned in closer to smell for feathers.

"Ah, and this must be the amazing doctor to the dragons. Yvet, I believe?" Macklin oozed gentility and took her hand, gracing the back with just the whisper of a kiss, pausing in the closeness to confide in a whisper, "There is no after scent of the previous shape, or I would also reek of salmon and herring."

Flustered, Yvette accepted the proffered seat and resumed the table. With her mind whirling with images, thoughts, ideas; her head was starting to ache from trying to take in what her eyes had seen landing in the yard, and the man who was now sitting beside her, while her scientific mind told her that they were two different things.

In reaching for the biscuits as Jon held out the basket, Macklin gingerly placed his right hand reassuringly on the doctor's hand. "Even though you have had months to adjust to the idea of dragons and others, I realize my appearance could have been a little unsettling. Maybe I could call on you two," catching himself as a cold nose pushed against his hip, eliciting a warm stroking of Scout's head and playful fondling of his ears. "My mistake, three; and perhaps I would be able to cast some illumination on the many questions I know you all have." His golden eyes twinkled with concern and warmth.

"Cert," Jon answered for the still stunned doctor. "We have our evening meals vulgarly at an early six-ish when Yvette comes from the clinic; and you already know when the biscuits are out of the oven." He then raised both the coffee carafe and his eyebrows in the universal offer.

"Oui, s'il vous plait," as he offered out his mug to be filled, "And I must comment that this is the most wonderful smelling table I have been at in a very long time." Once the brown elixir was treated with cream and honey, he raised his mug, "May I propose a toast, to new friends, whatever species they may be."

Thousands of miles away, a mug of coffee rose to furry lips, as the deep brown eyes that were almost black with the dark, watched through a now closed window at a certain patch of dark night where he knew there were hostas and on one leaf, a small gold claw print. The mind of a bear is a slow churning thing, quick when needed, but brooding as it stirred the very large pot of memories. Guff quietly sat sipping coffee and stirring memories during his lone vigil in the dark office.

Not so far away, two ice blue dragons also sat vigil with two other larger dragons that were even closer to the tiny gold dragon that now slept soundly in the forest. The talking, and Q'Nt's motherly fretting, had long worn down, the four were left sitting around the table staring numbly and glassy eyed at each other and at nothing. The smallest hand on the clock over the stove crawled from second to second in seemingly hour durations. Each tick sounded in the room like eggs slowly dropped for dramatic effect.

In the forest, from under the duff and rotting detritus, a dirty pink foot slid out, touching the china mug and the warmth within for reassurance. Then as if in realization of the heat produced by the little dragon and shared with the mug, a matching dirty foot joined the first and they rested flatfooted on the smooth porcelain for warming and connectivity.

Macklin reached for another biscuit as he caught the look in Boomer's eyes. "Don't worry, my friend; I will be no more a weight on your back than your brother. For me weight and size is irrelevant."

Mindfully applying the creamy butter and honey he half turned to Yvette, "So, to answer your question, yes, it was the end of the Fairy Wars that brought about the separation of the species; no longer speaking to each other. Each species walked away, on its own path, without looking back." Reaching down to scratch behind a fuzzy warm ear causing a groan and a slow roll to one side, "But there were certain exceptions, of course." Smiling, Macklin slowly bit into the biscuit as his eyes drooped closed. He focused sensuously on the scent and flavors.

The table littered with the results of the extended morning meal made Jon happy. He leaned back in his chair and thought about the recent happenstances that had changed his life: the wonder of absolute communication with his old friend Scout and the many new companions brought into his now full life. His good hand worried the mess that had been his other hand for more than half a century, as he thought of prices paid. A slow smile washed along the good side of his face as he thought about how it had all been worth it to get to this place today. A soft tender hand quietly reached over and rested on his arm. *"Home and family,"* he sighed, *"No matter what they look like."*

Looking at her watch, Yvette cried out, "Oh, it is time that I get to work, so if you would excuse me please." The man with the golden eyes mirrored her rising.

"We must be off as well, as we have an important meeting to attend." As he started clearing the table, Jon came up to speed as to the shifting circumstances.

"Non, non, please, I'll clear the table." He scowled half of his face and fluttered his hands as he gestured to put the crockery back down. Turning to Yvette he conferred patronal, "Mon cher, we will see you tonight, I am thinking that turbot are by the docks lately and would be a good meal, so I will see you then."

Macklin kissed her hand, shook Jon's and ruffled the now active Scout, "It has been a truly a pleasure to meet some of Tink's special family. Next time I come," he winked at Jon, "I will remember to bring you some fresh Cardamom and show you how to grind it." Turning to Boomer, "Shall we walk the good doctor out?"

In the yard, Boomer and Yvette embraced in farewell, and then he slipped once more into the harness eyeing an interesting colored rendition of his brother. Both he and the doctor laughed as he noted that the blue and brown-green trim made Macklin look like a blending of Tink and Skth both. Yvette wasn't so comfortable with the shape-changing thing, but shrugged and thought that after so much else, what difference was it now; it would just take a little more time to get used to it, that's all.

Boomer adjusted the harness as Macklin climbed into the cone and gripped the holds. "Does it really make one queasy when you hit Mach 3?"

"Tell me when we get there," Boomer laughed as they exploded off the front sidewalk leaving the trio waving goodbye and a few neighbors looking around in wonder at the sound. Out over open water, Boomer could feel Macklin assume Tink's characteristic wing stance as he had promised, so Boomer turned up the speed and raced for his favorite altitude, as he hurried to catch up with the trailing edge of night and then dawn, he also felt that fourth biscuit with honey. *Cardamom, huh?* He made a mental note to tell his mother as he could feel Macklin respond to the effects of busting through the third barrier. He would have smiled, but just glowed inside instead.

An atomic submarine was sitting beside a tender as they transferred some personal and hardcopy mail. The radar personal turned to her Executive Officer to report a small supersonic bogie on her screen at 300 miles out, but by then it had translated across and off her screen on the other side. An anomaly she thought; it had not pinged as metal, but more like a life form, something she was used to seeing in the sonar baths instead. She glanced at her watch to confirm that it was time for her lunch. The streak continued transitioning deeper into the shield of night.

For many, the night was dragging in a slow pace of nerves and worry, not the supersonic 2,000 miles per hour Boomer was racing to get home. Slowly the great fuzzy paw reached up and scratched behind a large brown ear. The drooping dark brown eyes rolled like slow steel marbles as Guff looked out the window that would glow as it heralded the coming of the new day, and the arrival of someone who, he hoped, had dealt with this problem before.

His right paw reached out and retrieved an overly used and probably abused mug filling with fresh aromatic coffee. Sipping the warm reassuring liquid, he looked, for the umpteenth time that night, at the small piece of glass, as he walked again out of the forest. The whole concept was amazing to him; but then, so was the computer that sat in the design room. Not that he considered them even in the same class, one being technology and the other maybe organic? To Guff, they were just the same; something he could just marvel at forever. As he sat back in his chair, he also remembered a certain small painting on a bisque lozenge that they had framed that summer for a trio of gnome brothers; and again his mind whirled in that eternal question of *"How do they do that?"*

The large bear stared out the one window that mattered to him right now, and took another sip of his coffee. *"Rocket fuel, hah! I'm falling asleep, and they call it rocket fuel."*

The little gold rocket turned in his mug, as he traded arms to rest his face on and drool. A tiny pink toe twitched at the movement in the porcelain upon which the foot rested.

A large blue dragon snuggled deeper into the arms of an obsidian dragon as the two dreamed uncomfortably in the dark. Their one son was now gold, and the other was somewhere in the night air.

A small blue dragon slept exhausted, curled in the protective hollow of a larger blue's fetal curl, as her head lay in the lap of a sea chameleon whose eyes were anything but sleeping. M'Ree, for probably the first time in her adult life, was having many thoughts, but not one entailed chocolate.

Meanwhile a coffee, eggs, bacon and fish fueled rocket was closing the gap as the crest of dawn drew across the eastern horizon, and the bear stirred. To his credit, Macklin had matched Tink's configured wing arch as promised, and had never moved. The two were on track to arrive earlier than promised and Boomer, even as tired as he was, was happy to be home.

The crack of dawn, was more of a "Boom!" as the supersonic duo exploded overhead in the early light of the day. Circling around, they were just touching down as Guff stepped out of the front door of the picture frame shop, followed by two blue missiles from deep in the atelier and M'Ree's lap, which was still trying to make headway and follow.

The tiny dragon sprang from Boomer's back and landed as Macklin the Merciless on the flagstones of the patio. Looking about, he stretched and smiled at Guff and Twill, "Great to be back. I like what you've done to the place," he added in his light sarcastic humor in reference to the never changing nature of the building and setting.

"So good to see you, Macklin," Twill shot back, as only a half-hearted sarcastic shot at the old friend and original owner of Paws & Claws Atelier. She did surge forward to kiss his two cheeks, and whisper a soft, "Thank you for coming, M'Loree."

He confided back, "I hear we have some work to sort out."

As if on command, the center of attention raised a sagging hosta leaf and stepped out onto the patio blinking at the morning sunshine. Taking in the solid bright gold nature of the tiny figure, Macklin drew in a breath, "Oh my."

The large bear stepped next to the man, "Hmm," he hummed, "Kind of nice in the sunshine, don't you think?"

Twill noticed it first. She was about to say something when a tiny voice from the rotting forest floor pointed out, "Tink! No foot prints!" Duff then shook out of the rest of the forest floor, and she examined the hosta leaf Tink had moved, "No claw marks either!"

Tink turned, and looking at the large hosta leaf, he sneezed, "Choo," but a tiny puff of gold came out of his nose, and spattered the leaf in a light sprinkling of gold sparkles. A few new freckles of gold were even on Duff's cheeks and nose.

"Uh oh," started Boomer, but Tink shot him one of his mother's looks, as he stepped over and dusted the speckles of gold glitter off of the leaf.

Turning, he looked to Skth and Twill, "I figured it out," he said, "and now, we have a frame to make for a very special customer." In so saying, he reached over and hugged Duff while leaving no marks, except a gold kiss left in her hair to match the new permanent gold freckles.

The rocket fuel was bubbling away, the glue pot was stinking nicely and the shop was full of people who had little or no business being there, but could see no reason to be anywhere else at the time. M'Ree was looking into nooks and crannies until Twill laid a claw on her and sadly shook her head with the news about the now-empty secret stashes consumed the night before. Guff was wheeling his chair back out into the workroom for its second time that day, as he offered the seat to Macklin. The stage was set on the largest of the worktables. Everything had been cleared, and the center not only dusted and wiped off, but also washed. The richly aged rock maple shone in the glow of work lights and dragon lights, and the three characters took their places.

Hours later, Guff and Macklin sat in the middle of a fall pasture, both introspective and replaying the sight of watching the glass ooze out of the flame of Twill, forming into an amazing lacey filigree of flowers and leaves that formed a small picture frame that echoed the style of Chippendale, but had the organic sense of the Art Nouveau period. Twill's flame danced like a will-o'-the-wisp in the light breeze of a spring evening; a glass leaf here that blended into a glass flower petal, and all as the sparkling broken Schabin gold that matched the little dragon's eyes, seemed to appear in the hot glass with an eerie shimmering colorless transparent flame. The third flame, a semi-transparent purple, licked here and there, freezing the radiance of the hot glass, and securing the illumination in and around each fleck of floating gold in the frame. Finally, as the frame was complete, Twill had floated a thick plate of glass into the middle of the frame. Once it had cooled, it was Duff's turn. She had thought long, then had placed her hand on first Guff's chest, then Tink's and finally Skth's before setting her hand on the glass as all had watched it sparkle and glow. Tiny sparklers had silently shot about and between her fingers as the glow under her hand matched the glow of the beautiful picture frame that was exactly what she had dreamed of. When she removed her hand, what she revealed was a perfect image of the forest outside, just as a blue jay had flown by both outside, and in the image.

Macklin reached out and retrieved another fish and rice ball, dipped it in plum sauce and popped it in his mouth. Slowly, chewing on the delicacy and his thoughts, he asked the bear lying beside him, "So you talked to Boomer?"

"Yes." The large bear scratched slowly behind his ear.

"And he said he didn't know?"

"Correct."

"But he still passed the test." The man processed another ball.

"When I asked him who of the three he would be willing to lay down his life for, he snapped his answer; which I have to accept as the truth." Guff rolled over on his side, scooped out a half dozen balls, and dragged them through the sauce on their way towards his open maw.

"Any of them," Macklin grabbed his hair in one hand and shook his head back and forth, pulling his hair with his hand. "So, he is the Patron, but will defend any of the three. Oh, we have a problem," he sighed, lying back into the dry grass, "No Reveal, no Princess."

The other Princess rumbled as only an 800-pound bear can, as he sucked the sauce from his paw and reclined into the pasture. Thinking, he commented, "Of course, there is the wedding thing. It's been a few Princesses, but it is still valid . . . "

Macklin thought about it as he pointed at the late afternoon sky wagging his finger, "There is that." His massive friend was past listening; the snoring had already started.

High overhead a strange aircraft with a large round saucer attached to its top, slid through the air as a human with headphones and boom mike talked to others on the radio, as she stared into several illuminated screens. The plane did not even leave any condensation trail across the sky to give any evidence of its passing. Far below, a blue heron, late to migrate, flew towards the small lake she knew that would be her resting place for the night. The chill in the afternoon's waning sun reminded the ground squirrel to finish making that other tunnel's exit sheltered from the winter snows. The ants marched, following a scent trail through the dried forest of grass stalks that gently moved in the light fall breeze.

"Well, it has been pleasant, as well as interesting," the man shook the bear's paw, and then turned to hug the large ice blue dragon waiting patiently next to the large work bench strewn with the tools and products of gold frame manufacturing. The great windows stood open in possibly the last days of temperatures pleasant enough to leave the air to freshen the workroom. The full staff was hard at work with the coming late fall orders sure to swell to long days and hours of overtime in the coming holiday season falling on top of the presents for the newly revealed Fairy Princess; which everyone was waiting to find out.

"How will you be going back?" asked Twill, always the sensible thinker of the team.

"I thought I would make a leisurely loop of it and enjoy some of the fall colors."

"No, I didn't mean what route, but how; as what?" Guff persisted.

"Oh, I thought about renting one of those RV things, and driving until I get bored. Then probably fly the rest of the way."

"You need a passport these days."

Macklin thought about it for a moment, and then reached in his back pocket and produced a diplomatic passport from Norway. "Would this do?" Smiling as if he had eaten the whole nest, cage and canary, he smirked at his friend.

"Smart ass," Guff reached out, hitting the man lightly on his shoulder . . ..

"Look out!" Two wild missiles came screaming through the open window followed by a red streak that came to a frozen halt mid-air as the other two crashed into Jeeter who was walking quietly past with a fifty-pound bag of whiting powder. He was hit square in the shoulders and knocked out past the worktables, whereupon the bag exploded into the exact space occupied by Tink and Skth.

As the huge cloud of fine white dust cleared, standing there on the work bench were what looked ever so much like two white plaster statues of dragons playing tag; one dodging and the other, reaching out with a wing to tap the other on the head. Both were blinking with tiny eyes at the gathered crowd of dragons. There was silence in the shop as nobody but Jeeter moved. The poor elderly dragon picked himself up by grabbing the edge of the table.

Slowly, one little dragon mouth started to open, maybe to say "Oops" or maybe to apologize or maybe because they recognized the large ancient blue dragon that was materializing next to Macklin the human.

Jeeter blinked at the two unmistakable tiny dragons now covered with the white powder, and he began to laugh. "You two," he giggled and pointed, "Look like you are getting bonded." Then realizing he was the only one laughing, he swung his head around to see that every other dragon was in attendance as well as Guff, and the human. Then he noticed the transparent dragon that was slowly becoming corporeal.

As she became more and more corporeal, she took a step forward and raised her hands in supplication as she looked intently at the two before her. The two whited dragons looked with blinking eyes at each other. Two heartbeats were one as they turned and nodded. The dragon gained more solidity as she began to chant, and they took each other's hands and faced the Chancellor and gathering of their closest friends and family.

The twins poked each other and quietly giggled, until they noticed Twill's twitching tail rudder, snapping decidedly to the right. M'Ree, totally forgetting about chocolate, removed her red marble stone-rimmed glasses as she caught her breath and began to shudder into a weeping mess. Only Boomer had forethought and screamed, "Wait! Nobody move!" and exploded out the window, only to return a couple of minutes later followed by a large blue-green dragon, and her black with red trimmed husband. Both entered and then froze in astonishment.

Nobody had moved, only Twill had twitched. Tink had whispered something out of the side of his mouth and Skth had leaned deeper into his shoulder. Or was it Skth that had whispered and Tink had . . . it was kind of hard to tell with them both being all white at the moment.

"OK," allowed Boomer, "everyone is here now; you may continue." Then feeling a tug on his trailing tail, he looked down at the last person to attend. Hovering down to the floor, he picked up Duff and placed her on his shoulders, "OK, now go ahead."

The ancient dragon nodded without looking back and continued. And with the end of the short chant, she looked about for some water. Understanding the ceremony and the nature of the two, well at least one, dragons' penchant for rocket fuel, Guff offered out his large mug of steaming coffee. At first the ancient looked at the mug with consternation and at the larger size of her claw, and then she looked back to the bonding pair and the size of their foreheads. Smiling at Guff for his unique solution, she dipped just two claw tips into the coffee, and turned to the pair of whited dragons. Chanting the final offering to long lives, large families and fair skies to fly in, she dabbed the two fingers on first one than the others foreheads, leaving them anointed, with the jewels clean of water to be first to clear and reveal the path of the bonded pair. Reaching forward and lightly kissing the tips of the two noses and smiling she turned, and stepped out of the way and stood next to the now dashing obsidian dragon with the glowing red trim and gold eyes, who stood where the human had been previously standing. Tink and Skth braced as the host of dragons began the Wind. Whiting and gold sparkles blew out and away through the open window, as well as a few other places in and about the workshop, to be found for years to come.

The party after consisted of coffee and quickly rustled up fish and rice balls. Macklin reassumed his old human persona, as he and his sister took a quiet walk in the moonlight before returning to get the recipe for the balls and sauces from Q'Int, with a promise to come and visit, cook and share secrets soon.

Guff and Macklin stood looking at the newly bonded tiny dragons as they stood on the workbench talking to Duff about things that probably only those three could talk about. Slowly a red dragon hovered up from behind the two past Princesses and rested his arms along some of their shoulders asking, "So, the kids are wed." The two Princesses nod slowly and dully and look at the proud beaming face of the newest Patron, whose eyes were only for the three on the bench.

"Now, who's your Princess?"

Epilogue

Tink sat in his mug beneath a young tender hosta. There was another young spring hosta off his left shoulder that was quietly snoring a very good rendition of an old favorite pixie snore. He smiled with a small smirk as his attention returned to the envelope in his hands as his finger carefully sliced it open and a letter fell out. Slowly he opened the fine rice paper.

Dearest Great Uncle Tink,

I am very sorry to have missed you at Aunt K'lee's recent hatching. I had so wanted to finally meet you and see Great Aunt S'kth again. I have heard for years about how you have labored under the belief that you are the very smallest dragon and wanted to stand eye to almost eye with you. For you see, I am now 40 years old and have stopped growing for the last ten years. I haven't added even a cat's whisker of growth. For my new job with the ministry, I have just returned from my physical exam; which gives me an outside confirmation that I am in fact 1.2 millimeters smaller than you are.

Looking forward to you and Skth, and Boomer too, visiting us next spring, it has been way too many years since Skth and I played seek and tag in the hollows

My best friend Myrth (who is 2 millimeters taller than I am) is very eager to meet both you and Great Aunt S'Kth.

Until next spring,

Your grandniece N'li

Tink lowered the letter. 'Really? Someone smaller than me?' He chuckled at the thought, being almost overwhelmed as the warm sun heated the green leaf above his head. The pungent scent filled his nostrils as he took a deep breath and slowly let it out to the accompaniment of a soft pixie-ish snore. Maybe he and Boomer would have to make a quick weekend trip to the north end of Norway this spring too . . .

Life was really something. As his gaze glanced at the open windows of the office where the many gifts resided, he thought of the first frame he had ever designed; the one that housed a special painting of a very special mountain, given to him by three very special gnomes. Who could have ever guessed that he would turn out to be a Golden dragon, the new Princess, bonded to a great dragon who had clutched twice for three great children, and best friends with a pixie who snores and would rather hang out with you in the hostas; it just didn't get much better than that he thought; as he blew another ring of gold smoke.

Maybe the old mug was really not too small after all. Maybe just a light coat of fresh gold on the inside to kind of "dress it up a bit"; nah, the dirty old gold felt just fine, as he lowered his jowls onto his crossed arms and joined Duff in a little Royal Nap.

Made in the USA
Charleston, SC
11 January 2012